LOVERS
OF ISIS

Romantic and Erotic
Vignettes from

Red Mirror Series

THE RED MIRROR
THE EMERALD TABLET
THE BLACK SCROLL

S. L. GORE

2014.10.03 Edition

ISBN: 978-1-940304-05-2

Published by Tajine Publishing, Las Vegas NV

Author website: www.SLGore.com

There are many kinds of love

Lovers of Isis

THE RED MIRROR – PHARAONIC EGYPT

River God
Goliath
Hector
The General
Antinous

THE EMERALD TABLET – GREEK EGYPT

Hektor
The General
Jason
Black Falcon
Tony

THE BLACK SCROLL – ROMAN EGYPT

Gareth Greene
Hector
The General
Rasheed
Antinous

PART ONE

The Red Mirror

PHARAONIC EGYPT

ISIS

Obsession

S heets tangled between my thighs, pillows tossed all around, I woke in a sweat in my wide, lonely bed. I had dreamed again of the Red Mirror. The vivid images were still playing in my mind when sunlight shattered the glass and the lush tapestry of my dream unraveled. Finally, all that remained was a crimson glow.

It was a rainy afternoon, an ordinary Tuesday, when the red aura first lured me into the shadows deep in the antique mall. There at the end of a long maze of neon beer signs, crystal goblets and sequined dinner jackets was a dark, dusty stall choked with jumbled figurines and castoff books.

The mirror whispered, and I paused.

Almost breast high, slightly taller than wide, the mirror leaned backward against a Chinese screen aflame with yellow chrysanthemums and orange-crested songbirds. Faint traces of blue and white flowers with glints of silver here and there peeked through layers of grime.

I stepped around fragile vases and toppled statues until I stood just in front of the red lacquered frame. The faint aura was subtle, but glowed brighter as I drew nearer.

I could see that once cleaned, the frame could be beautiful, but it wasn't the artistry that bewitched me.

"*Come,*" the Red Mirror beckoned. "*Taste of a life more sensuous than any dream.*"

River God

I sis!"

I had a name, the name of a goddess. I also had a man, or at least I saw one coming right at me. And what a man he was—a River God of bronzed flesh and white linen. The snowy stiff kilt wrapped tightly around his narrow waist and ended just above his knees. His thighs and calves were taut, the elongated muscles of a runner.

Broad, straight shoulders tapered in a triangle to muscular, lean hips. He wore nothing above the waist except a wide, beaded collar. In the sun, his chest glowed like burnished stone. I wondered if he, like me, also was without underwear.

He held out his hand to help me up, and I rose to my feet, almost no space between us. One step forward and we would be touching, his bare skin, bronze and smooth, on my gauze-covered breasts. His exotic scent went straight to my head. I craved to touch him, to fondle him, to make him quake with desire.

Never this bold on the other side of the mirror, I reached out to run my fingers over his bronzed chest, down his flat belly and under the snowy kilt.

He grew instantly hard, but instead of encouraging me, he took my hand teasing his manhood and raised it to his lips. I touched his moist tongue. His dark eyes, outlined in thick, black *kohl* lines drawn almost to the temple, never left mine.

His angular face, framed by a blue and white striped headdress, might have been too sharp on another man, but not River God. There was nothing about him that didn't sear me. I felt his heat right down to my bones.

We stood with barely a breath between us. His mouth, exquisitely carved by a master sculptor in a softer stone, was at the same time sensuous and hard. I would die if I could not feel the perfection of those lips explore every inch of my body, yet he made no move. Could he not feel the waves of my desire crashing on his shore?

My fingertips, light as the wings of a butterfly, stroked across the smooth muscle of his chest. I barely touched him, but I know he felt the spark. I saw it in his eyes. I saw it in the subtle upturn of his lips.

I was too mesmerized to appreciate what the combination of cool half-smile and smoldering eyes might mean. The omens of my heartbreak were there from the beginning, but I chose not to see.

Slowly trailing my fingers down his biceps and along his forearms to the wide gold bracelets at his wrists, I watched the tiny hairs rise. Gooseflesh rose on my own skin, like a chill across my shoulders in spite of the heat.

He leaned in close, his full lips at my ear, his breath hot and moist on my neck.

"Not now, Isis. Not here."

He stroked once across the hollow of my throat. His touch was utterly real; I couldn't be dreaming. I felt the wet on the inside of my thigh and guided his fingers to the damp.

With his lips at the curve of my neck on the magic spot that opens all doors, he breathed, "I shall come to you after the second meal and taste of your nectar. You shall fly to the stars with my tongue on your lotus."

He stepped back then, his body morphing into a kind of military posture with arms a bit rigid at his sides. Even his voice took on a commanding tone.

"Where is your Nubian slave? You are expected at the Temple."

Temple?

I scurried around in my mind, frantic and desperate for direction.

What temple? What would I do when I got there?

I looked carefully at River God. If he noticed anything different about the woman I had become, he didn't show it. There was plenty of promise in his eyes and half-smile, but no hint of suspicion. He didn't see me at all; he saw only Isis. And he very much liked what he saw.

The Temple

Watching me from the shadows were two men. I could just make out the whites of their eyes. I felt their heat and smelled their scented sweat. My oiled, naked body gleamed in the low lamplight.

There was a heavy new scent here, a narcotic smoke that blurred my vision and made air rush in my ears. My head pounded. I felt dizzy, and for a brief moment, I was afraid I would faint.

The inner sanctum shimmered in gold around a white alabaster statue of a seated goddess wearing a solar disk headdress identical to mine. Her right hand resting on her thigh held a large golden ankh. A dozen glowing lamps at the feet of the Goddess cast a soft light that barely flickered.

Without any conscious direction on my part, my hand moved to a musical instrument in a wooden case atop a black marble pedestal. A graceful silver loop held three delicate rods, each one mounted with dozens of small metal disks. The gleaming silver handle formed into twin heads of Hathor, the cow-eared goddess sitting on the altar throne.

High, chiming notes teased as I lifted the sacred *sistrum* from its ebony box inlaid with ivory. The men stirred when the seductive music broke the silence. The chamber was electric, and so still I could hear them inhale and exhale, together as one person.

Every action was as natural to me as breathing. I held the necklace out from my throat toward the statue, shaking the *sistrum* in a slow, even rhythm that grew more and more feverish. When I opened my lips to sing, the words flowed from me without effort.

"O Hathor, O Divine Cow and giver of milk,
O Goddess of Fertility,
O Goddess of Wine, Music and Dance,
O Goddess of Love.
We adore you.
We ask your blessings for this Son of the Pharaoh,
this First Prince of Egypt."

My voice, strong and husky, vibrated in my throat. The crown of my head pulsed. I no longer felt the weight of the headdress—or the ground under my feet. I felt light as air, floating in a velvet sea.

"This Royal Prince, beloved of Horus,
comes to dance.
He comes to sing;
His bag is full of great offerings,
His sistrum is of gold,
His necklace of malachite.
His feet hurry to the Mistress of Music,
He dances for her;
She loves his doing."

The two men moved right next to me, one on each side. The tall one took the *sistrum* from my hand and returned it carefully to its wooden case. The slighter one, the royal insignia hanging from a thick gold chain around his thin neck, removed my headdress and set it on the altar at the Goddess Hathor's feet.

My heart pounded in my chest; the heavy scent of musk filled my shallow breath. I swayed slightly on my feet while they each stroked my body, four hands caressing my breasts, my buttocks, the insides of my loins. The heavy scent of musk filled my shallow breath.

Together they led me to a divan and lay me down on my back on soft fur. In perfect unison, they started at my feet and began to suck each toe, one after another. Then their wet mouths moved to my ankles, licking the small bones there. They trailed up my calves to the inside of my loins, where like preening cats, they lingered with darting tongues.

A well-practiced team, they lifted my feet to rest just next to my buttocks, slightly on the outside. I lay on fur, spread full open, inviting them to enter.

They licked and sucked and nibbled at the tender skin on the backside of my thighs. Tremors moved through me as they edged closer and closer to the moist valley of desire, taking their time, teasing me, enjoying the straining of my hips and my low cries when they came near, then moved away. I was overcome with need. My womanhood begged for their mouths.

But just before their tongues found my sacred lotus, they rolled back on their heels and chanted in unison.

"O beauteous one, O great one,
O great magician, O splendid lady.
The Pharaoh reveres you;
give that his Son may live!
Behold him, Hathor, flaming one,
His manhood is straight,
The Son of Pharaoh reveres you,
O Gold of Gods,
Give of your milk that he live!"

With that they came to me again, each suckling my breasts, hands kneading like babes at their mother's teats. I lay on the divan, electric shocks rolling through me, moans reverberating in my throat and chest.

The Royal One mounted me while the other licked my open lips with his broad tongue. He did not kiss me, though.

I felt a thick penis slide deep inside. The Prince began to rock slowly, his chest rising each time his hips moved forward, thrusting deeper, then pulling out almost all the way, then thrusting again, never looking into my face, but only at his companion.

The pendant insignia on the heavy chain swung toward me and back, toward me and back. *Would he spill his royal seed in me?*

As if on cue, he rose up and lay his manhood on my stomach as a flood of white milk spewed. The taller one quickly bent and lapped it up with his tongue. Then they leaned forward and kissed each other, the Royal One taking back the semen with an open mouth.

They chanted once more.

"His bread is in his hand,
He defiles not the bread in his hand.
Clean are the foods in his arms,
They have come from the Prince of Egypt,
He has cleansed what he offers to Her."

And then it was over. I realized that they had never removed their kilts.

They knelt before the statue of the goddess Hathor, and the Prince's Scribe placed a carved, painted chest on the altar. Not looking back, they opened the heavy golden doors and disappeared.

I lay panting and stunned on the low sofa, aching and throbbing. I put my fingers between my legs and rotated on my screaming lotus. I had to have release. I didn't think I could stand.

The doors opened again, and the Ancient Ones entered, wearing thick, shoulder-length plaited wigs with twinkling gold chains. Not saying a word, moving silently across the basalt floor, they came straight for me in the dark.

"The Goddess is pleased," the old woman with scarred cheeks assured me. "The Pharaoh shall be pleased. The spell of Seth the Destroyer on the First Son of Egypt, the son-of-Horus, has been broken. The Golden One has given the Crown Prince back his manhood."

"Not very likely," I muttered under my breath, deciding it was best to keep my doubts to myself.

Goliath

He startled me, the old eunuch priest Qeb-ha, coming from nowhere to stand in my path.

"We sail at dawn," he told me in his squeaky, repugnant voice, but at least he spoke out loud this time and not directly to my mind.

It was late. The sun cast long shadows. I brushed past him in a panic to hurry back to River God and his promise of flight to the stars. I would have one last night to caress his smooth, unquestionably male body. One night to knead like bread his swollen nuggets and watch his throbbing organ swell with desire.

Waiting just outside the gate stood Goliath the Magnificent as tall and still as an Aswan statue. Striated scars from some age-old Nubian ceremony covered his cheeks. His oiled ebony skin gleamed in the sun. His biceps were ripe as melons; his thick thighs bulged. So as not to look directly at me, his onyx eyes stared straight ahead.

My own eyes traveled from the white triangle of his headdress to the white triangle of his kilt, drinking in his muscular chest and hard belly along the way.

I moistened my lips, envisioning the dark places I would taste, feeling my tongue slide up and down his giant's swollen rod and my sharp teeth nibbling at the glistening tip. In my mind, my long nails scratched his balls while I sucked him dry. But not too dry.

Yes, I would command the Nubian to service me if River God had come and gone. Goliath would do just fine.

The Bath

He was silent; I sensed his presence rather than heard him. My first sight was bare feet and sturdy ankles not a yard away. My eyes travelled up straight runner's legs to feast on an engorged penis standing erect, head glistening in the lamplight.

O Hathor! You are indeed the Highest-of-High.

River God was in the water before I could move, straddling me, pushing me back into the unyielding stone of the pool wall. I didn't complain.

I kept trying to get my head down, to taste him, but he teased me and traced his hard penis along the bridge of my nose, brushing around my lips, over my chin, down my neck and then rubbing back and forth across my nipples. He held my hands and wouldn't let me touch him. I was maddened by the need to draw his pulsing manhood deep into my throat.

He eased into the water on top of me, his hardness pushing against the softness of my belly. The back of my neck pressed on the unforgiving edge of the pool. I stretched my tongue to lick at his swollen knob, but his mouth was at my ear.

"Isis, do not move, or my seed will issue. I want it to last."

Releasing my hands, he pulled me full into the pool; I floated on my back, white lotus blossoms with dazzling yellow centers swirling in eddies around me. My nipples rose from the water; the aureoles of my breasts were dark circles just at the surface. On his knees beside me, his erection pierced the clear water.

He started with my closed eyes, then my eager mouth, his lips not touching me, but blowing warm puffs of air like a gentle wind across my skin. His breath was sweet with a trace of myrrh. He blew softly in my ear, down the side of my neck, and across the base of my throat.

I floated on a cloud of divine pleasure; the water was warm on my back and the air warm on my face, shoulders, and breasts. His breath, warmer still, moved to my nipples. He blew round and round each taut tip, never touching, but lingering until they rose so tight and tall that they stood like miniature obelisks.

His hand slid between my thighs. I opened wider, but that was all. I was content to do nothing, to exert nothing, to have no will of my own. His finger came from underneath and stroked my swollen bud in small circular movements, with almost no pressure. I drifted in a timeless dream.

Strong hands encircling my ankles, he pulled my knees past his ears, draping my legs over his shoulders. I still floated among the sweet-scented blooms. His hands cupped my buttocks while he lowered his head and raised me to his lips. His tongue swirled my throbbing lotus.

He sucked, and then played with his tongue, and then sucked again. When the roll of spasms swept through my womb, the walls of my vagina contracting over and over, a long, vibrating cry escaped my throat into the deep silence around us.

River God's mouth was on mine in an instant.

"Sh-h-h, Isis. The household is awake and nearby."

Too late for that. By now, every eye looked to my rooms. Every ear strained to hear more.

He stood up in the pool with the water reaching mid-thigh. His body had gone tense and his erection slack. I could feel every taut nerve in his body. River God knew he tasted forbidden fruit.

My hands in his, he drew me slowly to my feet. We stood inches apart, water streaming off our skin aglow in the hazy light of the alabaster lamps. The air was sweet with perfumed oil.

The sound of my heart pounded in my ears as my breasts rose and fell with each breath. I wanted nothing other than to feel him inside me—filling me, sucking me—the way the prince had stretched me in the inner sanctum.

"They will stay away," I assured him in a throaty promise. "I have given orders to be alone."

He hesitated. Slowly the corners of his mouth turned upward in his secret half-smile, and he was mine again.

His lips were full and dry and covered mine with ease. His tongue slipped into my open mouth, exploring slowly, never hurrying, always taking his time, relishing every touch. He sucked gently on my tongue and drew me to him with his muscled arms. My breasts crushed into his broad chest; his nipples were hard points. I arched my back, pressing my pelvis into his. His erection was back and between my clenched thighs.

I found myself outside of the pool, with no memory of exiting. We glided backward, two bodies moving as one, as he led us to the bed with billowing sails. The curtains brushed our bare flesh but didn't cling; our skin had dried in the desert night air.

We sank together onto the cushions of a bed designed more for pleasure than sleep. Smelling the mating scent, Pehtes purred round my ears.

I lay spread on soft linen, my shaved head resting among cool silk pillows and warm cat fur. River God's mouth was on mine again in a deep lingering kiss probing with his tongue. His touch was more sensual than sexual. He savored me as one does a fine wine, something precious you loathe to finish.

I had a sudden thought.

"Sail with me tomorrow. With you in my bed by night, I can face anything by day."

Startled, River God stopped his caress and stared at me in shock.

"I cannot do that. I am as bound to my duty as you are to yours."

His voice was incredulous. I might have asked him to fly.

He changed in that moment. I felt him begin to pull away. When he spoke, his tone was already distant with a note of patience that one uses with a child.

"Isis, sweet and dangerous Isis, you know that our destinies were foretold when we came from the womb."

Time slowed. The nightingale sang sweetly, unaware that the world had changed. The air, now utterly still, was abuzz with the hum of insects. The cries of night creatures carried from the Nile.

I panicked as I felt him slip away. Reaching out, I traced my fingers lightly along his forearm. The hairs rose, and I took hope.

He stroked my face, then along the bone at the base of my throat out to my shoulder. I was like a cat before him. Pehtes tried to crawl into my armpit; I wanted to follow her there.

"I desire you more than any woman I have ever known or seen." His voice was gentle and low, barely above a whisper. "But I must place myself away from you. The Gods have set us on separate paths. Mine is to serve the Pharaoh, yours the Goddess."

He paused to watch his fingers trace the mound of my breast. How could he touch me while saying goodbye?

"The great glory of a wise man is to control himself in his manner of life"

I hated those words. I wanted to put my hands over my ears to keep them from entering. It was my fault. I was too needy. I had gone too far.

He bent and kissed my lips with lingering tenderness. A chisel split my heart in two as cleanly as a piece of granite. The pain pierced my soul.

"The fate and fortune that come, Isis, it is the Gods that send them."

I had been taught a thousand ways to make a man desire me. Now there was nothing I could say or do to make him stay. He was gone as quickly and silently as he had come. I had a terrible feeling that I would never see him again.

Rasheed

I saw Barb at the bar at the same time she saw me. Tall and thin like a model, with a shiny helmet of platinum hair, she's easy to spot in a crowd. She smiled and waved discreetly. Perched on one of the high, leather bar chairs, she faced two men standing with their backs to me. One was blond, the other dark-haired. I already liked the square of their shoulders and the cut of their suits. Money and confidence. I could see it from across the room.

"Hi, Barb! I made it." I kissed her on the cheek before turning around.

My knees went weak, and I gasped out loud. Barb grabbed my arm and kept me on my feet. Standing just in front of me, dressed in a charcoal silk suit with a blue paisley tie, was River God

Well, River God with green eyes. I had the sense to realize I was staring at him with a gaping mouth and snapped my teeth together. If he recognized me, he didn't show it, but had the same amused half-smile on his face as the morning I first saw him on the banks of the Nile.

Tailored to fit perfectly over his broad shoulders, his suit narrowed at the waist. It took no effort at all to visualize the triangular torso underneath. He looked straight at me, or I would have glanced down at his muscular thighs to picture the generous, good parts between.

His sensuous lips had been carved by the same master sculptor. He had thick black hair now, styled in an expensive salon cut. He was shorter. No, he was the same. I was wearing three-inch heels, and my eyes were on level with his luscious mouth. I stared at him. The other three stared at me.

"You look exactly like someone I used to know," I said lamely. I couldn't think of anything else.

His half-smile was amused, but inviting. He might not recognize me, but he was definitely interested.

"You look like you could use a drink." His voice was incredibly, impossibly, the same.

In fact, everything about him was the same as River God, except his suit and hair—and the green eyes. Barb introduced him as Rasheed. His blond Nordic friend was Lars.

We settled in one of the small rooms just off the lounge, semi-private, with walls covered in traditional oil paintings in gilt frames. An ochre velvet sofa was against the wall. Plush velvet armchairs, one on each end, formed a U around a low, gleaming mahogany table.

I sank into the down-filled sofa cushions and crossed my black-silky legs. My skirt rode up to mid-thigh. The red patent of my heels shone in the yellow light. Rasheed eased into the chair at the end of the coffee table, just to my left.

He radiated an energy that was both animal and sensual. Just sitting next to him rendered me without a will of my own. I sensed that he knew it.

He didn't try to make conversation, but looked around, observing. I decided to be silent and mystical—like Isis. I glanced slyly at the muscles of his thighs stretching his silk trousers and barely resisted spreading my legs, opening myself to his touch, inviting his fingers to my wet.

Sipping my Plymouth martini, toying with the olive on a plastic stick, I studied him from under lowered lashes. It was not my imagination. Rasheed looked exactly like River God. But more than that, he *felt* like him. It was the way he moved and his voice—and the way his eyes probed for secrets.

I thought he'd forgotten me. Then he suddenly turned and caught me staring at him. The corners of his lips curved up again ever so slightly, and he leaned into me, the silk fabric of his suit tightening across his shoulders. He didn't try to hide the bulge in his pants. I could smell his cologne, faint but exotic.

His look was magnetic. I couldn't have torn my eyes away if I wanted to.

"I know," he breathed, tracing his middle finger lightly over my knee and up toward the hem of my skirt at mid-thigh. "I really feel you, too."

An electric shock ran straight up the inside of my loin.

"Listen to me. Don't say a word." His voice was low and urgent. "I want you to come with me to my hotel. I don't want you to say no."

I felt a twinge of fear. He looked and sounded like River God; he even *felt* like River God, but could I trust Rasheed to *be* like him?

Intense heat radiated from his body; I burned as if next to a furnace. The power of his muscles pulsed in his silk suit.

He put his hand on my upper thigh, very close to the Gateway to Pleasure, searing through layers of fabric and stocking. I envisioned a brand on my flesh in the shape of his palm.

"You don't have to worry about anything happening that you don't want," he said.

I looked at his mouth only inches from mine and knew there was only one thing I wanted.

When he leaned forward and brushed my lips with his he was tender. He put his fingers in my hair and kissed me again. His tongue found mine. He was gentle and full of longing.

"I desire you more than any woman I have ever known or seen."

His words riveted me; they were precisely the same as 2,500 years ago—or was it only five hours? I couldn't make sense out of this; it made no sense. But he had said those exact words to me before, and then walked away. I wasn't going to let that happen again.

"Okay," I whispered and nodded my head. "Okay."

The Wynn

Rasheed had a suite at the Wynn, in the tower with private entrance and check-in. We rode the elevator in silence to the top floor. Ceiling-to-floor windows looked out on Trump Tower and the blazing lights of Vegas Valley. I was aware of nothing but the heat of Rasheed's body. When he put his hand on the small of my back, my flesh blistered. Quiet words were exchanged with Gamel and Marcos, and they disappeared.

"They will stay away. I've given orders to be alone," he breathed in my ear as his arms went around my waist, pulling me back into him.

Hadn't I said the same words to him in my pink marble pool with white lotus blossoms?

He lifted my hair with one hand and held me tight with the other. He kissed each vertebra down the back of my neck and between my shoulder blades. How did our bodies just melt into each other?

I still had on my heels; my pelvis tilted into his. I felt him grow hard as stone against my hips while his hand moved from my waist down across my belly. He pushed hard on the tip of my womb with the base of his palm, his hand cupping my mound, burning hot through the knit of my dress.

I moaned low in my throat. I wanted him to stroke me like a cat. I would roll onto my back and give him my belly, my legs spread wide.

His hand traveled down my loin to the knee and then up the

back of my thigh to caress my buttocks, all the while kissing the nape of my neck and my shoulders. He let my hair fall. His free hand found my breast. When he touched my erect nipple through my bra and my dress, I cried out.

We stood like that for an eternity, my back to his front, his hands stroking me all over. We swayed back and forth, something primordial coursing through our veins.

Then he turned me in his arms and kissed me long and deep. I pressed my thighs against his and felt him huge on my belly, an iron post. When I put my hand down to fondle him through his trousers, it was his time to moan.

Low lights burned in the room; a mirror covered an entire wall, reflecting our silhouettes against the Vegas night sky. I glimpsed a lush king bed through an open double doorway.

He eased the zipper of my dress, the slider inching slowly past each tooth. I unbuckled his belt and unzipped his pants. He slid my dress off my shoulders and it dropped to my ankles, bunching on top of the shiny red heels. I slipped his trousers down his thighs, and they fell to his polished loafers.

We didn't say a word. We didn't even kiss. We wanted no distraction from the unveiling.

I helped him out of his jacket, loosening his tie and lifting it over his head. His starched shirt was snowy white in the red and black room. I undid every tiny button and slowly unfastened the gold cuff links at his wrists. When the shirt came off, I had my first sight of his bronzed chest and flat belly. No doubt about it, this was River God. I licked his erect nipples just once.

My fingers tugged at the elastic band of his trunks and pulled them down. I labored to breathe. Heart pounding and blood rushing all around inside my head, I went to my knees and took him in my mouth. He filled me almost to the throat. My head slid back and forth, pumping. His body shook, every muscle tense and rock hard.

"Do not move," he whispered with his hands on my face, lifting me to my feet. "I want it to last."

More words from the past. Was this real or a dream?

His hands slid around me, undid my bra and eased the straps off my shoulders. He was slow, deliberate, not in a hurry. My breasts were swollen white mounds with blushing halos, nipples aflame. He took one in each hand and a sound caught in his throat. His face took on a new light.

He moved his thumbs back and forth, back and forth, across the inflamed tips. I arched my back to bring my hard, aching nipples closer to his lips, begging him silently to take me into his mouth. At the first touch of his moist tongue, I would explode.

Instead he slid one hand under my panties and between my thighs. He brought back his hand, looked at his dripping fingers, and spread my own wet on my breast.

The first rolling wave of an orgasm washed through my womb. I moaned louder with each surge. If he had not held me fast, I could not have stood.

Without hurry, he eased my panties down past the slim garters to join my crumpled dress. Panting, near sobbing, I lowered my head to his chest. I didn't know a body so limp could still stand. He held me stable, dragging my clothes away with his foot as I shifted balance from one leg to the other.

At last, I stood naked in black silk stockings, black and red garters and red patent shoes.

He kicked his own clothes away and faced me, swollen knob glistening, erection probing the air. His hands were on my hips, pulling me forward, sliding his rod between my clasped legs. I locked my thigh muscles and rocked back and forth, astride him, riding at a slow pace. His hardness was pressing on my swollen bud throbbing again with life.

Engorged beast between my clenched legs, he walked me backward to the bed, moving us as one person. Like dancers in a waltz, our eyes locked in a spinning room, he lowered me, his eyes fixed on mine.

He kissed my forehead, then each eyelid, the tip of my nose and then full on the mouth, his lips smothering mine, sucking languidly, his tongue penetrating and unhurried. Lingering long over each kiss, he still took his time.

I was wild to feel him inside me, to fill me, to pound me. But I surrendered on the lush covers of the bed and let him do with me what he willed. He knew every sensitive spot to touch and exactly how much pressure to bear. He knew my secret places and laid claim to them all.

His finger hooked under the elastic of my left garter and slipped it slowly down the long length of my leg and over my foot. He rolled the stocking carefully over my knee, along my calf, and past my toes. One kiss on the arch of my foot, and just as slowly, he removed the right garter and then the stocking, ending with his lips on each toe. He kissed the shallow red marks left by each garter, first high on the left thigh, then on the right.

When I first felt his tongue on my clitoris, I actually relaxed— home again after lifetimes of being lost.

He sucked and licked and sucked more. His teeth teased while shocks jolted my body. An electric current pulsed through the soft under-bottom of my buttocks. When he sensed my need unbearable, he pulled himself up the length of my body, and I felt the tip of him at my gate. I wrapped my arms around his broad back and thrust my hips toward him, begging him to plunge deep.

And then, at last, he was full inside me. We both exhaled deep at the same moment, a long sigh echoing across eternity. At first he didn't move. We breathed in and out together. My vagina pulsed, on fire, swallowing him whole.

Like a starved beast, he began to devour me. He pounded and pounded, his hands grasping my buttocks to give him more leverage and better control the rhythm. I raised my legs high into the air so that he could plough deeper still.

Lust replaced tenderness. Animal sounds growled from our throats. A wave crested and a rapid succession of endless contractions of pure ecstasy rolled through me. His body convulsed, froze, and then shuddered. He collapsed on top of me. I could feel his heart throbbing in his chest next to mine.

We slept. I slept. The sky was barely light when he woke me. Rasheed was dressed in a fresh shirt, pressed suit, and a blue tie. His eyes were shiny bright, glittery like emeralds. I looked up at him in surprise.

He sat on the bed next to me and traced my features with his fingertip as if he were memorizing each one.

"I have to go now."

"But—" I started to interrupt him.

He placed his finger on my lips.

"Sh-h-h-h. Listen to me. There are things I can't tell you. Things you mustn't know. It's better this way."

I stared at him in disbelief. He wanted secrets after last night? We'd been like one body, no division, nothing separating us.

"When will I see you again? I don't know anything about you. I don't have your cell number—or your email." I was in a panic. For a microsecond I even thought of Facebook.

"I know how to find you." He smiled his secret half-smile, not of amusement, but sweet with longing.

He could walk away though; he had the strength for that. He leaned down and kissed me with such tenderness my heart cracked, again with the same chisel. The pain this time was also the same.

"We have known each other before, Isis, and we will know each other again."

"No-o-o-o!" I cried out.

But he was gone.

Not for long, though. I knew where to find him. I had the Red Mirror.

The Nile

The air was utterly still except for a hum in my ears. I drifted with no birdsong, no sound of hammer on stone, no rustle of wind through the palms. The hum was not constant, but more a repeating subtle rise and crest, a kind of "swoosh," somewhat like the sea trapped in a conch, but without any hint of a roar.

The Nile! The sound was the current swirling under and all around the cedar hull. I was back.

Golden sunshine filtered through saffron drapes. Not even a faint breath of breeze relieved the heaviness in the air. A light layer of perspiration swelled on my skin.

Behind Qeb-ha, the old eunuch priest, I saw Goliath rising from the afternoon sleep, his skin glistening like polished ebony in the sunlight. The muscles across his shoulders rippled as he adjusted his white kilt and headdress. His legs were twice as long as Qeb-ha's and powerful enough to break the eunuch's neck with one squeeze.

The pleasure from my River God was great beyond compare, but yesterday's drunkenness does not quench today's thirst. I needed satisfaction, and I would have it with Goliath.

"Qeb-ha." I tore my eyes away from the Nubian. "When we moor for the night, I wish to bathe in the Nile. The day has been long and hot."

Qeb-ha stepped quickly forward to the curtain.

"Isenkhebe Nefrusobek is aware that the God Seth waits in the shadows for the innocent to lose their way."

"I shall take the Nubian for protection. He looks as if he could battle Seth Himself and emerge the victor. Please arrange it."

But even as I spoke, I saw by the mob of merchants trading mountains of Egyptian grain for ivory tusks from Sudan—or earthen jars filled with oils and wine from Cyprus—that there would be no place I could bathe in the rushes with the Nubian.

I had daydreamed all afternoon of the cool of the Nile on my skin, of rising from the water, my body wet, my nipples erect. I would order Goliath to follow me into the grasses and lie on his back. I would lick him and suck him until he was a stone post. He dare not touch me; he would be too afraid.

And then straddling him, slowly—so slowly—I would lower myself onto his giant pedestal. I could never sink all the way. My throbbing lotus would scream out each time I moved up and down his shaft. I would dangle my ripe breasts in front of his thick lips, teasing him with a forbidden fruit he must never taste. And when my aching bud fully flowered in its lust, I would throw back my head and call out to the Goddess as tsunami waves crashed in my surf.

Oh, it would have been divine. But even I could see it was not possible this night, in this place.

Why couldn't Goliath with his glossy taut skin stretched over bulging muscles be here close to me instead of this puffy old eunuch?

"I am who I am, not by my own choosing," Qeb-ha said as solemnly as possible in his high-pitched voice. "Man, even a godly man, cannot alter the life the Gods assign him."

My face went hot; he had read my thoughts. I busied myself with a sip of wine, avoiding his eyes.

"We sail in the morning for Khent-min. May the Goddess protect Isenkhebe and bring sweet dreams."

He bowed low and then moved clumsily through the break in the reed curtains. I was left alone with my own ideas about sweet dreams.

Temple of Min

After massaging perfumed oil into my skin until it glowed, my ladies lined my eyes with *kohl* and dyed my lips and nipples deep red with pomegranate juice. The slim cut of my sheer gown molded to my breasts, hips and belly. Nothing was left to the imagination. I chose a shoulder-length wig doused with gardenia essence and plaited with yellow silk tassels.

With Goliath leading the way through the busy streets of Khent-min, I went straight to the Temple of Min, the god of male fertility. It was easy to find. A wide, crowded street lined with billboard-sized paintings of Min with his sacred erection led straight to the pylon.

Just outside the pylon gate, I stopped at a stone vendor's booth.

"Would the priestess care to trade a blessing for a fine statue of the God Min?"

The vendor gave me lewd smile showing black teeth. His hungry eyes didn't hide his lust. They traveled from my nipples to my ankles and up again before meeting my eyes.

"Give me that small basalt statue," I teased him, "and I shall bless you with a faience crocodile charm to make your Min rise. Let us pray that one charm is enough to aid such a needy member."

He laughed. Even more black teeth showed.

The Min statue fit neatly in my palm. I stroked the smooth, glossy stone with my index finger. Jet black and naked, the city's patron god held a flail in his right hand and an erect penis in his left. All Goliath, my own black god of fertility, needed was the whip.

Would I use it on him or command him to use it on me? Which would bring the greater thrill?

"The priestess has her own Min, I see," remarked the vendor with a smirk. He nodded his head in the direction of Goliath. "If the Nubian is the lady's taste, she can find more like him at the Temple."

The Temple was eerily quiet after the din of the city—and dark. Long shafts of dust-filled sunbeams angled to a polished stone floor. Vast murals covered the walls. Most depicted the giant-phallused Min seated at a banquet table piled high with *cos* lettuce oozing white milk from its tall leaves. White bulls and barbed arrows covered a forest of square columns.

A nine-foot statue carved of black basalt with a phallus as long as a man's arm and as thick as a log towered over our heads. Kneeling at the stone altar, I placed a garland of lotus blossoms at Min's massive feet and sang a hymn of praise.

Min, Bull of the Great Phallus
You are the Great Male, the owner of all females.
The Bull who is united with those of the sweet love,
of beautiful face and of painted eyes,
The goddesses are glad, seeing your perfection.

The room was hot and the air thick with frankincense, but not thick enough to mask the smell of sex. Two priests in a trance ejaculated into silver bowls like the dozens already at Min's feet. The worship of Min must take many enticing forms, the best hidden in secret sanctuaries behind closed golden doors.

I wandered down a narrow corridor, lit by torches in niches shared with basalt Mins with his erect member. Goliath followed close behind. If I didn't stumble on an obliging priest, then I would find a private corner and measure the Nubian's bounteous manhood against the new standards set by these black statues.

We turned a sharp corner, and the hallway dead-ended in a closed wooden door decorated with brass studs. I heard lyre and pipe music on the other side, and the sound of chanting. These voices were deep, not at all like the high-pitched chorus in a Hathor Temple.

I quietly lifted the latch and eased the heavy door open a crack.

A dozen men or more, all nude, engaged in the worship of the almighty phallus. One bent over, sucking the engorged penis of one man, while another penetrated him from behind. Another penetrated the second man until they formed a complicated endless Gordian knot of copulating men, who at the same time performed *fellatio*. Even I, trained in a thousand ways to give pleasure, had never seen anything like this.

A low dais dominated the far end of the small chamber; two men lay back in low chairs. I recognized them at once as the Crown Prince and his Scribe who had shared me in the temple.

The Crown Prince, his face in a trance, was being serviced by two pubescent boys busy at his crotch. A great wreath of lotus blossoms draped his nude chest. His companion, the Scribe, lounged in a chair of carved phalluses with a young child not more than ten between his legs.

Their depravity had certainly not been cured by our ritual in Hathor's Inner Sanctum. With the boy's hair gripped in his fist, the Scribe jerked the child's head back and forth, back and forth, in a wild, ruthless rhythm.

Maybe it was my thought of the Goddess that disturbed his psyche. I'm certain I didn't make a sound. But the Scribe suddenly looked straight at me. His eyes widened, and he sat up, pushing the boy's head away. His evil rushed at me like a thousand buzzing hornets.

I shoved the door shut with my shoulder, leaning into it for just a moment to stop shaking. My heart hammered; my palms sweat. I turned to Goliath to motion for us to get out, but it was not the Nubian who stood behind me. The metallic insignia of the Royal Guard flashed in the torchlight.

A hand went over my mouth; another grabbed my upper arm,

dragging me around the corner and pushing me through an open doorway. There were no windows and no lighted lamps. It was black as the darkest night. The flicker of torches cast dancing shadows in the hallway outside.

I struggled to free my arm, but the weight of the soldier's body crushed me to the wall. Sobbing from terror, I tried to bite the hand on my mouth.

"Say nothing, Isis," he whispered. "Nothing at all."

O Hathor, I worship at Your feet for the gift You have brought me!

The voice in my ear was River God. My whole body trembled so violently, I'm not sure I could have stood if he hadn't held me up against the wall. Instead of sobbing from terror, I burst into tears of relief.

"Listen to me—and listen to me carefully." His fingers dug into my upper arms. "These are dangerous men—capable of any evil. You must leave now—no hesitation—now! This is no time for your foolishness."

"But I thought you were in Thebes," I whispered. His touch felt real enough. His scent was real enough. But I still feared I was dreaming.

"The Pharaoh commands me to escort the Crown Prince to Saïs."

I heard the words but was only aware of his heat. I kissed the base of his throat, above his leather chest armor. He tasted of sweat and myrrh. In spite of the tension, I felt him harden against my womb. Our bodies were so taut that one flick of a finger would shatter us into a million small pieces. I was as fragile as glass.

I put my hands on the back of his head and lifted my face to his. He resisted for a brief moment, and then gave in. The hardness in his mouth softened; he was as tender as the night of the bath, as tender as the night at the Wynn.

My life force flowed into him; I was hardly aware of where he ended, and I began. Our need for each other bound us so tight, we might have been shackled in chains. But he had the strength to break away.

"Now go. Go! You were never here. Do you understand? You were never here."

He released me from the wall, took my arm more gently, and steered me down a new corridor, the Nubian on our heels. I heard voices in the distance calling out, "Guard!"

Bright sunlight blinded me when he pulled open a small red door in the rough stone wall. It was a tiny side street, not more than four feet wide.

"Do not speak of what you have seen to anyone, Isis. Do you hear me—anyone?"

He didn't follow us into the alley but closed the door without a word of goodbye.

O Hathor! River God and I traveled the same river. We both sailed to Saïs. The Universe wanted us together. My feet didn't touch the pavement all the way to the boat.

The Hunt

As much wine as I'd consumed, I couldn't fall asleep. I saw myself riding in a fast chariot—bow and arrow in my hands, jewelled dagger at my waist—bouncing over the shining stones under a cloudless sky, hooves thundering on the hard ground with the power of the horses vibrating along the shaft, rising up through my loins to thrill me.

I throbbed at the memory of River God's lips, the pressure of his manhood against my belly, his chest on my breasts.

Rising silently, I padded softly across the deck. My ladies slept in the corner; no one stirred. I slipped without a sound through the bamboo curtains into the night. The yacht harbor was quiet. Even the gamblers had gone silent.

It took a few moments for my eyes to adjust to the starlight. The crew lay forward on the deck, wrapped in linen sheets, some curled on their sides, others lying on their backs like mummies. Goliath should have been easy to spot among the Egyptians; his mass was double that of most. How delightful it would be, at last, to feel his 'double' manhood probe my womb.

But the Nubian was not to be seen. Mosquitoes buzzed round my ears. One bit me on the forearm, and I squashed it. A tiny spot of blood showed black on my pale skin.

"Does Isenkhebe Nefrusobek require something?"

Qeb-ha startled me. Curse of Seth, I hated his squeaky voice.

"Where is the Nubian?" I asked boldly.

Goliath was my slave. Could I not do with him as I pleased?

"He is with Ankh-hor's men preparing for the hunt."

Even in the starlight I could see Qeb-ha's small smile at my disappointment.

"Is there something I can do?" he asked.

I glared at him. He knew what I wanted and that a eunuch was useless.

Swirling my swollen lotus with my fingertip dipped first in my wet canal, waiting for sleep that wouldn't come, I pleasured myself with images of muscled Nubians and bronzed Egyptians pounding me against the rail of the chariot.

All the while, sniffing the mating scent, tossing their silver-twined manes, massive stallions snorted and pawed the ground.

Anything could happen. Something would happen. I would make sure it did.

Tomorrow was the Hunt.

Hetmus-hor

Welcome and Blessings, Isenkhebe Nefrusobek! I am Hetmus-hor, son of Ankh-hor, and honored to lead you in hunt on this most magnificent of days."

Hetmus-hor stood a head taller than the other men. He was as handsome as Tutankhamun and covered in as much gold. A white triangular headdress framed a bronzed face with a straight nose and shining red-flecked brown eyes outlined in *kohl*. His dazzling smile flashed perfect white teeth.

He bent low and kissed the lapis Hathor Ring on my hand. I could easily envision his broad shoulders wrestling a lion to the ground. I could easily imagine him wrestling me. When he straightened, my eyes were on level with his wide chest clad in an elaborate leather vest patterned in gold sunbursts. Ra rising over the mountains was not brighter than Hetmus-hor.

"You shall have my best charioteer," he announced. "My chariot will be in the lead. You shall follow directly behind with your Nubian in third position."

He still held my ringed hand when he lowered his voice and leaned so close that his speckled eyes were only inches away.

"If that is agreeable to you, Isis?" he asked with a hint of tease. His eyes twinkled when he said "Isis." He had the expression of a naughty boy delightfully testing his boundaries. He dared use my private name, and he knew me not at all. Hetmus-hor was indeed a confident man.

I pulled my hand back, but not in such a brusque manner as to discourage him. Only to rein him in a little. My eyes told him everything he needed to know.

"You move as fast as your chariot, Sir. Do not spend all your strength at the beginning of the hunt."

He laughed, a great booming sound, throwing his head back. It was all a game to him. He had been born to the hunt. There would be other moves. He looked forward to them with pleasure, as did I.

"By Horus, I love a woman with wit. If you hunt as well as you speak, we shall come home with enough trophies for another feast."

Never dimming his smile, he took my hand again to lead me to the shade of the sycamore grove.

"Bring wine," he called out. "Let us toast our honored guest, Isenkhebe Nefrusobek, who graces us with her beauty and intelligence."

He certainly knew how to flatter; charming words came easily to him. He clearly noticed how his compliments to my wit had pleased me, and he adapted his game quickly. I had the feeling he'd never struggled for anything in his life.

If the rumors the sloe-eyed woman whispered in my ear at last night's feast had any truth, he certainly never struggled to win a woman's favor.

"*Hetmus-hor is as charming as a courtesan,*" she had confided with a knowing smile. "*He is quite known in Hermopolis for his powers of persuasion. There are more than a few wives and daughters who would attest that to be persuaded by Hetmus the Great Hunter is most pleasurable indeed.*"

I had no objection to being persuaded; we clearly both wanted the same thing. I already envisioned us alone in the desert with the aroma of wild herbs in the hot air. I would twist my legs around his slim waist and hang from his broad shoulders. Then we would see if Hetmus the Hunter lived up to his reputation.

Servants appeared with tin goblets of unwatered Delta wine. The morning air was splendid in the crisp sunshine; there was no trace yet of the heat that would come.

Hetmus lifted his goblet to me and recited:

"May thou spend millions of years,
thou lover of Thebes,
Sitting with thy face to the north wind,
thy green eyes beholding felicity."

He had stolen the words of from the chalice of Tutankhamun but substituted green eyes for me. I gave him the favor of a smile with a bold look that left the door wide open for possibilities.

"A toast to the kill!" a nobleman shouted.

Another called out, "Isenkhebe! Isenkhebe! Queen of the Hunt!"

Everyone, including the servants with the horses, cheered. I never felt more alive.

Lion of the Desert

O n your face, Egyptian whore, before the great General
Sher, Lion of the Desert and Beloved of Cambyses, King
of the World."

The guards pushed me first to my knees and then shoved my face
into the dusty rug. The General reclined on cushions, his uniform
replaced with a robe, silk like mine, but deep green.

"Bring her up to her knees. Let us see her face washed of desert
filth and tears."

They pulled me to rest on my haunches, the gown flowing around
me, shimmering gold in the yellow of the oil lamps. The women had
cleaned my wig and covered it with a long scarf of emerald silk,
woven with gold thread in an intricate arabesque pattern. It cascaded
around my shoulders in stark contrast to the yellow of the robe. My
amethyst earrings dangled from my earlobes.

The men who had grabbed me after the sandstorm scattered the
hunt were there. And a bevy of fierce-looking officers, all with the
same ribboned beards and long, coiled hair. They stood while the
General lounged. Unlike Egyptians, the *kohl* around their eyes was
drawn to make them appear perfectly round. They stared at me. I
didn't need a mirror to tell me how I looked. I saw it clearly by the
lust in their eyes. But I saw hatred, too.

They talked to each other without looking away from my face. I
understood Persian well enough to hear them discuss if I should be
killed now and taken down to the plain and dumped. They reasoned

that a search party would find me and take my body home. They would have time to finish their mission for Cambyses.

The General rose from his seat. The others fell silent. He loomed over me, a great bull with a massive chest and legs like the thick columns of a temple. I looked up into his eyes and saw a slight spark of something human. I stared straight at him and refused to blink.

Seconds passed. No one spoke or moved. The wicks in the lamps spluttered, making small hissing sounds like a thousand serpents.

"Leave us.'

It was all he said. He never took his eyes away. We had locked into battle; he was not accustomed to defeat.

When the last man had exited, his face relaxed just a fraction; an ironic smile curved his lips. He stared at me still but with less intensity.

It was he who turned away first. He reached for a goblet on a brass tray set on a short wooden tripod and sank again onto his cushions, contemplating me from across the carpets.

"I shall call you *Ishtar,*" he said idly. "You are the glittering evening star in a lavender desert sky."

"I am worth much to my people, Your Excellency." I thought it wise to use a title of respect. This man held my life in his thick fingers. My voice, strong and clear in the small space of the tent, reflected none of the terror I felt.

His face registered shock when I spoke, perhaps that I was fluent in his language, or perhaps that I dared speak without permission. He studied me for what seemed like an eternity. I was deciding if I dared say anything else when his eye went to my hand.

"What does it mean that you wear the ring of the Goddess of Love?"

"Hathor is more than the Goddess of Love, esteemed General," I answered, hoping to convince him of my importance. "She is the Solar Goddess, the Gold-of-the-Gods."

His face turned hard in an instant; his upper lip curled, exposing yellowed, square teeth, big and strong enough to grind raw flesh.

"Do not presume to instruct me about the inferior gods of Egyptian dogs," he snarled. "Why do you wear the ring?"

"I am a High Priestess in the cult of Hathor. I assure you the Temple will pay whatever you demand for my return, safe and untouched."

"And if you are *touched*? What then, High Priestess of Hathor?"

I didn't answer but met his eyes, cold and soulless as a predator's, directly and without flinching. He was a hybrid of bull and lion with only occasional glimpses of man.

"I am not in need of a ransom from effeminate Nile priests." His voice was as frigid as a winter wind.

He sipped his wine, studying me over the rim of the goblet. He waited for my response. Everything depended on the next moment—my future and my life.

"Could it be possible for a lion of Persia to have needs not met?" My voice was both coy and bold with the tease of promise.

I saw his pupils dilate, even surrounded by his coal black iris. His eyelids jerked slightly; I had touched a nerve. He tried to keep his face stone, but revealed all in the blink of his eye. No matter his words, he was a man of many needs, some never met.

He sipped more from his goblet and drew smoke from his pipe. I smelled the same sweet odor as in the women's tent.

"I have a proposal for you, Ishtar," he said as casually as if he invited me to tea. "I sense you like a challenge."

He paused and drew deep on the pipe, slowly exhaling the smoke in a perfect ring.

"I hear that certain priestesses of Hathor have—what shall we say?—exceptional talents. Your reputation reaches as far as Persia."

He hesitated only long enough to gauge my reaction. I showed him nothing.

"If you please me, you will belong to me and me alone, but only as long as I am pleased. When you no longer please, I shall return you to the women's tent, where you can please the other men. And when you please them no more, I shall have you killed."

I watched his lips move in his impassive face. How easily he talked of my inevitable death. It had been decided; it was only a question of when.

"What do you say to that, Ishtar?"

Not more than one minute passed. Instead of answering, I rose from my knees to my feet in one movement. I no longer felt the pain in my body. I moved slowly toward him. The emerald scarf slipped from my head to the carpet; the gold in my black wig glittered. The bells on my sash jingled seductively, like the tinkle of the *sistrum* in the temple.

I fixed my eyes on his and knelt at his feet. I took the goblet from his hand and placed it on the brass tray beside his cushions.

They teach in the temple that there is a sexual power inside us that when summoned, oozes from our pores. It's an animal energy that conjures up base desire. But the magic of Hathor is special; it transforms raw lust into a promise of pleasure and satisfaction known only by the gods.

I turned on the Power. My body radiated animal sex mingled with the potent allure of intense sensuality—and deep mystery.

"I have secrets," my aura teased, "wonderful secrets that only I can share."

Electricity sparked in the air. Great sensuous waves rolled over the General. Mesmerized, he barely breathed; his eyes fixed on my every movement.

I slowly untied the purple silk sash of his robe. I pulled it free in one long motion and dropped it carefully next to the pillows. His eyes blinked when he felt its slick slide across the small of his back. I opened the front of his gown, folding the cloth back without hurry. I never took my eyes from his. His breathing came shallow and fast.

He was nude under the robe. I let my eyes wander. I caressed him with only my gaze, appreciating the muscles of his broad chest, the mass of thick, curly hair, like a beast. His nipples were already erect. I looked long at each one, but did not touch him.

I followed the line of hair down his hard belly. It crossed his navel and descended into a great black bush. His thighs were thick tree trunks. His manhood stood erect and hard, an obelisk to the sky. It looked as thick as my fist. I leaned back on my heels to study him. My eyes followed the vein down the underside to the huge swollen sacks at its base. The man was truly a bull.

I started with the sacks. I took one in my mouth while I gripped the other in my hand—hard. The General gave an involuntary cry. I sucked harder and gripped harder. The rougher my touch, the more he moaned.

When I felt him near the edge, I stopped and traced my tongue up the vein. I massaged his balls gently, a new caress, light and ethereal. When I arrived at the head, I eased his foreskin down with my fingers. I pulled harder and harder, the glossy bulb erupting out with each downward tug. I could see the skin stretching almost to breaking point; small droplets of clear liquid bubbled from the tip.

I pumped him up and down, up and down, while squeezing his shaft in my fist. The rhythm was steady. He thrust his hips for me to go faster, but I stayed in control. I took my time, tormenting him with his own urgency.

I slowed and put my tongue to the head, exploring the surface, licking its smoothness, biting with my sharp teeth. I stuck the pointed tip of my tongue into the small opening there. One hand held the shaft; the other was back on his balls, pulling and kneading, first rough, then gentle, then rough again. As full as his sacks were, I managed to have both in one hand.

The General twisted and panted. Each time he came close to exploding, I stopped. How many times could I bring him to the edge before I let him go over?

Putting my knees between his thighs, I forced them apart. I lowered my open mouth onto his manhood and took him in as far as I could. I sucked him with all my strength. I rocked him hard, my hands on his hips to give me more force, his shaft thrusting deep into my throat.

And then when I sensed he was just there, I pinched his erect nipple hard and put my finger at the lip of his anus and plunged in.

He erupted with a great shaking and bolting like a wild horse. I held on to him, my finger in his anus, twisting his nipple without mercy, his manhood filling my mouth until he collapsed and breathed in great gulps.

He had never touched me, except to hold my head when I sucked him. I had never opened my robe. He lay spent, his massive chest rising high and falling. I rolled back on my haunches and to my feet to stand over him. I said nothing.

The General opened his eyes, looking up at me. There was something new there. Just a flicker, but it was a start.

Reaching down slowly, I folded his robe across his bare chest and loins. I handed him his goblet of wine and stepped backwards, folding to my knees again on the carpet, in front of him. Not one word had been spoken since his life-and-death challenge to me.

I waited. I looked straight at him, unblinking. I believe my face was expressionless. I tried hard that it was. Inside I quaked. I had given it everything I had.

When he spoke, his voice was almost human.

"You have gained yourself a night, Ishtar. The reputation of Hathor is well deserved." A tiny spark of delight twinkled in his eyes. "Maybe even more than could be imagined."

He started to dress.

"Go to the harem and sleep. No one will approach you."

A soldier appeared to take me to the women's tent, but not before I saw something glint on the table. It was the jewel-encrusted hilt of my hunting dagger.

Emerald Sash

Would this be the last dawn of my life in this world? A soldier shook my shoulder and barked for me to get up. I still had on the yellow gown, my wig on my head. Sleep had taken me the moment I lay down, and if I journeyed to the land of dreams, I was too exhausted to notice.

When we came to the General's tent, the guard pushed me roughly through the flap. I immediately prostrated myself. I didn't want my face shoved into the dusty carpet again.

When the General snapped his fingers, I rose to my knees and faced him.

He was drinking hot liquid from a ceramic cup, his massive feet clad in heavy sandals propped on a cushion. He had on his leather tunic with a short kilt. Did the man ever sleep?

"My officers want me to kill you, Ishtar. They say you are endangering the mission. What do you say to that?"

His tone was lazy, as if he casually mused over the fate of a goat.

Did he want me to beg for my life? Would that elicit pleasure— or scorn? One should not give way to the tongue when not asked. I would not give way to my tongue, until I knew *why* I had been asked.

He continued in the same casual tone.

"I told them that it would be a pity to destroy such a creature as you. But then, they do not know you as I do."

He waited. He expected a response. I had to gamble. I had no choice. I modulated my voice carefully in a tone confident with the hint of challenge.

"You told me that I would be yours as long as I pleased you. Have I not pleased you? Or are you not a man of your word?"

He actually laughed. He threw back his head and gave a mighty roar of a laugh. He smiled at me. I saw his strong, yellow-stained teeth. His eyes crinkled in the corners.

"I am certain, Ishtar, that there are few men you would not please."

He refilled his cup and settled back; he appeared utterly at ease.

"I value beauty, and I value brains, but I value talent most of all. And you, beautiful and clever Ishtar, have been given an extraordinary talent. It would be a crime to waste it."

For the first time I thanked my mother for developing my special abilities with all the skills of her cult. My father's tutors gave me language, so I could understand and spar. And of course, I thanked Hathor for giving me the Power. I owed my life today to all three.

I waited for a signal, a sign of what he wanted next. He wouldn't tell me, of course. He played the cat to my mouse. He wanted me to squirm, and then he would pounce with his great paw when he was ready.

The General watched me, never taking his eyes away. I looked all around the tent. Neither of us spoke, each waiting to see what the other would do. I saw a whip—the kind Persians use on horses—on top of a pile with saddle pads and a bridle.

I moved the tray of food between us to one side. His pupils dilated. He stopped smiling. I stood up before him and untied the emerald green sash with golden tassels and tinkling bells. The yellow silk gown fell open in front, not all the way, but enough that he could see the curve of my belly, my shaven mound, and a hint of my breast. Taking the sash in my hand, I doubled it, forming a loop.

As fast as a striking cobra, I slipped the loop around his neck and yanked hard. I caught him totally off guard. The little bells tinkled; the tassels swung back and forth. He went wide-eyed with shock. I released the pressure so he could breathe.

"You go too far!" He bellowed like a bull.

My voice cut through the air.

"I have not begun."

I held onto the end of the noose with one hand and reached for the whip with the other. My robe fell open when I stretched, revealing my full breasts, crowned with dusky roses and tightened nipples. He didn't try to remove the sash from around his throat.

Gripping the whip, I lashed him across his biceps; the leather thongs stung his flesh. I jerked hard at the noose at the same time.

A great moan heaved from his bull chest. His manhood rose under the kilt. I lashed him again, on the other arm, harder this time. Angry red welts came up on his skin. His erection grew larger still.

I whipped his thighs, still tightening and releasing the noose with each stroke. He snorted like a wild bull. I expected him to rise up and paw the ground.

I only struck a half dozen times, but each blow was more forceful than the one before. He grabbed the whip with one hand and seized my hand holding the noose with his other. He pulled me on top of him, my soft breasts crushing into the stiff leather of his vest, the metal lions and mesh imprinting a pattern on my skin.

He flipped me forward on my knees like I was a loaf of bread and dragged me backward. I felt his massive rod ram deep into me. Could I survive such a weapon? I feared I would split apart. Thank Horus, he had chosen the canal of my womanhood and not the other.

But he exploded the moment he entered me. He lost control. He held my hips flush against his groin and breathed hard like a runner after a race. Then he released me, shoving me face down on my stomach while he fell back onto the cushions.

I could see through a crack at the base of the tent that Ra had vanquished the serpent of the underworld and begun once again his journey across the sky. I wondered again if this was the last sunrise I would see.

Deadly Bite

C overed in dust and stinking like a stable, the General stomped into the tent, his hungry eyes searching for me. I looked for my death sentence in his face, but if he had decided I must die, I couldn't see it there. He hurried toward me, shedding his armor with each step.

"You smell like a horse," I said calmly. My strength came from somewhere outside me. Inside, I quaked from anxiety and fear.

He stopped short—speechless, his leather vest half on, half off.

I relaxed on one elbow, slightly on my side, accentuating the curve from my shoulder to narrow waist that rose again along my hip. My legs stretched out, ankles resting gracefully one on the other, knee slightly bent, toes pointed. The sapphire blue silk folded on every contour of my body. I stared at him boldly from under half-closed lids and dialed up the Power.

"Water!" He bellowed through the closed flap. "Bring me water for a bath. And food."

He pulled off his thick sandals and tossed them aside, standing in his loose shirt and kilt. Sweat made rivulets in the pale powder on his skin. Stripes from my whip still flamed bright red on his arms and legs. I wondered what his men thought when they saw those.

Pots clanged and voices rose as the camp prepared for the evening meal. Ra was retreating under the western horizon. Other night sounds echoed through the canyon, subtle but different vibrations that went with the changes of texture in the late evening air. I felt it slightly cooler in the stifling tent.

The General grabbed a jug of water and poured a stream down his throat. It spilled into his beard, caked with dust. Why don't Persians shave like civilized people? All that hair was so unclean.

The food arrived first. He sat on cushions in his dirty shirt and kilt, stuffing slabs of fatty meat into his mouth. Bits of it clung to his beard. And he says it's distasteful to eat with women who chatter while they chew.

I saw him as raw animal. I envisioned him returning from battle, covered in human blood, ravenous for the taste of rare meat.

Twilight had settled when they brought the steaming bath water in brass jugs with large copper bowls. Stacks of coarse cloth arrived with it. Small decorated beakers of perfumed oil stood on a round brass tray.

"Do you wish me to bathe you?" I asked politely.

"Do you see anyone else here?" His voice was gruff, but not threatening.

I took several lengths of the cloth and spread them over cushions.

"Lie here," I told him.

He called the guard.

"Do not disturb me. Do not enter unless there is news of the Egyptians."

The guard fixed on the General when he spoke, but I could tell he looked at me out of the corner of his eye. I wondered what camp gossip whispered about me. There must be wild speculation about the Egyptian sorceress who had bewitched their General.

The General settled on the cushions, his massive frame bending with a grace I wouldn't have thought possible in a man his size.

I pulled his shirt over his head and put it aside. Then I removed his kilt and put it on top. He was already erect, but I ignored it.

Beginning with his arms, I wiped the layers of dust away. I moved to his thighs and stroked downward to his calves and ankles, dipping the cloth from time to time in water. When the cloth became too brown, I took a clean one. When the water became brown, I poured fresh.

I rinsed his hair and long beard and wiped the grime from his face. I washed his feet, and between his toes. I bathed him as I would a small child. I did not turn on the Power.

His body relaxed, the erection melted. He closed his eyes and I thought him asleep. But when I started to move away, he opened them and asked, "Where are you going?"

"To get more towels and the oil, Excellency."

I dribbled scented oil into fresh water and swabbed his entire body, now clean of dust and sweat. Only when I gently washed his testicles and penis, did the erection come back.

It had to be dark now. The lamps in the tent gave off a mellow glow. I could hear the camp laughing around the cooking fires, eating the evening meal, enjoying the soft night after a fierce day.

When finished, I took away the jugs and the dirty cloths and put some clean fabric by the bed. The General lay with his eyes closed, relaxed. I brought him his pipe with the sweet smelling smoke and lit it for him. He leaned up against the pillows and drew deep drafts; the muscles in his face calmed even more. He was quite handsome really, in a brutish way.

I slid out of my robe and pulled the caftan over my head; both tumbled to a lush pile. Deliberately, slowly, I straddled him, unhurriedly stretching forward, only the tips of my erect nipples grazing his flesh. I took my time to slither from the black bush nesting his stallion manhood, past his thick waist, to his gorilla chest.

I kissed him deep and caring, my tongue probing the inside of his mouth. No urgency, just languid, very tranquil. The last hint of tension in his massive bulk evaporated into me, and then flowed through me into the thick, hazy air.

My nude body lay full on top of him. The warmth of his skin burned into mine; the beat of his heart reverberated into my chest. My lips pressed softly on his again. He floated up from the cushions.

I kissed him on his broad chest, everywhere, in a language that said, "I adore you." I kissed the red welts on his arms. I kissed his hands and put them to my breasts. He squeezed me, but gently. Expecting pain, I got tenderness.

His hands moved up and down my body; he stroked me, his palms rough and calloused. My skin, still chaffed from the blasting sand, was velvet compared to his battle-worn flesh.

I whispered in his ear, "Let us go to the bed."

He picked me up while still reclining and then stood. My feet dangled in the air. He kissed me as he lay me down. The power and sensibility of it surprised me. I was breathless. He began to make love to me, not animal sex, but a kind of raw passion with tender emotion that moved me.

I stirred; I couldn't help myself. He was overwhelming me.

I stretched my neck so that he would find the trigger points that ignite my fire. He found them. He found them all, and he tasted them all with his wet lips, broad tongue, and sometimes his teeth.

It was building in me. I didn't want to believe it, but I was so wet that the damp was on the inside of my thighs. My nipples were rock hard and pointed. Animal sounds rumbled deep in my throat like the low growls of a lioness.

No more touching. My hand found his stone pedestal, so thick I could scarcely close my fingers around it. I guided him to me and placed him at the gate. He moved his hips slowly and probed a little deeper with each thrust.

My juices flowed so that even he, in his great size, was gliding with ease. He filled me and stretched me, and still I wanted more. I couldn't get enough of him inside me. When he lunged into me, my hips rose to meet him. I hung onto his broad neck while he pounded me amid cries of pleasure, his and mine.

"Deeper," I pleaded. "Deeper!"

My words electrified him. He came to his knees, lifting me with him. He had the strength of ten bulls. He stretched his legs out and held me in his lap with his Min manhood so deep in me that it crushed against the tip of my womb.

My legs locked around his hips. My own weight pushed my swollen bud against his iron shaft.

He rocked me back and forth, and I could only hang my head backwards and plead for mercy. But when he slowed, I begged for more.

When I could bear it no longer, a comet erupted up through my cervix and out the crown of my head. I soared to the stars.

Contraction after contraction pulsed in my womb. It went on forever; I wanted it to go on forever. I held onto his massive arms, my nails digging in his flesh. I would not let go.

He lay me down and moved inside me, slowly. All the way in, and then almost out, before sliding deep again. I stopped swirling and came back to earth. I reached between his legs and took his sacks in my hand, squeezing with each thrust. I stretched for his neck with my lips, and he lowered himself.

I bit him in that place that is my own trigger point. I tasted a drop of blood.

It was the bite that brought him over. His body convulsed; a long, protracted howl escaped his throat. I feared the guards would come, but they didn't. They knew now was no time to enter.

He collapsed on top of me, struggling to catch his breath.

"You are too heavy. I cannot breathe," I whispered into his chest.

He rolled off me and lay spread-eagle on the bed. His eyes closed. His massive chest rose and fell. His manhood lay limp against his thigh.

The jeweled hilt of the dagger was cool to my hand. I didn't think; I didn't hesitate. I grabbed his beard and plunged the blade deep, drawing it across his throat from ear to ear, just like the doe. It took all my strength.

My hand found the green silk scarf, the one that matched my eyes, and I stuffed it in the gaping hole. He choked. His eyes were immense and bewildered. He looked at me in utter disbelief.

"I'm sorry," I whispered to his lips quivering in death throe. "I'm so sorry, but you would never have let me go."

I covered his nude dying body with a blanket. I wanted to dress him but didn't dare take the time.

Grabbing the sandals, I tied them to my feet, my fingers shaking so hard I could barely hold the thongs. After pulling the turquoise caftan over my head, I grabbed the cloth with the bread and water bag and at the last moment, threw the General's dark cape around me; it would blend into the night. I ran to the back of the tent, opened the flap and crawled through. I was out.

Stars filled the night sky. The moon would rise in less than an hour and turn the rocky hills white. I found one of the trails in the cliff face that ascended more slowly, and began picking my way through the gravel and rocks, as silent as I could be. I hardly dared breathe.

The sounds of the camp, the laughter and talking of men, echoed through the ravine. They might even be joking about the General, making lewd suggestions about the Egyptian witch who pleasured him. Of course, they never imagined in their wildest fantasies that he lay dead in a pool of his own blood.

I clutched the bloody dagger in my right hand. If captured, I had to drive the blade deep into my own throat. My own imagination was not wild enough to describe what the Persians would do to me now.

Regret

As Sit-hathor spoke, the Hathor energy flowed through me. I felt the General again—the pain and the ecstasy—and then finally the ride on a comet. I shuddered and exhaled all the air in my lungs; my breath rattled my chest and vibrated in my throat. To my ears the sound was a wail.

"I killed the General, Mother," I whispered. "I made love to him, and then I cut his throat."

Her black eyes opened wide in horror before her lids nearly closed, and she exhaled a long hiss, not unlike that of a cobra.

"He bled to death, Mother. I watched his *Ka* leave his body."

My voice took on a flat quality devoid of emotion. I heard myself speak, yet was detached from the meaning of the words.

"His blood spilled down his chest and onto my hands. It was everywhere. I tried to staunch the bleeding with a green silk scarf."

"Listen to me!" she commanded. "Do not *ever* again speak of love with this animal. You owe him nothing, do you hear? Nothing."

"He had to die, Mother," I sobbed, "but I did not want him to. Can you understand? I did not *want* him to die!"

Sit-hathor leaned forward until I saw nothing but her face. I'd never seen her eyes so glittery, like black glass. Her fingers dug into my shoulders.

"Stop, Isenkhebe! I forbid you to have feelings for that monster!"

I closed my eyes and saw his lifeless eyes. I felt dead myself.

"I had no choice." I said flatly. "It was him or me." At last I was resigned to what was and couldn't be changed.

She relaxed her fingers and kissed me lightly on the forehead. When she spoke again, her voice was matter-of-fact, as if she commented on a household chore.

"Of course you killed him, my daughter. And I hope you cut off his filthy balls and stuffed them in his vile mouth."

Hector

L eaning casually against the frame, Carla's Argentine boyfriend, Hector, waited by a floor-to-ceiling picture window in her bedroom. The Stratosphere looked close enough to reach out and touch.

"Hello, Isis."

I walked right up to him, put my hands on his chest and leaned my head back. He was so tall.

"Hello, Hetmus. I never expected to see you here."

Hector took me by the shoulders and pulled me tight to him, my hands still on his chest, my elbows crushed between us. He was like a man who had thirsted on the desert for days. He wrapped his long arms around me, nearly lifting me off my feet, kissing my lips, my neck, my shoulders, my throat, everywhere he could find flesh. His breath was hot and moist on my skin. An image of him devouring me flashed in my mind; he could have swallowed me whole.

I slipped my arms under his dinner jacket and pulled myself into him, burying my face in his broad chest. I smelled starch and the faintest scent of soap. He was rock hard and huge against my waist. I leaned further into him and swayed back and forth, feeling his hardness roll on my belly.

With no effort at all, he lifted me into his arms, my feet dangling down, just as he had held me in the desert under the shadow of the circling falcon.

"I've waited a few thousand years for this," he breathed in my ear as he carried me to Carla's bed.

There among the silk pillows and pile of guests' fur coats, he lay beside me and ran his long fingers down the length of my body from my face to my ankles, his eyes soaking up my every curve. The heat of his hands warmed me. He stroked me all over; I stretched and purred.

"You are perfect, Isis. I could never tire of touching you."

The bulge between his impossibly long legs grew larger. I slid down the zipper and slipped my fingers first inside the light wool and then through the gap in the soft cotton of his briefs. He throbbed hot and thick in my hand as I milked him.

My fingers swirled on the smooth wet skin of his engorged knob. When I pulled the skin back down his shaft, the knob popped larger and swelled more.

I nibbled him and sucked him and licked the small glistening drops.

Another man might have lain back and let me pleasure him, but not Hector. All the while I fondled him, his hands roamed my body, exploring my every curve.

"Let me pleasure you," he whispered.

Then his long fingers went deep into my canal and straight to a place no other man had ever found. The spot that I'd heard of but believed was a myth. The G-Spot. It existed, all right. O Hathor! Does it ever exist!

Time stopped. I forgot Hector's swollen shaft. I forgot the party outside. I forgot everything except the feel of his fingers rotating on that magic spot. Burning heat radiated deep into my buttocks and loins. My knees relaxed outward. I was spread wide. I floated on the velvet sea with sensuous, rolling, undulating waves crashing on my shore, one after another washing over me, drowning me in pleasure.

I never wanted it to end. I wanted never to move. I wanted Hector's finger on that spot forever.

I would never have left Carla's bed if not for Barb.

She appeared in the doorway with her lips pursed like an angry schoolmarm. All that was missing was her hands on her hips. Waves of rage filled the room.

"I, uh, hate to break this up, but Carla is looking for you, Hector."

She spoke to Hector, but glared at me, her eyes shooting daggers. *What are you doing? Have you lost your mind?*

"Go to her," I told him.

Thank Hathor, it was Barb who had come in and not Carla. There was no telling what Brazilian Carla might have done. What would I do if I found my boyfriend fingerfucking one of my friends in my bed?

"I am not giving you up," Hector said as he straightened his clothes. "I will do whatever it takes to have you—*cualquier cosa.*"

When he disappeared through the doorway, Barb looked at me with disgust.

"God, could you be more obvious? Both of you disappearing like that? And in Carla's *bed?*"

"I need a drink." It was the only answer I had for her.

Later that night, when Hector opened the door to my condo, Aisha was there immediately, rubbing against his legs. He picked her up, stroking her black fur. She didn't struggle at all, but relaxed into his arms and purred louder.

"Please don't say anything to Carla," I pleaded. "Not yet. It's too soon."

"It's not too soon for me, Isis."

He wrapped me in his arms, but this time he held me without crushing. His lips lingered on mine, his tongue gentle, penetrating, but not devouring. He didn't stroke me; he didn't explore me. He didn't use his hands at all except to hold me.

But I felt his need all through his body. My body responded with a will of its own. The heat of a sudden flush warmed my skin. I pressed into him and felt him rock-hard again. I wanted so badly to touch his hardness, to fondle and stroke him, to make him grow larger still, but I didn't. I wanted to please him and for him to please me. But not now.

"Hector, I'm not ready."

He was gentleman enough to stop, but I could see he was confused and frustrated. And why wouldn't he be?

"It's too soon," I said lamely.

He took my face in his hands and raised my chin so I looked straight into his eyes. The little red specks sparkled in the brown.

"It could never be too soon for us, Isis."

He stroked the side of my cheek, then stroked once across my forehead as if to wipe the tension away.

"Put every worry out of your mind. Nothing will happen to you when you are with me."

He kissed me again, very lightly, just a brush on the lips, and then whispered in my ear, *"Hasta mañana."*

Dream

S ometime in the night, warm hands moved across my breasts and over my belly, caressing my hips and the slope of my thighs. Fingers climbed my mound and descended into the wetness. They lingered until my bud swelled, and then moist lips explored all of me, leaving no place unkissed.

Soft music drifted from a hidden spot under the arbors. A gentle breeze moved the palm fronds. There was a faint scent of myrrh. I moaned in my sleep; Pehtes purred in my ear.

"Isis," a low voice breathed my private name, but I wasn't sure who. "Isis. Isis."

I didn't open my eyes. I wanted it to go on; I didn't want it to be a dream.

Antinous

Hermes Trismegistus turned his head and spoke into the shadows. "Do you not agree, Antinous? Is my daughter not both beautiful and quick?"

I was thrown a bit off balance that Hermes hadn't told me that we weren't alone.

"Your daughter is indeed beautiful, Hermes."

Antinous had the voice of an educated Greek, deep, musical, trained for oratory and theatre. He apparently wasn't ready to concede my wit.

He leaned against a wall, muscular arms lightly crossed. A blue *chiton*, belted at the waist, ended halfway up his wrestler thighs; fabric draped in soft folds from his broad left shoulder across his muscled chest. The right shoulder was bare, as were his magnificent biceps and perfect forearms. The contour of his muscles ended in strong wrists and graceful hands.

His beauty was so perfect, he might have been sculpted from marble. A Greek statue, but clothed.

A mane of waves with streaks of gold crowned his head; ringlets fell on his brow and around his ears. He had hair you wanted to run your fingers through and watch the curls spring back. He had a body you wanted to run your fingers over and watch the gooseflesh rise.

When he took the third chair at the table, I saw he was even more beautiful up close. His pale skin was flawless. I didn't think it possible for eyes to be so blue.

He watched me a little too intently, making me mildly uneasy. There was a reserved and concentrated air about him that was just a little cool and impossible to read.

Both Hermes and Antinous studied me, Hermes with a bit of amusement in his eyes, Antinous quite serious. They seemed to be waiting for me to say something.

"You have called me here for a reason, my father. Am I to guess, or will you tell me?"

"A sharp tongue like your mother!" Hermes laughed out loud and poured himself more wine.

Antinous didn't laugh. In fact, his eyes narrowed just a bit, and a rather deep crease appeared between his eyebrows.

With the grace of an athlete, he rose from the table and returned with a package about the size of a laptop but much thicker. More like a heavy atlas. I wondered wildly for a moment if it were a suitcase bomb.

Under the soft leather wrapping was a glowing slab of green faience covered with Greek letters. I made out a few phrases.

The following to be the truth. As it is above, so it is below. All things come from the One.

Hermes swallowed my hand in his. How unlike his touch was from that of my mother Sit-hathor with the Hathor energy that aroused in me a hot frenzy. His energy flowed into me and filled me with calm.

"You are the chosen one, my daughter. It is your destiny to protect the Emerald Tablet. You understand that it must not fall into the hands of the Persians. The very future is at stake."

I must have given him a bewildered stare. Was he saying that the fate of the world depended on *me*?

He hesitated, looked over at Antinous, and then back at me. This time he took my hand in both of his. His tone was soft and patient, like a doctor giving a patient startling news and trying to deliver it in the gentlest way possible.

"You shall be the wife of Antinous; he will take you, with the

Tablet, home to Greece. All has been arranged."

Wife? I would've pulled my hand away if Hermes hadn't held it tight.

"A woman cannot travel alone. A woman cannot live alone," he said patiently. "This you know to be true."

What I knew is that I didn't know the Greek, at all. He was handsome, even beautiful, but cold and aloof. I sensed wariness on his part. How convinced was he of this marriage?

As uncommon as it was for a man not to desire me, I couldn't see that he was in the least attracted to me. His eyes told me nothing.

Would he expect me to be faithful to him? Surely they both understood that impossible for a priestess of Hathor. And I wanted River God. I still held out hope.

River God. Would I ever see him again—in this life or the other? Hermes claimed to know the secret to the cosmos. He must understand how souls could meet each other on both sides of the Red Mirror.

"Hermes, have we known each other before? Will we know each other again?"

"We shall know each other until we have learned what we need to learn," he answered. "But do not think, my daughter, in terms of have known or will know; they exist at the same moment. Time is a continuum that loops back on itself."

Antinous had said nothing all this time. What secrets did *he* know? I still couldn't read anything in his eyes. His face was a mask.

I sighed. My choices weren't limited; I had none.

"When do we sail?"

I followed Antinous up the spiral staircase, each of us with a torch. Neither of us spoke; I could only guess what was going through his mind. The tension between us was electric. We hurried down the long tunnel, but he stopped at the bottom of the steps that lead up to the little chapel with the false door.

The torches in our hands blew a little sidewise. After the

stuffiness of the damp tunnel, the air seemed almost fresh.

Antinous stood inches away. White Atlantean symbols danced against the blue dome behind his head. He smelled of lamp oil and slightly of male sweat, without any hint of perfumed oils or myrrh. His skin glowed. I'd never seen a man so perfectly formed.

His eyes were the color of the sky over Thebes on a spring morning. His lashes were thick like brushes. Leather bands encircled his wrists; he wore no other adornment and no *kohl* around his eyes.

The gold highlights in his curls shimmered in a halo around his Adonis face. His lower lip was slightly fuller than the upper, which was shaped into a bow; his mouth almost formed a pout. His chin had a deep cleft. A muscle in his jaw knotted and unknotted.

Antinous didn't speak; he didn't move. My breasts rose and fell as I breathed; the sheer linen clung to their curve. The emerald eyes of the serpents coiling around my arms glinted in the torchlight when I reached out to trace my long nail around his lips.

He put his free hand on the nape of my neck. His grip was more forceful than I had expected; it didn't fit with his aloof demeanor. His eyes locked on mine, but I saw none of the hunger I see in men's eyes.

My fingers combed through the short curls on his neck. I traced around his ear with my fingertips. My eyes invited him.

Finally he lowered his face toward me, but didn't close his eyes until his lips were on mine. His tongue went deep; he penetrated me as far as he could. I opened my lips and took him in, sucking on his tongue, urging him on. My heart raced; heat surged through my veins. I felt hot as the sun.

He was rock hard and big enough to please anyone. I cupped my hand around the swollen bulge of his *chiton*, leaning into him, rubbing my breasts against his chest, pressing my thighs into his.

How far were we from the wall? I envisioned my back against the cool damp stone, one hand guiding his steel rod to my wet chamber, the other holding a torch. Would the torches stay lit if we lay them down on the stone floor?

But instead of responding to me, he drew back while still gripping my neck. He pulled his lips away in the middle of the kiss and left me with my lips open, swollen, hungry for more.

His manhood slowly shriveled until I finally dropped my hand to hang awkwardly at my side. His eyes stayed locked with mine, but they revealed no secrets; they told me nothing about what was going on behind them. It was as if their blue depths had no connection to the changes in his body.

The torches in our hands burned evenly in the still air. There wasn't a sound in the domed chamber except our breathing.

He was my husband and my future. With the tip of my index finger, the one that traced his ear, I eased the strap of my dress aside. Slowly, deliberately, oozing with promise, I revealed each seductive inch of bare flesh. My breast was a pale mound in the yellow light, the dark nipple erect and throbbing.

Antinous looked down, blinked once and then looked into my face. Taking his hand away from the nape of my neck, he slid the sheer fabric back into place, covering me, never taking his eyes away from mine.

I jerked as if he had slapped me.

He switched the torch to my right hand and then took my left hand into his right.

My breath caught when I saw the kind of wistful yearning that I often see in men's eyes. But I also saw doubt.

"I know you can satisfy me, Isis. But can I satisfy you?"

Then gripping my hand just as firmly as he had gripped the back of my neck, he said, "Come," and started up the stairs.

The Commander

A hand pressed down on my mouth. I tried to sit up, but couldn't move my head. There was no moon. I could see nothing in the darkness except the form of a man directly over me. I kicked, and I thrashed, but could not dislodge him. Bile came up into my mouth.

"Sh-h-h, Isis," River God breathed in my ear.

I clutched him to me, digging my fingertips into his muscled back, hoping to draw strength from his power. His lips replaced his hand, and he tried to kiss me, but I sobbed too hard.

I felt his muscles tighten over the full length of my body. I wanted to melt into him, to become one with him. I could walk out of here, and no one would see me.

River God waited for me to calm. His lips and tongue traveled slowly down my neck, across the hollow of my throat and up to my ear. He took the lobe between his teeth, gently, and then sucked with long languid pulls that I felt right down to my throbbing lotus. His lips were hot and moist.

His fingers went in my mouth, stroking my tongue, wetting them before going to my swollen breast to stroke my nipple in small gentle circles. My saliva was slick on the throbbing tip.

His tongue was in my ear; he breathed life into me. He took his time, unhurried, savoring my need. His touch caressed me as tenderly as a breeze. My breath was so shallow, I scarcely took in air.

He ran his tongue around my ear and licked down my neck. His finger massaged my lotus in his slow, languid rhythm that teased me to life, but never hurried to finish.

No one had a touch like River God.

My hand found his hardness; I felt him swell as I squeezed the first droplets from the tip. The head was moist and smooth in my palm. I licked my hand and made him wetter still, rubbing his bulb with gentle circles, caressing his shaft in my hot palm, pumping up and down, up and down, slowly, slowly, until he grew hard as the stone phallus of Min.

He moaned. The sound of his pleasure was sweeter than the softest love song. The muscles in his thighs and butt grew hard and taut like carved marble. I sucked on his navel, exploring deep with my tongue. Then like a preening cat, I licked his hard nipples until he pulled my face up and finally kissed me, his tongue plunging to my throat, his lips pressing on mine, devouring me.

He was almost, but not quite, brutal. The palm of his hand crushed along my ribs, across my soft belly and dug into my mound. I opened up to him.

His fingers slid up the dark damp and pushed against my cervix. My wetness soaked the bed linen. I whimpered at each stroke, spreading my loins, shifting my hips to open wider, to welcome his touch, to give him everything.

When his lips left mine and began their trail of kisses to my breast, I arched my back, raising my throbbing nipples to his lips, begging for his mouth, aching to be suckled.

His tongue was wet and warm when he sucked. His teeth brought me to the edge of pain but never took me there, always hovering at the extreme threshold of pleasure and not crossing over. I gripped his head and pressed him into me, but he moved to my other nipple and teased with his teeth and wet tongue.

My hips rose and fell as his fingers possessed me, plunging into my wet, rotating on my lotus, exploring every part of my dark valley. I rocked on the palm of his hand.

My cries must have wakened the household, but Maia didn't

come. She knew those sounds well. Pehtes curled at the top of my bare scalp, purring a lion's roar, wallowing in the animal scent.

The sleeping potion fogged my senses. I floated above the bed yet could still feel his touch. The night stars disappeared; the open balcony faded. Las Vegas sparkled through the tall windows of the Wynn.

In one breath, he was River God, in the next, Rasheed. Our souls glided back and forth between two worlds.

"Why did you not come back to me?" I whispered. "I came back for you."

Of course, he didn't think of my coming back though the Red Mirror. River God knew nothing about the future. He stopped his caress and let his hand rest on my thigh for just a moment until he rolled onto his back.

"I came for you in the desert," he said in a flat, cold voice.

"But you allowed Hetmus-hor to carry me out and be praised as my savior," I pleaded. "It could have been you. It *should* have been you."

He got up from bed. The spell was broken, like the night of the bath in Thebes. Words are always the spoiler with River God.

His silhouette against the open night sky moved quietly in the room to find his sandals and his sword.

"You must leave Saïs," he said. "It is not safe for you, even here in the Temple."

I listened to his voice in the dark, telling me the real reason he had come.

"I have heard rumors at Court. The Persians will pay any price for your capture. Cambyses wants revenge for General Sher's death."

I closed my eyes and saw the General's startled face, eyes huge with disbelief, blood gushing from his slit throat and spilling onto my hands. I went icy cold. The Persians are masters of torture. It takes days for their victims to die.

Eben the fortune-teller's warning at Carla's party screamed in my ears. *You have to go back, Isis, or you will suffer. You can't imagine the suffering.*

River God sat on the edge of the bed. I couldn't make out his features in the dark, but I clearly heard his worry.

"You must leave for the South, maybe as far as Kush."

"I cannot go south."

River God gripped my shoulders and pulled me into him. I winced from the pain of his fingers digging into my flesh. His eyes flashed in the dark.

"You will do exactly as I say. Do you hear me? This is no time for your foolishness."

River God still thought of me as the pampered, impetuous girl I once was, but I was not the same woman. I had survived the desert. I had survived the General.

"Make ready to leave at sunset tomorrow," he ordered in his Commander's tone. "Look for a ship under my banner."

I took his hand in mine and covered my mouth with it, drinking in his fragrance, tasting my own fluids. He pulled away gently and raised my fingers to his own mouth. His breath was hot; the tip of his tongue wet my fingertips.

Was this the last time in this life I would feel his lips on me?

I had said nothing at all to him about Antinous and Greece; I couldn't. It was too dangerous to tell anyone, even River God. One could never tell what one didn't know. Even under torture. So I lied to him with my silence.

"Make yourself ready," and not "I love you," were his last words as he headed toward the balcony.

"Why do you always leave me?" I cried out as he slipped over the side and was gone into the night.

Two Men

We stood in the shelter of the doorway for a few brief moments. I saw soldiers everywhere, but not close by. Hector, in the body and mind of Hetmus as I was in Isis, stepped outside and kept his back to the wall. I watched his tall figure move away from me before I dared step out myself.

A hand came out of the night and closed over my mouth. I started to scream, but stopped; I wanted no attention drawn to me. An arm pushed me back into the dark recess around the door. I struggled, but the man held me fast.

A halo of pale curls glowed in the lights of the harbor. I bobbed my head up and down rapidly, relaxing my body to let him know I recognized him and his hand dropped from my mouth.

"Antinous!" My voice was a breathless whisper.

Hector didn't make a sound when he came up behind Antinous, but his long shadow fell across the wall behind me. Antinous pivoted to face the Egyptian, drawing a sword as he turned. I grabbed his wrist to keep him from striking.

"No, Antinous! He saved my life. But for him, I would not be here."

I couldn't tell him the whole truth—that not only had Hector saved my life, but he had come through the Red Mirror to do it.

There was a long moment of tension, no one speaking, the two men staring at each other, measuring the other's worth. My left hand on Hector's arm and my right on Antinous burned as if I touched fire.

I sensed that Antinous sized up one of my lovers with whom he must compete. Hector judged the man who would take me from him.

Finally, Hector said begrudgingly, "Greek, you are the luckiest man alive."

Then he smiled at me in the most sweet and tender way and put his palm on my cheek. His love flowed into me, giving me strength.

"Let us get you on that ship."

Antinous carried a hemp sack with green wool, lengths of silken cord, and a Greek wig. I took off my black waves with gold ankhs and pulled the dark blonde plaits and curls over my shaved head.

While Antinous tried to sort the yards of wool fabric, Hector wiped *kohl* and mica from my eyes and eyebrows with my Egyptian linen gown. Then he took the green *peplos* cloth from Antinous and draped it around me expertly, fastening it in place with the pins and silk cords. When he saw my surprise, he smiled.

"Hetmus-hor knew a few Greek ladies in his day," he said through a blaze of white teeth.

Hector's sandals crunched on the loose rock as he walked away toward the quay to find the Commander. Antinous stayed with me, but neither of us spoke. He was here; he had lived up to his promise, but more than ever I was aware of his doubt. And he didn't even know about the General's child.

Three Men

Quiet words were exchanged. I heard River God's voice, low, giving orders. The footfalls on the deck of the ship sounded hollow; there must be a space below. We descended a short flight of steps, very steep. I could hear the river rushing past the cedar boards; then someone untied the sack and it fell around my ankles.

River God reeled with shock. I'd forgotten I wore the dress and wig of a Greek and no black *kohl* on my eyes. My naked face must have been pale as white sand in moonlight.

"Do not utter one word." His tone chilled me. "The sound of a woman's voice on this ship will carry all the way to the Crown Prince's ear."

His voice was cold. There was no affection at all in his eyes. Was it only last night that he caressed me with such tenderness?

How could I beg him to take me to the sea, if I couldn't speak? His face was black with jealousy and rage, but I saw longing under his anger. This time I was leaving him.

We stood in a tight circle, the four of us—blond and muscular Antinous, Hector so tall he could not stand fully upright in the low space, and fuming River God, rigid and tense in his military vest with the Pharaoh's golden insignia. And me, facing the three men who controlled my destiny.

Hector held out his right arm to River God. There was nothing in the way he looked that hinted that this new Hetmus-hor was anything more than when the two men had confronted each other in the desert. The change was in his demeanor.

"We are agreed then? You will take Isis and the Greek north to meet the Phoenician ship."

At first River God refused to look Hector in the eye. When he finally faced him, he didn't try to conceal his contempt for the man who had lost me in the desert and then was praised as my savior. And now the spoiled son of a useless nobleman arranged my escape, but not to the south as River God planned.

Hector gripped River God's shoulder; his long fingers dug into the hard muscle. I thought for a moment he might shake him, as if to bring him to his senses.

"I know exactly what I ask of you, man. But there is no other way."

I actually thought River God would refuse. The muscles in his jaw were so knotted I could see them flex even in the poor light. His left eye twitched in a tic.

"Do you think I would give her up," Hector insisted, "if I thought there was any chance I could have her?"

River God glared up at Hector; his black eyes were hard as obsidian. I thought him so handsome, but tonight the bones of his face formed harsh, ugly angles. His mouth, so lush when he kissed me, was tight and cruel.

I held my breath. I think we all held our breaths. At last, he gripped Hector's forearm, just below the elbow, and laid his left hand on Hector's shoulder to signal the pact. A man of his word, River God would not betray his pledge.

The air in the narrow space below deck was as charged as before a sandstorm. My heart raced, and my head pounded from the suspense.

Antinous stood silently to one side, almost out of the ring of light. He was no fool. He understood the drama he witnessed and the role he played. One wrong word from him and this scene could end in tragedy.

Hector stroked my cheek with the back of his fingers. The red specks in his eyes were iridescent. I couldn't look away from them.

"I shall never find another woman like you, Isis."

Then he kissed me, long and deep. He didn't hurry. He was oblivious to River God and Antinous standing next to us. When he pulled away, he leaned down and whispered in my ear.

"You owe me one. *Hasta Las Vegas.*"

He kissed me one last time, lightly, just a fleeting touch of his lips, and then disappeared up the steps.

River God stood absolutely frozen, like a quartzite statue in a tomb. When he finally looked at me, his glare was full of accusation. I saw betrayal in his face and wounded pride. I hadn't said anything to him about Greece—or Antinous, whom he ignored. He wouldn't look in the Greek's direction. Raw pain sharpened the planes of his face.

I wanted to reach out and tell him this was not goodbye. I wanted to say the words he had said to me in Las Vegas, *We have known each other before, and we will know each other again.*

But River God knew nothing of the future; he knew nothing of himself as Rasheed.

This was the last time I would see him in this life. I edged close to him, my body yielding, his more rigid than ever. I was desperate to reach him, so I did what I'd never before done with a lover. I summoned the Power.

My skin flushed with heat. A hot aura pulsed from my body. I believe my flesh glowed in the dim light.

"You told me in Thebes that the Gods set us on our separate paths," I crooned in the softest of honey whispers. "This is not the path I would have chosen; this is not the path I want."

Still he didn't respond, not to me, not to the Power.

"I would have lain in your arms until you left me," I breathed. "I would have been there waiting for your return."

Balancing on my tiptoes, my breasts pressing on his leather chest, I put my lips to his. Chiseled from stone by a master sculptor, they did not yield. My desire burned so bright, I would have lain with him right there on the rough planks, even with Antinous standing over us.

His pride wouldn't let him hold me. He stared straight ahead, refusing to look at me, trying to make of me a non-person, to have me no longer exist.

Only the twitch in his eyelid gave him away. He would show no pain or weakness; he cut me out of his heart at the same time he cut my heart out of me.

Invisible fingers tore at the connective tissue in my chest. Not even the Persians could invent such torture.

He moved past me and up the steps, not looking back at me, never looking at Antinous. *I* couldn't bring myself to look at Antinous.

I leaned my back against a pole and watched my heart, ripped from my chest, pumping on the wood planks, spewing blood, the dark red stain spreading in a wide pool around my feet.

The warship pulled away from the wharf, oars moving crisply in the water. I heard the sail unfurl with a sharp snap, filled instantly by a brisk wind. River God was true to his word; we entered the swift current flowing north toward the Great Green.

Antinous and I didn't speak. We didn't look at each other. I curled up on two bales and tried to sleep. I was even more exhausted than in Sit-hathor's tent, after the desert. I wondered how living flesh could endure such tension and pain.

Antinous Thrice-Greatest

When I woke, it was dark. Antinous sat at the wooden table in the cabin of the Phoenician ship, concentrating on an open scroll in the light of a single oil lamp.

"What are you reading?" I asked idly from the shadows.

"It is the treatise by Thales that introduced Egyptian geometry to Greece." He sounded enthusiastic; there was a new shine to his eyes.

Thank you, father, for my years with math tutors. How long ago did Hermes make his plans? Since my birth? Since before?

"What is your opinion of Pythagoras and his postulates on deductive reasoning?" I asked.

"Pythagoras takes Thales to new levels," Antinous answered quite passionately. "He hypothesizes that mathematics is the key to the cosmos."

He looked directly in the direction of my voice. I felt the first contact.

"Pythagoras sees numbers in everything," he added.

He sat in a halo of light in the quiet cabin. The lamp sputtered. The night was silent except for the sea washing against the hull, carrying us west along the coast of Africa to Greek Libya. Even the seagulls slept.

I enjoyed that we spoke Greek together. It's a lilting tongue that tickles the ears with vowels. No guttural sounds or hiccups, it's all music and poetry, easy to modulate—easy to insinuate other meaning.

"I regret I did not meet Pythagoras while in Saïs." My voice, resonating like the low notes of a lyre, filled the small cabin with promise.

His eyelids flickered. The glow of the oil lamp lighted his face, casting delicate shadows on perfect bones. He took a sharp intake of air when I came into the ring of light. His pupils were large and black; all trace of blue had disappeared.

The cut of my gown was loose, but designed to fall on the curves of the body, along the rise of my breasts and the slope of my hips. The hormones of early pregnancy were rounding out angles. I was fast becoming a curvaceous Greek.

He sat sideways to the table. His long legs with tight loins and rounded calves were stretched out and crossed at the ankles. The fabric of his *chiton* draped on his muscled thighs. His body was indeed perfect, exactly proportional, every muscle toned. He must have wrestled all his life.

I glided smoothly and silently toward him. When I leaned over him to ease the scroll from his hands, my swollen breasts pulled at the yellow linen. My nipples rose.

Ever so slowly, never taking my eyes from his, I pulled my gown past my knees and straddled him. My soft loins squeezed his hard thighs.

Antinous was so still, he might have been a statue. He didn't blink; he didn't breathe. I placed my palms on his chest. His muscles were so tense, his skin so smooth, he even felt like marble.

But heat rose off him; the tang of salt mixed with his strong scent of male. I could feel the warmth of the sun in his flesh.

In one day at sea, his skin had turned golden in the way of fair Greeks who reflect the sun. His eyes were transfixed on my face. Would he reject me tonight as he did in the tunnel?

"Husband," I whispered, and leaned to brush my lips against his.

I had no warning. He was on his feet in one movement, his hands on my buttocks, my legs straddling his thighs. The chair crashed to the floor. The table rocked. I expected the lamp to fall and splatter oil and fire on the carpets.

Antinous drove me straight to the wall. It happened so fast, I could only throw my arms around his neck and hang on. His mouth was on mine and his tongue down my throat. My head slammed against the cedar paneling. He held me with one hand and dragged my caftan up past my waist with the other. Then he jerked his loincloth off and flung it across the room.

He plunged into me and pounded me, both hands back on my buttocks. The rough edges of the wood paneling scraped my back as he banged me and banged me against the wall. He must have rocked the whole ship.

When he took his mouth from mine and allowed me to breathe, I used my cheek to force him to turn his head, and then one hand to hold him there. I put my wet tongue in his ear and blew and sucked gently, enough to torment, but not enough to damage.

He went wild and climaxed with a jolt that wracked his whole body. Collapsing against me, he pressed me into the wall, his forehead on the cedar close to my ear, his breath coming in gulps. He never loosened his grip. I was sure the flesh of my buttocks would forever show an imprint of his fingers.

His melon biceps bulged when he walked us to the bed, my thighs squeezing his thighs, his manhood still inside me. Then he tossed me down and flipped me over in one swift movement, dragging me up on my hands and knees. He ripped the Greek wig away and yanked the linen gown over my head. I heard seams tear.

Not possible, but he was iron-hard again. He thrust into me, holding my hips in both hands and lifting me up and into him. My face buried in the blankets, I reached to grab the back of his thighs and hold on. The two of us rocked with such force, the joint where the bed met the wall creaked with strain.

He pulled out of me and rolled me to my back. His tongue was deep in my mouth at the moment he entered me again. I wrapped my thighs around his waist, locked my ankles, and lay back, eyes closed, surrendering to pleasure.

My arms over my head, stretched out on the bed, palms up, I let him ravage me. He was tireless. He pounded and pounded until I feared the bones in my pelvis would separate. But I didn't stop him. We were both drenched in sweat.

Like a master choreographer, he turned us on our sides and pulled my hips into the curve of his belly, sliding again into my wet. I lay limp and helpless as a rag doll.

His hands massaged my tender, engorged breasts; I had a wild vision of milk spewing forth. He rolled my nipples aflame from new hormones between his thumb and finger, relentlessly, not quite rough, not aimed to hurt me, but not gently. I cried out in pain, but put his hands back when he stopped. I'd never felt such raw sensitivity. Agony and ecstasy in the same moment.

I gasped when he slid his finger onto my engorged bud and rotated hard. Moans reverberated through my chest and vibrated in my throat. My bud flowered. My womb contracted and contracted. The muscles in my vagina sucked his hardness.

Antinous cried out and went rigid, shuddering twice, then a third time.

We lay panting, completely spent, sweat glistening on our bare skin in spite of the cool sea night, my full breast filling his warm palm. I nestled my hips against his flat stomach and felt his lips cool on my bare scalp, his breath warm on my skin.

When he rolled over to his back, he turned me with him, holding tightly, never letting go. I burrowed into his side, my shoulder in his armpit, my cheek on his chest. We didn't speak; the sound of our breathing was louder than the swells of the sea.

I thought only to shower him with affection, but when I eased on top of him and began nibbling his lips around their fullness and licking the deep cleft in his chin, he hardened again.

Three times! Oh, this Greek indeed had many talents!

Pushing myself up on bent knees, I straddled him, one leg on each side of his waist. Just at the moment my hand found his swollen manhood and guided him inside me, the flicker of twinkling sparkles flashed in the dark. Lamplight reflected off the fragile golden charms of my necklace. He reached up and touched a tiny rabbit.

Fecundity. I knew his character by that choice.

I laughed lightly, a sound like small golden bells, and rocked slowly back and forth, in a steady rhythm, milking him. He caught my tender breasts in his hands, gently squeezing their fullness before pulling them to his open lips.

There was no doubt in his eyes now.

"Antinous Thrice-Greatest, my husband, we are going to have a wonderful life."

I didn't need to summon the Power at all.

Cleopatra's Barge

I chose a sleeveless red satin dress that hugged my bust, waist and hips. Flesh-toned, sheer stockings ended in scarlet stilettos with thin ankle straps. I even wore the red and black garters from the night of the Wynn. I topped it all off with a white mink that cost me $600 in my favorite vintage shop. I didn't hold anything back.

The traffic on the Strip at this hour would be a nightmare. I took Koval and turned left on Sands, driving past the Wynn with its bittersweet memories of Rasheed in the penthouse suite with stunning view. I used the back entrance to Caesar's, the one only cab drivers know.

A blond valet with nice shoulders took my keys, and I stepped out—long legs, red satin, white BMW. The look in his eyes told me everything I needed to know. *Bring it on, Rasheed.*

It was early for Vegas. No one else sat at the bar. I eased onto a padded barstool and ordered a Plymouth martini, up with an olive. I had already finished half of it and no sign of Rasheed. I checked my cell again. The only message was from Barb asking me to meet her at the Stirling Club.

"I'm at Caesar's—waiting for Rasheed." I said it very cool, as if meeting him was a common occurrence.

"Rasheed! Why didn't you tell me?"

"I was afraid I would jinx it. Besides, I know you don't like him."

"Don't let him jerk you around."

Actually Barb, I'm looking forward to him doing whatever he wants.

"And it's not that I can't see he's hot. He's just a little too unavailable for my taste."

"I'll call you tomorrow, Barb, and tell you all about it."

I put my phone down beside my martini glass. A man took the stool next to me, but I didn't look up.

"Looks like you're expecting someone," he said politely. "May I buy you a drink while you wait?"

I nearly knocked over my glass when I heard his voice. Antinous had traded his Greek *chiton* for a powder-blue oxford cloth shirt. He had the clean cut, preppy look of a Brooks Brothers ad. His face was golden tan except for the white around his eyes, like a pair of goggles. He must be a skier.

His hair was a mass of shiny curls. The same deep cleft split his chin. Gorgeous as ever, he outshone any of the statues at Caesar's.

"My name's Tony." He held out his hand for me to shake.

I looked at his outstretched hand and remembered how it gripped my butt so hard on the Phoenician ship that I bruised. For an awkward moment, his hand hung suspended in the narrow space between us, and then he put it on the bar.

"Excuse me if I was out of line," he apologized. He shifted his weight away from me. He didn't recognize me at all.

"I'd love another martini," I said with a warm smile. "I just wanted to make sure you weren't a salesman."

"You can tell I'm not a salesman?"

"Believe me, I can tell."

I didn't embarrass him by saying I also could see he wasn't local; he had that out-of-towner expectant look, *This is Vegas. Anything can happen.*

The bartender put two icy Plymouth martinis with plump olives in front of us.

Tony was so beautiful, it was criminal he was male. I knew a lot of women who paid a fortune to have blond-streaked curls like his. I almost regretted I was meeting Rasheed. I'd love to see if this Tony was as ferocious a lover as Antinous.

"I'm from New Jersey," he offered without my asking.

"New Jersey?" The thought of Antinous ending up in New Jersey saddened me a little.

"Well, from Princeton to be exact."

That was more like it. He had to be the best looking professor in the Ivy League. His preppy clothes didn't hide his muscles at all. He had the same wrestler's thighs and powerful arms that had crushed me on the ship.

"What about you?" he asked.

"I live here."

"You *live* in Las Vegas?"

I don't know why people are always so surprised when I say that; there are 2 million others like me.

"Living here is like living anywhere, except I get to dress up. I like wearing my high heels."

The male in Tony couldn't resist looking the length of my red satin dress all the way to those heels. I had no trouble imagining him ripping my clothes off as he drove me to the wall of Cleopatra's Barge.

That's when Rasheed came down the concourse. I could spot him in a crowd of a thousand. Like a lioness in heat, I sniffed his pheromones from afar.

He walked with a group of tough-looking men in pricey business suits. Some scanned the room while the others talked. His two bodyguards, Marcos and Gamel, walked close by him.

"It was great talking to you, Tony, but I see my date."

"Sure, I understand. Here's my card. If you're ever in Princeton, look me up. It's quiet there, but I know a couple of places to get a good martini."

He paused for a second as if waiting for me to say something. "You never told me your name."

I only hesitated a moment before answering, "It's…uh…Isis."

"Isis? Isn't that the name of an Egyptian goddess?" Something sparked in his eyes. "It seems like I knew an Isis once, but I can't remember where."

Rasheed walked up behind me, put one hand on my shoulder and moved my hair away with the other. He touched his lips to the trigger point on my neck, not a real kiss, just a fleeting brush that burned on. He breathed in my scent like an animal before mating. The heat from his hand seared my skin through the satin.

He took the empty stool on my other side and faced me. His legs were spread open; his knee pressed into my calf.

"You look good enough to eat," he breathed in my ear.

I thought the same thing about the bulge between his thighs.

His chiseled lips wouldn't reject me tonight. I wondered if there existed a Hathor Power for men. I wanted to jump him right there at the bar.

"Let's have dinner in the room." He was cheerful for Rasheed, almost buoyant. His eyes, warm with affection, glowed like polished jade.

But then his face hardened. His skin actually darkened. He had seen Tony. There was no doubt about him recognizing the Greek. Rasheed's face took on the black rage of the night below deck on River God's ship.

I put my hand on the inside of his thigh. High up, to get his attention.

"Rasheed, he doesn't know. *Trust me*. He has no idea."

He scared me; I didn't like the way he looked at Tony. I slid down from the stool and took his hands, leaning into him, between his open legs, pressing against his bulge. My breasts were soft and full against his hard chest.

"Let's go up to the suite," I breathed in his ear.

It was like I wasn't there. Rasheed glared at Tony with cold hatred in his eyes, the warm jade frozen to green ice. Then Marcos the bodyguard appeared and spoke so low that, close as I was, I couldn't hear what he said. Rasheed nodded, but still glared at Tony who was walking away.

For one wild crazy instant, I thought that Rasheed might be ordering a hit on him.

Taking me by the arm, Rasheed guided me across the empty dance floor, saying, "Why don't you take a seat in a booth over here? I'll just be a few minutes."

We passed a group of hard-looking men seated around a table, and I flashed on mafia bosses deciding who will live and who will die. They stopped talking. I felt their eyes following us.

Rasheed helped me into a red leather booth and then leaned down and kissed me on the lips in a way that said, *This woman belongs to me.*

Everything with Rasheed has to be mysterious and high drama.

Bodyguards milled around with no attempt to be inconspicuous. This was Caesar's Palace; the mob had been coming here since the days of the Rat Pack.

Tony's card read 'Anthony Callis, Ph.D., Director of Cosmological Research, Institute for Advanced Study, Princeton NJ.'

He was legit. It fit my sense of cosmic order that Antinous the mathematician was reborn as Tony the astronomer or cosmologist, or whatever the difference was. I wondered if he were married, had kids. I wondered about his life with Isis in Greece. I wondered about the General's child.

A waiter set a flute of champagne in front of me at the same time a large man slid into the booth on the opposite bench. He moved fast and sat there before I looked up.

He had a salon haircut, styled back on the sides with neck hair too long for an American. He was clean-shaven, but I would have known him anywhere. His massive chest and biceps stretched the expensive Italian-looking suit. I visualized the thickness of his thighs bulging the cashmere of his pants.

My eyes fixed on the green silk tie with arabesque pattern at his throat. Dark red blood began to bubble above the knot as I stared.

"Hello, Ishtar. It has been a long time."

He called me by the name he'd given me in his Persian tent in the desert.

I couldn't avoid his eyes any longer. I took a deep breath and exhaled.

"Hello, General."

Goodbye Rasheed

Rasheed arrived at my side in seconds. I didn't need to look at him to know his mood. His energy field was like the strobe of a pulsar.

The General smiled smugly at both of us and said, "Your lady friend is most charming, Rasheed. I envy you."

They knew each other! The shock of it slammed me. But it was in this life, not the other. River God and the General never met in the desert.

"Let us celebrate," the General suggested in a somewhat teasing tone, the smirk still on his face.

As if by magic, a bottle of *Cristal* champagne arrived.

"To relationships—past, present and future." He looked directly at me when he said it.

Rasheed fixed his unblinking, hard, glittery eyes on the General.

"I sense that your beautiful friend and I have met before." The General sipped his champagne and gave me a knowing look.

I couldn't help my eyes widening. Surely he wouldn't bring up what happened between us, not in front of Rasheed. I didn't want to think about what Rasheed would do if he realized this was the Persian who had tasted me—if he had the slightest hint of my ride on the comet.

"You have the most stunning eyes," the General continued, nodding his massive head at me in approval. "I have always had a weakness for emerald eyes like yours. They have been my downfall on more than one occasion."

He enjoyed himself, happily watching me squirm, waving a red cape in Rasheed's face. But it was the bull goading the matador.

Electric shocks ran from Rasheed's body into mine.

"Rasheed and I are business partners, did you know that, *ma bella*? You must find that a fascinating turn of events." The General's tone was far too intimate.

The impact of his words on Rasheed was obvious. He hadn't spoken; he barely breathed. He was like the cobra in the desert, eyes fixed, head almost swaying. I had to do something before he uncoiled and struck at the General's throat.

"What kind of business are you in?" I tried to sound polite and disinterested.

"The world is a dangerous place. Everyone feels he must protect himself. I help people do that. I am—what might you call it?—a broker."

"What is it exactly that you broker? Or is it a secret? Or maybe it's secrets that you broker?"

He threw back his head and laughed. It was the same laugh as in the tent when I accused him of not being a man of his word.

"You've got guts, I like that. But then I've always liked that about you, Ishtar."

Rasheed turned his face to me, icy eyes narrowed with suspicion and distrust. *You didn't tell me about your plan with the Greek. What other silent lies have you told?*

Standing out of the booth, the General said to me, "*Á vedeci, bella.* It was my pleasure to see you again. I look forward to our next meeting, wherever—and whenever—that might be."

Then as quickly as he'd appeared, he walked away, his bodyguards around him, devastation in his wake.

Rasheed's aura had gone black. His left eyelid twitched in a spasm.

With each heartbeat, he pulled back from me, retreating as fast as one of Tony's galaxies hurtling through space. I was losing him.

I would gladly have lied, but my mind was a blank. I couldn't explain away the General.

Rasheed's expression was so frigid, I thought his face would shatter with one flick of my finger. He always could turn his feelings from hot to cold like a shower faucet.

"I'm going home now." I said it quite simply, without much emotion in my voice.

He slid out of the booth and stood. I slid after him. He didn't help me.

I folded my white mink coat carefully over my arm. I forced myself to relax the hand gripping my red clutch. Every movement was concentrated not to show my desperation.

But as hard as I tried, I couldn't stop my eyes from filling with tears. My three-inch heels put me on level with his once lush mouth. It seemed impossible that those hard lips had pleasured me and made my soul sing.

I wanted to kiss him, to warm him from stone to man, but his granite mouth was cold. Just like the night below deck on River God's ship, there would be no melting Rasheed. He refused to look at me, trying once again to make me a non-person. I didn't bother to summon the Power.

"Maybe you'll call me when you can let go of the past."

I walked away. He didn't try to stop me. He hadn't said one word since he first came to my booth and faced the General. I don't know how long his eyes followed me before I disappeared in the crowd.

Hector and the Tablet

Late the next morning, Hector picked me up in his white Range Rover. He wore faded tight jeans with a yellow polo shirt and lizard cowboy boots. A worn bomber jacket lay on the back seat.

"*Á donde vamos?*" he asked with his blazing white smile. "Your wish is my command."

He looked so like Hetmus-hor in that moment, the confident Hetmus on the morning of the hunt, before he lost me in the sandstorm and everything went wrong.

"You decide. I just needed company." What I really meant was that I needed to be with someone who wanted me.

He smiled in a way that said he was pleased, but he didn't comment. I stared out the huge windows of the Range Rover and told myself Rasheed didn't deserve me.

"You have many beautiful things in your home. *Muy impresionante.*"

I rarely brought men back to my condo, but when I did, they weren't much interested in the furniture.

"Show me where you find such treasures in Las Vegas."

"Seriously? Most men don't like shopping."

"I am not most men."

He was certainly not most men. I'd never believed in the G-Spot until Hector, but he'd made me a believer.

"You're not married, are you?" I asked rather out of the blue.

I'd never asked Rasheed if he were married. I'd never asked

Rasheed anything.

"No, Isis, I am not married. I have been waiting for you."

"I'm not very good at commitments either," I answered.

He locked eyes with me for a just a second.

"We will have to work on that," he said.

His look told me that working with Hector could be very pleasurable indeed. I studied his profile with strong Latin nose and head of chestnut waves combed back from his brow. His big hands with those long fingers that went straight to the Spot gripped the wheel in a relaxed, self-assured way.

He had crossed through the Red Mirror for me. I doubted Rasheed would do that.

"What's Argentina like?" I rather suddenly was interested in exploring my options.

"Buenos Aires is full of life, like Las Vegas. But I grew up on an *estancia*, a ranch."

The ranch accounted for his ease in the cowboy boots. And those powerful thighs. I imagined his long legs squeezing the horse's sides as he twisted and dipped in the saddle.

"So, what is it that you actually *do*? I mean, besides play polo."

"I used to chase all beautiful women. Now I chase only you."

Hector, the man who never struggled for anything, was back in his teasing mode.

"Are you telling me you're a playboy?"

"I prefer to think of myself as a man, not a boy."

We pulled into the parking lot of the antique mall on Eastern. Hector followed me down the aisles filled with armor suits, models of sailing ships, neon beer signs and embroidered Spanish shawls.

"Here's where I found the Red Mirror. It was just over there, against the Chinese screen."

No one was in the stall at the end of the maze, just like the first afternoon I saw the Red Mirror, and just like the day I bought it.

Hector pulled me back into him, slid his hand between my

thighs, and lifting me off the ground like I weighed nothing, carried me behind the yellow-flowered screen. He kissed my neck and my throat and nibbled at my ear. I gyrated my hips into his groin and whimpered while he stroked my breasts.

"I have wanted to do that since you first got in the car," he breathed into my neck as he turned me around.

His tongue was first deep in my throat, then in my ear. All the while his big hand with long, powerful cowboy fingers was between my legs. I was alive at his touch even through the thick denim.

He bent me slightly backwards and put his mouth on my sweater, suckling me through the wool. My hair swung in the air as I arched my back. Only the security camera stopped me from lifting my top. His strong hands, firm and commanding but without a trace of roughness, pressed on my stomach and down the inside of my loin.

The Spot burned like fire. Just the memory of his fingers there sent electric shocks through my buttocks, down my thighs and deep into my womb.

"You are so desirable, Isis. I want to touch you forever."

He stroked my breasts and the line of my hips. He suckled more. The pink of my sweater turned red where his mouth had been.

Iron fingers massaged me through my jeans. I was so wet I was sure there would be a stain. He eased down the zipper at the same time he leaned me back into a bookshelf. His fingers slid under my panties. I spread my legs to a V.

A vase fell first. Hector grabbed it in midair. But the bookcase kept swaying and when I reached back to steady it, I knocked a shelf loose, and a stack of dusty books, then something heavy, fell to the floor.

We both stared at the mess in horror and then at each other. Hector grinned.

"Look what you do to me," he said and kissed me lightly on the lips.

"Nothing's broken that I can see, so we're saved," I said.

Then I thought, it probably wouldn't matter to Hector. He'd just write a check. He wouldn't even think of cleaning up.

But Hector bent to the floor and picked up a canvas-wrapped packet about the size of a large, thick atlas. I recognized the size and shape immediately. Luckily it had fallen last and landed on a soft pile of books. He turned the crumbling fabric back, and a glint of shiny green glass shimmered in the fluorescent light.

"Isn't this something for you, Isis? Couldn't you read Greek on the other side?"

the following to be the truth…

The Emerald Tablet.

Hector slid his hand around my waist and pulled me back into him, but not hot with passion this time. His other hand reached across my breasts and around my shoulder to wrap me in his arms. He held me close but not tight. I could fly away and still come back to rest.

Leaning my head on his chest, letting him carry my weight, I relaxed into the cocoon of his body. Safe. Hector always made me feel safe.

"This tablet is something very special, Hector." I said cautiously. "More special than you could ever imagine."

"Then you must have it. It is yours."

He grinned his broad confident smile; I could see how much pleasure it gave him to please me. Being with him when he smiled was like watching Ra Rising.

When he saw how serious I was, he took my chin in his fingers and looked me deep in the eyes. His were the warmest of browns freckled with those reddish specks that picked up the highlights of his chestnut hair.

"Everything is yours, Isis, if you just let me give it to you."

I was tempted. Oh, how I was tempted. But did I really need Hector to give me what I wanted?

Now that I had the Emerald Tablet, couldn't I manifest everything myself? Couldn't I also have River God?

PART TWO

The Emerald Tablet

GREEK EGYPT

ATHENA

Yellow Silk Dream

I call it my yellow silk dream. It always starts out with buttery satin sliding on my bare skin. The room is bathed in white moonlight shining in from a terrace open to the stars.

Sometimes I hear gentle waves slurping pebbles from the shore. Mostly the world is silent.

Then the men come. Four of them. Their bodies are formed in every perfect detail, but I can't see their faces. Coalescing from the shadows, they draw nearer and nearer to cover my body with kisses before disappearing through green doors inscribed with words I don't understand. I know I am meant to follow and that it's crucial I choose the right door, but it's never clear to me exactly why.

What should be an erotic whimsy turns into a kind of mild, nagging nightmare. Instead of savoring the touch of the men's lips on my secret places, I wake up agitated and distressed.

I don't dream the yellow silk dream every time I sleep, but often enough that I lie in bed before I doze off and plan which door to pick. But in spite of my preparation, I never make a decision.

Even Aisha was fed up. She'd taken to deserting my restless bed to curl up a safe distance from whatever madness stalks my sleep. Seeing that I was myself again, she brushed her white whiskers across my cheek and purred a welcome-back melody in my ear.

Reflected in the Red Mirror was a beautiful blonde with a look in her eyes that said, I know exactly what I'm doing.

Yes, Aisha, I'm back—but not for long.

Hektor of Naukratis

The mood in the great hall of Aphrodite's Temple on the Akrokorinth switched quickly from somber and tense to light and playful. Young girls appeared with silver pitchers of wine and golden cups. The chorus of pastel-gowned priestesses strummed on their lyres again and sang softly.

Gliding with the grace of practiced dancers, the most accomplished of my thousand ladies flowed in clouds of musk among the men. Silver bells tinkled at their ankles; bells rang in their soft laughter. Trained singers all, their voices had a musical cadence.

A few teasing words reached my ear—they were setting up appointments for this evening. Now that the business portion of their visit had concluded for the day, the Alexandrians were intent upon enjoying the pleasures of Korinth.

Hector lost no time approaching me. I could see by his swagger and bold eyes that he didn't know me but intended to. He most certainly hadn't come through the Mirror.

His hair was the same rich chestnut, but instead of brushing the thick waves back from his brow, he wore barbered curls that fell on his forehead and around the ears. His white teeth blazed. Polished bronze greaves covered his long shins up past the knee. A scarlet cloak hung off his bare shoulder. All toned muscle, he had the rich mahogany tan that comes from training daily in the nude.

Surely Apollo the Sun God gave him his shine.

"Please accept my respects, Athena of Korinth. I am Hektor of

Naukratis. I had come today anticipating great beauty, yet I find myself more awed by your wit and grace. In beauty and youth, such intelligence is rare."

Charming words came easily to him. He delivered them in a most natural way, confident and without pretense.

He dared to touch my bare skin above the elbow, on the back of my arm. It had been a very long time since Athena had felt that thrill. I eased away from his hand, not a real rejection, but clearly signalling that he moved too fast.

Far from being discouraged, he seemed amused by my attempts at aloofness. He barely hid his triumph, arching his right eyebrow and giving me another of those bold looks implying intimacy.

In spite of his audacity, I found his virile self-assurance both galling and tantalizing. I suspected that, as much as Athena was accustomed to masking her thoughts, I didn't hide them very well.

"I am the houseguest of Xenon," he went on grandly, not missing a beat. "He begs you accept his invitation to an evening of music and poetry. The wine and the company shall be the best the city offers. And as the world knows, the best of all pleasures is found in Korinth."

He handed me a small scroll waxed with Xenon's seal. The neat script announced a *symposion* in honor of Hektor of Naukratis.

When I answered very coolly that I would perhaps drop by for a cup of wine, Hektor smiled without a trace of surprise. I'm sure that few women resisted his charms.

Just before he went through the door with his crimson cape swirling behind him, he turned back to catch my eyes admiring his broad shoulders and long thighs.

He nodded and smiled knowingly, again arching that eyebrow.

The spot on my arm where he'd touched me burned. So much for Athena the Ice Queen.

Symposion

Hektor was by my side at once. He exchanged a look with Xenon, arching his eyebrow slightly as he slipped the cape from my shoulders and handed it to a boy slave. I saw Xenon's wry smile as the look of a gambler who had lost a friendly bet.

This was not the first invitation I had received from Xenon, but it was the first I'd accepted.

Hektor's unashamed eyes travelled from my ripe breasts, down past my curvy hips and along my lush thighs to my pumiced and hennaed toenails before returning on my face.

"There are not words written to describe your beauty," he announced with a flash of white teeth, "so I shall seal my lips and let my eyes tell you what my heart feels."

We settled on a sofa of carved cypress covered by red cushions woven with yellow flying cranes. Crowded and noisy, the room was already too hot. I kept my feet on the footstool, my spine straight, and rested my elbow lightly on the high armrest.

A slave boy brought a gold chalice embossed with Dionysus capturing bare-breasted Ariadne in his muscled arms. Swan heads formed the two handles. Twin nude boys, carrying a silver *krater* inlaid with golden sunbursts, ladled wine into my cup. The wine was sweet, dark and hardly watered. Xenon intended for a wild night.

Hektor leaned back against the blue wall, drinking from his silver ram's head goblet and smiling at me over the top. His long legs, free of bronze greaves, stretched out along the divan. True to his word, he let his eyes speak; they said he was ready.

The room fell almost silent when a boy with chestnut skin and matching curls, nude body draped in garlands of poppies, plucked the strings of a *kithara* and sang verses from Sappho. His voice was that of an angel, high and sweet.

Here recline the Nymphs
at the hour of twilight,
Back in shadows dim of the cave,
their golden Sea-green eyes half-lidded,
up to their supple
Waists in the water.

Hektor's hand moved to my waist. I stiffened, and he moved his hand away. When I met his eyes, they still smiled.

"*Kallistei!*" Hektor toasted me. "To the most beautiful."

Each guest raised his *kylix* to me and then rushed to name another beauty. The toasts triggered a competition with the first man beginning an ode to his lover then passing the phrase to a second—then a third and so on—to complete the verse. The finish of each recitation ended with a toast. Xenon's guests were roaring drunk.

I sipped slowly at my own cup.

Immersing himself in the party, Hektor cheered out loud when merited and booed without pity when drunken words fell over each other and lost their sense. He joined in the heckling when young men competed in tossing their wine across the room to splash into a *krater.*

Although he often touched my arm and, more than once, the thigh band visible under my gown, he was patient, drawing me slowly from my shell with his confident and unhurried presence. Like a comet falling inexorably into the sun, I began to fall under his Apollo spell.

Small boys carried trays with stuffed dates, candied rose leaves, sesame cakes and raisins. The fish stew was flavored with fennel; a whole roast lamb appeared in an aromatic cloud of rosemary and garlic. It was most unusual to serve food at a *symposion*, but Xenon, too, made his own rules.

I had no appetite and scarcely took a bite. Both the unwatered wine and Hektor made me a little giddy.

Young men moved in close to older ones and let hands explore under *chitons*. A pair of nude youths wrestled in the center of the room, sweat glistening on their golden skin. The handful of *hetaerae* settled with their patrons to small acts of intimacy.

All the time, the musicians played double pipes and strummed the strings of lyres.

His palm warm and dry, Hektor stroked first my shoulder, then slowly down my arm and back up again. His touch was that of a master sculptor molding my flesh. I closed my eyes and let his warmth defrost me, one degree at a time.

His fingers on my cheek turned my face into his. Flecks of red gold floated in the warm brown of his eyes; shiny locks the color of polished cedar curled on his forehead.

"Athena of Korinth," he whispered, "why do you lock your fire inside marble? You have the face of a goddess but the too-serious expression of a woman past her prime. Have your duties aged you? Do you ever laugh?"

His words stung because they went straight to the truth. The Temple on the *Akrokorinth* employed more than a thousand women to be fed, clothed and cared for, even unto death. While the Goddess promised love and pleasure to others, my days were filled with petty squabbles, leaking roof tiles and unsettled debts.

"We do not always have choice in our lives," I answered too defensively. "I was a child when my father delivered me to the Temple. But I have worked all my life, and the Goddess has blessed me. When the Gods appoint, we must obey."

"You are far too intelligent to believe in that superstition, Athena of Korinth. Gods do not reward or punish—or ordain our lives.

Epicurus says that we are but atoms moving in space. We can only hope for pleasure and avoid pain. Why not accept pleasure for its own sake? Who can say that he will still live tomorrow?"

Sliding his arm around me, his hot palm moved onto the sheer bodice of my gown and took my breast in his hand. In one smooth, effortless motion, he reached down and eased my legs from the footstool to the divan, pulling me back into him, turning us on our sides, a little upright against the armrest. His manhood was a stone post at my back.

I held my breath while he cupped my other breast and his lips found that spot on my neck that opens all doors. I didn't try to suppress my moans of pleasure. I purred like a cat.

Hektor simply took me in his expert hands, doing exactly what I wanted but hadn't dared ask for. My nipples grew hard in an instant under his fingers and rose in tight peaks through the yellow silk.

He shocked me with a splash of wine on the mound of my breast. Before I could think to stop him, he sucked away the wine, leaving a dark circle. I ran my fingers through his curls, forgetting everything—where I was, who I was.

His long fingers eased up the back of my gown, sliding under the gossamer silk. He lingered for a moment to stroke the golden thigh band before caressing my hip, my inner loin, and then slipping into the wet. He went straight to a spot in my canal that only he, of all men, found.

Heat spread instantly through my pelvis and buttocks and down my loins. The atoms of my body, moving in space, melted into a pool of warm oil.

I gasped out loud when he rotated there with his finger; he covered my mouth with his other hand to still my cries. His lips and warm breath were on my neck soothing me with whispers in a low and husky voice.

"Sh-h-h. Relax, Athena of Korinth. You are so beautiful. Let me pleasure you."

I would have promised anything if his touch on that spot would never end. Surrendering all, I tumbled without sense of head or foot; rolling waves washed over me. The release was so needed, tears wet my lashes. Hektor kissed them away.

My mind stilled; I had no thoughts or cares. I lay utterly at ease with my body molded into his.

He had softened somewhat but was still hard. I reached back for him, but he stopped my hand.

"I shall take care of that later."

His tone sounded too matter-of-fact for a man lost in passion. He straightened the long skirt of my gown, pulled us upright and handed me the golden chalice. I felt dizzy and disoriented. I'd had too much wine and not enough to eat.

"You shall love Alexandria, and Alexandria shall love you," he was saying as if all had been decided.

I suddenly hated his smile. Rather than charming, I saw him as smug. Was this the strategy? Send Hektor to seduce me, and I would follow him back to Egypt? Did they honestly think me so weak that I could be tamed by an orgasm?

I willed my eyes to ice when I passed the golden goblet back to him. The lapis lazuli of the Hathor ring on my hand was almost black in the low light. Hektor's hands with knowing fingers were now occupied with his wine cup and mine.

"You have serviced me well, Hektor of Naukratis," I thanked him politely, frost hanging on every syllable. "You have most ungraciously reminded me that I must attend to my needs more frequently."

Turning my back on him, I called for my cape to cover my wine-stained breasts and bid good night to a sober Xenon. Then with my back straight as a sword and head held high, I followed the lamp boy up the steep slope to my sacred hill with the Temple that reveres women.

Trophy

The Ancient One scratched at my office door.

"Your Grace, Hektor of Naukratis requests an audience," she told me cautiously. "He is prepared to wait."

"Tell him that I am occupied with my duties."

"Do your duties ever allow you to enjoy the theatre?"

We both swirled at the sound of Hektor's male voice here in the most private of sanctuaries, my office. The Ancient One clutched her chest. I jumped from my chair to grab her arm as her knees hit the tile floor.

"How dare you enter my chambers?" I demanded. "Men are forbidden on the Temple grounds."

Mine was a small house at the back of a white-walled garden, the last building after a cluster of brick dormitories and storage rooms. My office with its window on the sea was up a steep flight of open stairs. Hektor had penetrated deep into sacred grounds.

His broad shoulders filled the doorway; he had to duck his head under the oak lintel. Leather sandals laced up to his knees. His *chiton*, ending at mid-thigh, fell on tanned, muscled loins. The scarlet cape on one shoulder was fastened with a golden lion that matched two armbands around his powerful wrists.

I resented that he was such a magnificent specimen of masculinity—and even more, that I noticed.

"You must leave at once," I insisted. "Your presence here offends the Goddess."

But instead of leaving, Hektor helped the Ancient One from the floor and settled her on a three-legged stool. Without any hesitation, he found the water urn and bent to a squat to put a clay cup to her lips, holding it for her while she sipped. She squeezed her eyes shut as if frightened to see what evil filled the room.

Her breathing slowed. He asked if she were hurt. She shook her head and opened her eyes. She actually looked at Hektor with gratitude, seeming to forget it was his audacity that had caused her to fall.

I glared at him, but he looked at the Ancient One, not at me.

"Do not blame her," he commanded. "I followed her here."

"I blame no one but you."

Satisfied the Ancient One was revived and unharmed, he rolled back on his haunches and faced me.

"I sail the day after tomorrow for Egypt, Athena. You shall not see me for weeks." He spoke as if we were long-time lovers. "Come to the theatre with me. There is a performance this afternoon of Menander's *Double Deceiver*."

I had to give him credit for persistence. He appeared oblivious to my position as Supreme Priestess; men usually cowered in my presence.

"You need a break from your work, woman. I fear your frown will etch itself into your brow."

The Ancient One turned wide eyes on me. It was clear she waited for my response. That surprised me—we both knew there could be only one answer. I had a thousand details to oversee before I sailed for Alexandria.

"I have no time to waste," I snapped impatiently. "You were at Delphi. You heard the Oracle."

"At last, she acknowledges the truth! Indeed, my sweet Athena of Korinth, you have no time to waste. Each moment that passes is gone forever. The difference in men's lives is simply how moments are passed. Do you choose to pass them in pleasure or pain?"

"And if I choose not to go to the theatre, does that mean I prefer pain? Perhaps time spent with you is more pain than pleasure?"

Hektor smiled. We both knew any pain he caused was born of the pleasure he'd given me. There was no point in pretending the *symposion* never happened.

He had a disarming and infectious enthusiasm about him that was almost boyish. For a moment, I envied his freedom to choose pleasure. My desk overflowed. Piles of scrolls and wax tablets nearly buried the floor mosaic of a nymph struggling in the arms of a satyr.

Yes, I was tempted, I really was.

"In any event," I said with more conviction than I felt, "we live not as we wish but as we can."

"Sad words from a beautiful woman who could have anything she wished. I ask you only to the theatre. Leave all this behind for one afternoon. It shall be here when you return."

"You do not strike me as a man who lacks for company. There must be many women who would be pleased by your attention. Why do you pursue me with so much persistence?"

"Why pursue you? Because, beautiful Athena, you beg to be pursued. Your signals are subtle but unmistakable. And I love a challenge. Is it not harder to conquer a woman than to subdue a wild beast?"

A challenge. And a conquest. I was used to that kind of thinking. What I didn't like was that he saw me as needy and begging to be pursued.

The Ancient One sat quite still and made no move to leave; she hadn't said a word. Did she hope to protect me—or that Hektor and I would forget her and play out our drama as if alone?

Her presence didn't at all deter Hektor.

"Life is too important to be taken seriously," he said taking my shoulders in his big, strong, warm hands. "We have only this moment—only here and now."

Hektor never once kissed me at the *symposion* but had conquered me with his lips on my neck and breasts. How easy it had been for him. I saw my own head mounted on a wall among his trophies of lion and wild boar.

I tried to move away, but he held me firmly without being forceful.

"Pleasuring you gave me pleasure in a new way. I want more. *You* want more. Listen, Athena—your need speaks to you now."

His hands stroked slowly down my back, his long fingers molding my waist and spreading across my hips. He cupped my buttocks in his palms and pulled me into him. I felt my arms slide around his neck.

Lowering his head slowly, holding my eyes, I knew he was going to kiss me, even with the Ancient One looking on. What I didn't know was whether, with the Ancient One looking on, I would open my lips and welcome him.

The General

"Tread carefully with Hector, Isis," Isabel warned. "My son is not the man you think he is."

I was standing a little in shock at Isabel's last words, watching her weave her elegant way through the tourists and gamblers in the Bellagio lobby, when a man stepped up behind me.

"May I offer you a drink?"

The General laughed just a little when he saw the expression on my face. Surprise and fear, I imagine, is what he read. That's what I felt.

"Somewhere safe?" he suggested. He glanced in the direction of the Petrossian Bar. "Here?"

I stood there like a dummy, trying to decide if I should run.

"Are you afraid I'll throw a cloak over your head and carry you off?" he chuckled.

"The thought did cross my mind."

Then his smile came—the same as in the tent in the Persian camp, the smile that crinkled his eyes.

"Come, Ishtar. No tricks. I promise."

He called me Ishtar again—the name he'd given me when I was his sex slave. My first impulse had been to get away from him as quickly as possible, but instead, I sat for the second time today at a table in the Petrossian Bar.

The waiter smiled big and said, "Welcome back." Isabel must have left a nice tip.

I ordered a Plymouth martini, and the General told the waiter to make it two.

He was more handsome than I remembered. His rough and pitted skin was appealingly savage; no matter how well-groomed, he couldn't hide his animal power. He had the chest of a bull, even in his tailored suit. He wore his hair a little long in the European way. His deep red tie at the throat brought vivid visions of gushing dark blood.

His tone with me was conversational, even friendly. He seemed perfectly at ease. I saw him reclining in his desert tent in silk robes, beard carefully curled and tied with colored ribbons.

He swallowed a gulp of his icy martini and took both giant olives in his mouth, chewing with a smile and studying me, nodding his head slightly.

"It would seem we move in the same circles. First Rasheed, and now Señora de Segovia. Las Vegas is a small world."

"Isabel—Señora Segovia—is mentoring me," I replied, although not sure why I felt compelled to explain. I wasn't his captive anymore.

"And Rasheed?" That's when his eyes got serious and locked onto mine.

"Rasheed is none of your business."

He raised his eyebrows and smiled a little. I couldn't tell if he knew Rasheed had dumped me that night at Caesars. I wouldn't give him the satisfaction of learning that his not-so-subtle insinuations had succeeded in driving Rasheed away.

"He doesn't know anything about us, General. I'd suggest you keep it that way—if you want to do business with him, that is."

My warning seemed to amuse him. I studied his face, trying to gauge what he knew, wishing that he might tell me something about Rasheed. Had he seen him? Had he mentioned me? *Would he ever come back?*

But before I could try to draw him out, he put his thick fingers under my chin and turned my face slightly sideways and up. His eyes travelled from my hair, around each feature, and ended by looking in my eyes.

I held my breath for one long moment while the scene in his tent played like a hologram between us—my ride on a comet. I felt it. He felt me feel it.

This was too close to what I'd feared would happen. I willed my voice to be firm, uncompromising and devoid of fear. I wanted to be absolutely clear.

"I'm not going with you—and you're not coming with me. This is not going anywhere."

Why was I sitting here? Why hadn't I run when I saw him?

He chuckled a little at my declaration, as if it were the last thing on his mind. Then he leaned forward the tiniest bit.

"I have a proposal for you, Ishtar. I know you like a challenge."

He had to know he used the same words a couple of thousand years ago when he gave me the choice of life or death.

"I am a collector of fine things. I find it more successful if I do not show interest in any item by openly bidding on it. I employ agents who do the buying for me. They earn a respectable commission on each purchase, and of course, I pay all expenses."

I stared at him. I'm sure my face was sheer astonishment.

"Are you offering me a job?"

"I am offering to pay you for your services. That should make a pleasant change for us."

I laughed. How could I not? He joined me, and I felt close to him for a breath. We had shared the most intimate of experiences—passion ending in death.

"Why would you want to hire me? Or do I want to know?"

"All you need to know is that I want to acquire a number of artifacts that will be more sought after if word gets out that I am interested. There are those who would outbid me simply for the pleasure of seeing me lose."

"And that's all there is to it? You want to buy something and don't want the price driven up? That's the reason for the cloak and dagger?"

'Cloak and dagger' slipped out quite innocently. I blinked after saying it. Until now, we'd never mentioned my slitting his throat and escaping in his cloak.

I hadn't meant to be funny, but for the second time tonight, he laughed out loud.

The General was a lot more relaxed in this lifetime. I laughed with him, and he signalled for another round of martinis.

The Petrossian Bar filled up. There was only one seat left at the bar. The hum at the adjacent gaming tables grew louder as evening players began to show.

"I do have choices this time, General. I don't have to accept your offer."

"No, you don't, but you will."

"How can you be so sure?"

"Because you accepted having a drink with me."

His eyes smiled at me across the table.

"That tells me that you are searching for something. Why else would you play games with a man you so feared that you killed him? You *are* playing games with me, aren't you, Ishtar?"

"I'm more interested, General, in learning why you are playing with me." I wasn't going to let him control the conversation. He'd taught me that. I'd learned from the best.

He surprised me with a flicker of tenderness in his eyes, saying, "I had forgotten why I find you so compelling. As afraid as you are, you show no fear. There are few who stand up to me—and no other woman."

His voice lingered over 'no other woman' in a wistful way. Then he smiled and raised his glass.

"I, too, enjoy a challenge, Ishtar. That's another thing we have in common." His eyes twinkled; he loved baiting me with unsubtle reminders of our shared taste for dark passion.

We sipped on our martinis. He relaxed back in his chair. He knew my decision, and I knew it, too.

I was sick of my job. I was tired of scraping by every month.

"If I decide to work for you, then work will be it," I cautioned. "Nothing more. Don't expect anything else."

"I expect you to be you. What else could I expect?"

I wasn't so happy with his response; it left open a lot of doors. He was skilled at easing the way, though.

"We won't tell Rasheed about our arrangement, *ma bella*. That *is* what you want, isn't it? For Rasheed not to know about us."

The General reached out again and slowly traced his middle finger down my cheek. His eyes were hypnotic. I didn't pull away.

"This will be our secret." His voice was low, soft for him, mesmerizing. "You can trust me."

He put a business card on the table with his cell number and email address. I couldn't take my eyes off the crocodile logo printed in the upper right hand corner.

The Crocodile spells the end and the beginning. The prophecy of the Oracle of Delphi to Athena. *Two Roads. One leads to honor, the other to slavery.*

"Send me an email," he went on, "and I will forward you the specifics."

When we stood to go, I repeated, "Strictly business. Expect nothing."

And then as if another person were speaking, I heard myself say, "Unless you can convince me otherwise."

I couldn't get to my car fast enough. I half expected him to follow me—or send his little army of bodyguards—but he didn't.

Barb was right. I was crazy. I don't know why I said something like that, except I seemed to have developed a taste for playing with fire.

Black Falcon

Metal rattled on the door. The sound was so slight, I wasn't sure at first if I heard it, but the creak of the wood from a step affirmed someone entered the cabin. It was so dark, there were no shadows.

My mind took a moment to realize I was at sea. I could hear waves against the hull and slow breathing, quiet and controlled. Should I lie still and pretend to sleep or sit up and confront the intruder?

The hand came out of the darkness, but instead of grabbing me, it reached for Jason. I clutched his thin body to me, and he awoke instantly, a young animal alert for danger.

"No," we shouted in unison, but the hand dragged him from my arms and stood him to his feet.

"Get out," Black Falcon commanded.

Jason, a wisp of a shadow, refused to move.

Black Falcon lifted him, pushed him across the threshold, firmly closed the door and moved a chest to block the entrance. I only saw vague forms; his eyes were more adjusted to the dark than mine.

When Jason's sobs came through the thick wood, I rose from the mat and put my lips to the narrow crack to soothe him.

"Do not fear for me, Jason. Go sleep with the Nubian."

But to Black Falcon I whispered, "Why do you come to me like this? Why do you frighten the boy?"

"He is a slave."

"He is *my* slave."

His fingers were in my hair, loosening the braid, releasing the thick waves to fall around my shoulders and down my back. He lifted a handful and buried his face in my scent.

I traced the deep lines in his cheeks with my fingertips and then outlined his lips, recalling with sweet memory every kiss of River God, each kiss of Rasheed.

Black Falcon's breath was hot and moist. I explored his tongue, tugging and pinching gently with my fingers. He bit down with equal gentleness and sucked.

The knot of his loincloth melted in my fingers, and the linen fell away.

Swaying on tiptoes, pressing my breasts into his chest, feeling him hard against my belly, I kissed his lower lip, drawing the flesh between my teeth, matching his soft bite on my fingers. I licked his throat where his Adam's apple bulged slightly.

His body was so tight I thought he might shatter into a thousand shards of glass.

Taking my time, my hands glided along his shoulders and down his biceps, caressing his forearms to his wrists. When I raised his thumbs to my erect nipples, he quivered and jerked. Hot semen sprayed the front of my gown.

Only steps from the wall, I nudged him with my palm on his chest to lean against the damp rough bulkhead.

"Sh-h-h, let me love you," I crooned in the soft, irresistible cadence of a lullaby.

All the while I breathed promises in his ear, my fingers loosened the tie at my right shoulder and then the left. The milky gown slid past my breasts and hips to pile silently on the floor around my ankles. The flowing waves of my hair were heavy on my bare back.

Mesmerized and breathless, he allowed his thirsty eyes to drink in my breasts glowing white in the starlight.

With the most loving of touches, with my lips hot on his bronzed chest, I took his hands in mine and placed his fingers in my hair.

There was no place that I didn't taste; I savored his salty sweetness with my tongue. I suckled first one nipple, then the other, my fingers toying at the thick nest of hair at the bottom of his belly. Entangled in my waves, his fists pulled and twisted. The low rumbles of his moans filled the silence.

His back muscles were as tight as knotted rope under my fingertips. I willed my hot palms to ease him, stroking down his back, past his narrow waist to his hips and hard thighs. I willed my lips to excite him. My wet tongue went into his navel, and his manhood swelled into my face.

I circled the engorged knob with my tongue, licking and nibbling. He writhed against the wooden bulkhead, his feet spread wide, hips thrusting toward me. But before I could take him into my mouth, he pulled my face up, his fingers still in my hair, and kissed me.

Only his kiss could carry me to that warm liquid world of rose-colored water and sky. I floated to the narrow mat on the floor, weighing nothing, nothing at all.

There was no rage in him now, only need. He vibrated against me; every cell in his body cried out for me, but still he resisted, refusing to flow into me as I flowed into him. I offered him my soul to meld into me.

Arranging me as an artist does a model, he spread my hair out around my head. He caressed first the length of one thigh and then the other, stroking between my loins, spreading my legs. His fingers dipped in my wet and then spread me on his lips before kissing me long and deep, his tongue probing mine.

My hands were everywhere; I couldn't stop touching him, couldn't stop exploring all those familiar places.

Not in a hurry—I have never known him to hurry—he rediscovered every inch of me. He kissed my toes, my ankles, the back of my knees, but waited to enter the gate to pleasure. He kissed my fingers, my palms, my wrists, inside my elbows, the base of my neck, but waited to touch my breasts. I thought of a thousand places I wanted him to taste but surrendered to his pace. He would find them all.

I cared about nothing else in that moment. I wanted to be nowhere else. If I could have changed anything, it would have been to give him two mouths, that he might kiss my lips and my body at the same time.

The swells of the sea rocked the ship in the languid, seductive rhythm of the Mediterranean. The night was mild and silent. I could hear my shallow breath mingling with his; the purr in my throat reverberated in my ears.

When his lips returned to that magic place in the hollow of my neck, the spot that opens all doors, I took his face in my hands and breathed, "Trust me."

I retraced with my own lips on his perfect body every kiss he had given me. I felt him hold himself back, struggling for control while my caresses opened the tiniest chink in his armor.

"I shall not hurt you," I pleaded.

I took him in my hand and pumped slowly, very slowly, the length of my body rubbing against him with the same rhythm.

We have this moment only; there is only here and now. Hektor's words were in my head—but not Hektor. For the briefest of instants, I saw his Apollo smile flash and felt his warmth, and then he was gone. Here and now belonged to Black Falcon.

Black Falcon gripped my wrist, stilling my hand. "I want it to last."

Waves whispered against the cedar planks separating us from the sea. Starlight gave just enough light for me to see the intensity in his face. His eyes smoldered; his arms were dark and lustrous. Long coils of my hair shimmered on my white arm and shoulder. Far away, in another world on the other side of the door, Jason snored lightly.

I wet my finger and traced around his ear. With his hands under my buttocks, Black Falcon lifted me into him and drove in one thrust to fill me. He stopped. Neither of us moved.

I felt him shudder ever so slightly—not in climax—but in relief to be home. No matter how many centuries and lifetimes passed, it was always the same between us.

I waited, breathless, until I felt him surrender. Every muscle in his body relaxed; he flowed into me, at last, as I flowed into him.

Back and forth, in and out, rocking with the hypnotic pulse of the sea, he moved my hips with his. I clung to the nape of his neck, my fingers stretched out on his shaved head. Our mouths were one, breathing each other's breath, mingling our cries.

I reached for his full sacks with my fingertips, and he exploded with a great shaking and trembling. Dropping his head, he sucked in air with huge gulps. The heat of his shoulders seared my palms; his sweat glistened.

"Touch me, please touch me," I whispered.

He stroked me like a cat. I stretched for him to pet me.

His broad, moist tongue on my nipple left hot saliva that tingled as it cooled. He circled and licked and teased before he sucked. I imagined my hot milk spilling into his mouth.

There was nothingness all around me; I heard nothing. The wave rose and rose, and I lost myself in the vast void until it crested.

"O-o-o-o-o," I sang, clinging to him, my lips at his throat relishing his salt.

The ship rocked; the wood creaked and strained. A seagull called out. We lay perfectly still on the narrow mat, breathing together, two bodies so entwined we might have been one.

When the stars faded and we saw the first lavender light of dawn framed in the cabin window, Black Falcon rose and put on his loincloth, tunic and kilt. As I watched him from the mat, the scene at the Wynn played in my mind. That day Rasheed had walked away with no word for the future.

Well, he couldn't leave me now. We were on a ship. He had nowhere to go.

Kneeling beside me, he lifted a lock of my hair and put it to his lips, kissing me through my hair. There was so much tenderness in his eyes. He stroked my face in exactly the same way as he'd caressed me the morning he disappeared two thousand years from now. I stiffened in dread of his next words.

"My man Goliath will move your things to my cabin."

O Aphrodite! I shall make sacrifice at your altar the rest of my days!

Still, I wasn't too spellbound to ask, "What about the boy?"

For the first time, I saw Black Falcon smile. Not a real smile, but the turned-up-corners half-smile of Rasheed.

"He shall not sleep with us."

And then he moved the chest, opened the door and stepped over Jason curled up outside.

As Heraclitus says, the sun is new each day.

Hektor

It was to Hektor's credit that he sent word in advance that he would pass by my guest villa on the Pharaoh's grounds in the early evening to hear if there was anything I required. He wasn't so forward as to invite himself to dine, but the rules of hospitality guaranteed him at least a cup of wine.

I sent Jason to bed with his papyrus scroll and Kallisto the kitten.

When Hektor arrived, crimson cloak over his shoulder, he looked around for the boy, and not seeing him, said, "I have brought your slave sweets."

He barely concealed his satisfaction that I had chosen for us to be alone.

We had settled on the tangerine sofas and taken a cup of Cypriot wine when he set a packet of emerald green silk on the brass tray set on a low wooden tripod between us.

"For me?" I asked innocently.

"For you," he answered, raising an eyebrow.

The folds of the silk revealed a heavy gold necklace with seven exquisite gold owls suspended from a thick chain. The owl is the symbol of Athena, my namesake, the Goddess of Wisdom. I recognized Macedonian gold work. The piece was worth a fortune.

"Do you hope to buy my attention?" My words were softened by a coy tone which held more than a hint of invitation.

"There is not enough gold in the world to buy you or your attention. I would not be so foolish as to think a trifle like a necklace would gain me favor. You require something much more than that."

He waited a few moments. The sun had set; the sky deepened to lavender, the color of my gown. Across the Great Harbor, the *Pharos*, fabled Lighthouse of Alexandria, blazed. Salt air mixed with the scent of jasmine. The only sounds were the waves breaking on the gravel beach and a nightingale. Another answered. A slight wind rustled the leaves of the myrtle trees, and in my mind's eye, I saw white petals float gently to the grass like first snow.

Hektor moved gracefully around the brass tray table to stand next to my sofa, towering over me, his shoulders so broad they filled the room. The Spot throbbed.

Taking my silence as consent, he scooped me into his arms, carried me across the pink granite tiles to my white marble bedchamber and lay me carefully on the linen spread. He removed his cloak, never taking his eyes off me. He untied the thongs of his sandals laced to his knees without once looking. But before he took off his *chiton*, he noticed Jason asleep at the foot of my bed with the kitten and the open scroll.

He picked him up, and then the kitten and scroll, setting both on Jason's stomach, and carried all into the next room.

I didn't move waiting for him to return. Would Hektor's expert touch help me forget Black Falcon? A delicate winged Eros, chubby and pink, smiled down from the painted ceiling above my bed. As I watched, he flitted among white doves, lyres and bunches of purple grapes. My mouth was incredibly dry, but not my secret valley. The Spot burned.

Hektor towered over me once more, pulling the *chiton* over his head and untying his loincloth until he stood naked, the long muscles of his glorious body highlighted by the glow of a bronze oil lamp with star and moon cutouts. Tiny stars and crescent moons reflected off the marble walls and Hektor's bronzed skin. His manhood swelled and rose in the air, head glistening.

"You are so beautiful," he whispered and then lowered himself next to me.

His strong hand with long fingers stroked along my shoulder and across my throat. He caressed the tops of my breasts showing above the lavender silk, not touching my erect nipples rising in the lustrous fabric. Would he spill wine on me again? My heart raced, and the peaks rose higher at the memory.

I watched him as he focused on my breasts rising and falling, enjoying his tease, waiting for him take me in his full lips, to feel his wet tongue on me. The amber glow of the oil lamps streaked his mane of rich waves and curls with fiery red. When he saw me looking at him, he smiled slightly and put his mouth to my breast and began to suckle me through the silk, leaving dark circles. The heat of his hands warmed me.

Tears welled in my eyes; my moans were soft vibrations humming in my ears. The Spot burned hotter.

He loosened the ties of my gown and removed the gold pins; the cloth tumbled from my bare shoulders. His hands again stroked only my bare skin. Then with the moves of an expert, he eased the top of my gown to my waist.

"You are so desirable," he sang in the lowest and huskiest of tones.

I reached out to touch his engorged manhood, to feel his smooth tip, but he stopped me—like the evening of the *symposion* in Korinth. But I had no doubts about his desire tonight.

"Let me pleasure you, Athena of Korinth."

I relaxed into delicious luxury. He required nothing from me but to enjoy his touch. When he slid my gown up my thighs, past the curve of my hips to join the cloth gathered at my waist, I parted my legs, inviting him, holding my breath in anticipation of what I knew would come next.

He focused wholly on my body; his eyes followed his hands as they caressed me.

"I could never tire of touching you."

Hektor stroked my stomach and down the slope of my thigh. He stroked my breasts and the line of my hips. His hands were strong, his touch firm and commanding without a trace of roughness or urgency. Always the master sculptor, he molded my flesh.

"You are more perfect than Aphrodite herself."

I drew a sharp intake of air when his finger went straight to the Spot. Draping my legs over his loins, I filled my hands with his thick cedar curls.

"O-o-o-o-o-o," I sang, the note rising and falling, louder and louder as his finger rotated on the magic spot that only he knew. Electric shocks spread through my buttocks, down my thighs and up into my belly.

With the sound of the sea in my ears, I let the wave slowly build, wanting it not to crest but for the sensation to go on forever. When I thought the pleasure could not be greater, his finger slid along my wet valley to rotate on my lotus. The dam burst, and I swept over the falls.

He kissed the tears from my cheek and whispered into my ear, "Beautiful Athena. There is more."

Pulling me back into him, both of us on our side, he slipped his hardness deep into my wet and then pulled all the way out again. I gasped. With one arm under me, his big hand with long fingers stroked my nipples, steady, sensual, patient. His other hand cupped my mound; the base of his palm pressed against the base of my womb.

I cried out when his manhood slid in—and again when it slid out. He sucked my insides out with him each time he left my canal. He kept me guessing when he would next enter.

His face buried in my hair, I felt his hot breath on my neck.

"I want to touch you and be in you forever," he crooned. "I could never have enough of you."

He never tired. His hands stroked me all over as if I were Kallisto the kitten. His long fingers massaged my lotus while his rod moved slowly in, and drew slowly out, as the waves of the sea suck pebbles from the shore. I pushed my hips back into his belly, gyrating slowly and rhythmically like a Persian dancer.

"Do not think of anything, Athena. Just feel."

A thrill shot through me when his tongue went in my ear. I pressed my thighs together, squeezing his hardness inside me, not letting him pull out, reaching back to grip the back of his thigh and glide with him. He filled me. We moved with a slow steady rhythm. I rode the buildup, feeling and not thinking, holding my breath until my canal pulsed, contracted and pulsed again.

Taking my face in his hands, he kissed me with a tenderness I would never have believed of him. His lips covered mine; his tongue probed deep. When he tried to pull away, I gripped the back of his neck and lifted my head to follow him, my lips clinging to his.

He laughed and kissed me lightly on the tip of my nose.

"Why do you laugh?" I had dared trust him; I had dared to trust again.

"Because you are such a delight."

When he smiled, it was not his usual broad flash of white teeth but a sweet half-smile. A new warmth in his eyes replaced amusement and all arrogance; if he saw me as a trophy, I was one he sincerely cherished. He kissed me most lovingly first on my lips, then on each eye.

"Now you," I breathed in his ear.

"Do not think of me," he laughed again. "I can go all night."

I believed him. He almost did. I heard the first cock crow when he left my bed. We had not slept.

The Golden Youth

When we knocked at the door to Antinous' office at the Library of Alexandria, there was no answer. I tried again and then pushed open the polished cedar door and stepped into a spartan white chamber lined with shelves overflowing with scrolls.

Antinous was in deep conversation with a golden teen who was impossibly more beautiful than Antinous himself. No barber could ever create those luxurious strawberry blond waves; they were a gift from the Gods.

Antinous looked up when I entered. He turned immediately back to the youth, put his arm around the boy-god's shoulder and smiled at him warmly. The familiar way in which they touched left no doubt as to their intimacy.

I felt foolish and embarrassed—and regretted that I hadn't waited for Antinous to answer the door. Everyone knew about these special relationships between Greek men and teenagers. *Erastes* and *eromenos*—lover and loved. But that didn't make it easy to accept with Antinous.

Most Greek women resented their husband's intimate companions. How could she compete? It was an inherently unfair playing ground. The wife remained sequestered in the home while the men trained for war, debated philosophy and attended *symposia*— all forbidden to her. She could never join one of their drinking clubs. Only entertainers, temple girls and *hetaerae* were allowed.

It was painfully obvious that Antinous was the youth's *erastes*, his teacher and mentor. If they were sexually intimate—and I was convinced they were—Antinous was the penetrator.

I felt an irrational, visceral reaction to the vision of Antinous screwing this beautiful boy. I had no right to be jealous, but I was. I suspected that the youth was the reason Antinous had declined my dinner invitation; he preferred the teenager to me. By the look of his touch and his warm smile, it was obvious he loved the boy.

The teen left Antinous to stand before me and bow his head just enough to show respect.

"Leandros of Ephesus, Lady." His tone was polite and not in the least obsequious. "Peace be with you."

His eyes were the most astonishing blue I'd ever seen. I was quite startled just looking into them. Alexander the Great was said to have eyes like these, eyes that mesmerized everyone he met.

I had thought perfection defined by Antinous, but Leandros was without flaw. I surrendered all thought of competing with him. I couldn't offer what he offered—their Y chromosomes spoke to each other in a way I never could.

He passed by me, past Jason, and out the door. The slave Ajax stepped far aside and bowed his head deeply, chin on his chest. This teenager was someone important, or the son of someone important, which is the same thing.

Antinous smiled at me and put his hand on Jason's head. He showed no discomfort at all.

"You may leave Jason in my safekeeping," he assured me. "I shall return him to you knowing how to read."

His blue eyes said nothing about what he felt about the teenage beauty with Alexander's eyes—or about me.

Tony

Packing my suitcase for the New York auction and my first job for the General, I went for a sophisticated look with a black Chanel suit, patent pumps and pearls.

When I emptied my clutch, a business card fluttered to the bed.

Anthony Callis, PhD
Director of Cosmology
Institute of Advanced Studies
Princeton NJ

It was the card Antinous—Tony in this life—gave me the night I ran into him at Caesar's Palace.

On a wild impulse, I sent a quick email asking if he remembered an Isis from Cleopatra's Barge in Las Vegas. The reply came from his Blackberry about one minute later.

To: Isis
From: Tony
How many beautiful women named Isis does a rocket scientist meet?
To: Tony
From: Isis
I'm going to be in New York. Is it too far from Princeton to meet me for a drink?
To: Isis
From: Tony
Martinis? When and where?

Tony and I spent the afternoon at the Metropolitan Museum and walked back through Central Park. It was one of those perfect New York days with the first hint of spring in the air.

There were a few moments of awkwardness in the lobby of my hotel before I decided to ask him up while I changed my boots and grabbed a warmer jacket.

We didn't speak or look at each other in the elevator. I kept seeing him as muscular *Diadoumenos* cast forever in marble. I wondered if he saw me as *Aphrodite*, and then told myself to stop it.

The door to my room opened with the keycard, and I stepped in. It all happened so fast, I didn't have time to turn on the light.

Tony pinned me to the door with his perfect body. He didn't put his hands on me but placed his forearms on either side of my head. The light from the city through the floor-to-ceiling windows was just enough to see his face. His features sharpened as my eyes adapted.

He asked me without words, looking intently into my eyes. His eyelashes were incredibly thick and curly. A halo of loose blond ringlets framed his face. He didn't make a move, waiting for me.

I bit my lower lip. *Don't do it! You'll be sorry.*

But I ignored the Light and nodded ever so slightly, giving my consent. Tony kissed me so hard I thought my head would go through the reinforced door. I suspected he hadn't slept with a woman since his wife died. The pent-up passion exploded into a force of nature.

Tony ate me alive; his lips crushed mine with his tongue down my throat. His hands on my shoulders, then my waist, and then my hips were those of a wrestler crushing his opponent. I cried out once or twice when he was too rough, and he slowed down, but not for long.

He ripped my sweater over my head and unzipped my jeans. His hands were under my panties in front, then in back, and then in front again. He kissed my neck, my throat, my shoulders and my lips. I could feel him hard as iron pressing against my stomach. Pinned to the door, I could barely move.

Pulling his shirt over his head without unbuttoning, his lips were back on mine the moment the cloth cleared his face. His chest was as perfect as *Diadoumenos*. My fingertips caressed his taut skin, and if I thought he had been wild before, it was nothing compared to the beast my touch unleashed.

With his hands gripping my buttocks, his fingers digging into my flesh, he lifted me with no more effort than he heaved a climber's backpack. My legs locked around his waist. I held onto the back of his neck with one hand while stroking his gorgeous chest and bulging biceps with the other. He carried me to the desk, shoving the lamp aside. It tumbled and crashed. I heard the shatter of broken glass.

Nothing slowed him. Using his toes on the heel, he pried off one of his sneakers, then the other. He unzipped his khakis with one hand while the other gripped my hip as if I might run away. I would have helped him, but he moved so fast and with such intensity, I was afraid to get in the way.

He pulled his slacks down to his ankles and kicked them across the room. He tugged my left boot off and then the right. I clung to the desk, else he would have yanked me to the floor. Peeling my jeans from me in one movement, he tossed them aside without so much as a glance.

I reached behind and unfastened my bra; he buried his face in my breasts at the same time he yanked down my panties. I had been stripped naked in less than a minute. His boxers disappeared somewhere in the dark room.

Then he stopped. He put his forehead on the top of my head and breathed heavily for a few moments, his chest heaving. I caught a faint whiff of locker room sweat—unabashedly male.

"I'm sorry," he apologized. "It's been so long."

I kissed him to let him know everything was fine, and he squeezed me all over, his hands so strong I knew his fingers left red marks. It felt wonderful to be ravaged in such a delicious, unthreatening way.

I rode the frenzy with him. He never actually hurt me, and if he went too far, he listened to my whimpers and backed off.

He pounded me, my legs locked around his waist, our bodies rocking the desk, slamming it against the wallpapered wall. I expected the phone to ring with a warning from Security to quiet down.

When he came, it was like a convulsion. His body shook, then trembled, then shook again. Gooseflesh rose all over him; I caressed the millions of hair follicles electrifying his skin.

Taking time only to catch his breath, he lifted me and carried me to the bed. He was already hard again. Rolling me to my stomach, he shoved a pillow under my belly. I reached out for the headboard and grabbed hold of the edge. With his hands gripping my hips, he plunged into me, over and over.

The bed rocked, and the headboard banged the wall. I held on, pushed back—and again feared the phone might ring. But I didn't try to calm him.

He dragged me to the foot of the bed, with my breasts squashed into the bedspread and my knees on the floor. His hands were none too gentle, but still he never hurt me. My cries, loud before, changed to wild shouts. Clutching the bedspread in my fists, I buried my face in it, thrusting myself back into him.

With a kind of wrestler-lover hold, he clutched me with one powerful arm gripped around my waist and the other tight around my chest and shoulders while he plunged. I cried out in a sound more cat than human as release rolled through my pelvis in waves.

Tony dropped me on the bed and rolled me over. My arms lay limp, stretched out, palms up. He thrust inside me again, once, twice, three times, and then his back arched, and he actually howled.

I started laughing; I couldn't help myself.

"That good, huh?"

He collapsed next to me, roaring as loud as a lion. We laughed until tears came, lying next to each other on the bedspread, stark naked, drenched in sweat.

"I'm starving," he declared. "Let's order room service."

When I came out of the bathroom, he sat with his back against the headboard, still naked. His perfect body glowed in the soft light of two shaded lamps; a giant smile spread across his face.

"Man, that was great!" he announced. "Can we do it again?"

I laughed and started to slip on the white terry cloth hotel robe.

"Wait!" he shouted, ripping the bedspread back and jerking a sheet off the bed. He draped the sheet around me, lifted my arms and adjusted my hips so I stood in the classic *contrapposto* position.

Raising the TV remote in the pose of an emperor with his scepter, he commanded in a theatrical voice, "I am the god Ares. You are my sex slave. I forbid you to wear blue jeans again."

I envisioned a laurel wreath around his head—the champion of the Games.

We managed another quick round and were under the sheets laughing and giggling when room service knocked on the door. We devoured the hamburgers and guzzled the cold beer; Tony threw most of the French fries at me. We slept on salty, stained sheets.

I woke to sunshine streaming in the windows, Tony's hands on my breasts and his hard-on against my butt.

"You're insatiable. Don't you ever get enough?" But I giggled like a college girl and only pretended to struggle.

He maneuvered me into one of his wrestling holds and ran his fingers over my body until he found where it tickled.

"Stop," I shouted. "You're a sadist!"

He beamed, relaxed his hold and then kissed me quite tenderly, asking, "Has sex ever been this much fun?"

"Order some breakfast while I hop in the shower."

But the hot water had just come when he slipped into the glass stall with me. His erection was huge, and so was his grin. He soaped me all over, and then I soaped him, massaging his balls and his penis until he exploded, his back leaning against the marble tiles of the shower. Hot water rained down on us.

"Go," I commanded. "I have to get dressed. Room service should be here by now."

Hair washed and hanging wet on my shoulders, I wrapped the

second white hotel robe around me and called out, "Tony! Has breakfast arrived?"

Standing in the middle of the room was not room service but Hector.

They faced each other—Tony, all wet from the shower in a white terry cloth robe matching mine, and Hector in his bomber jacket and jeans, half a head taller, an overnight case in one hand and a bouquet of red roses in the other. They both turned to me when I opened the bathroom door.

I'm not sure how Tony's face looked; I only saw Hector. He stared as if he didn't recognize me. Then he glanced around the room, and I saw it through his eyes—broken lamp, bed linen stained, tossed and tumbled, dinner dishes piled on the nightstand, clothes all over the place. I felt sick when I saw my panties by his big foot in tasseled cordovan loafers.

I started to speak, but the look in Hector's eyes stopped me.

"You!" Hector said to Tony.

There was no doubt he recognized Antinous the Greek. He'd given me over to him back on the Nile. Not because he wanted to, but to save me.

"Hector," I started, but what words could follow?

"*No dices nada,*" he snapped. "Nothing you say can fix this. Anything you say will make it worse."

Tossing the roses on the battlefield bed, Hector turned, strode to the door, opened it and walked out. The heavy reinforced door shut firmly behind him. The click of the latch was loud and final.

Gradually I became aware of noise from the street drifting through the double glass windows. I heard a siren, far away, as if from the end of a very long tunnel.

"Guess you weren't expecting him, huh?"

I was vaguely aware of sounds coming from Tony. I forced myself to make them into words with meaning.

"What did he mean by *you*?" he asked in a puzzled tone. "Should I know him?"

I could hardly tell Tony, world-respected scientist, that Hector recognized him from a previous life.

"I'm sorry, Isis," Tony was saying from the end of the same tunnel as the siren. "I'm truly sorry."

I stared at the closed door. *Should I go after him?*

"Was that your date from Cleopatra's Barge? He seems taller."

I shook my head, slowly and numbly. Rasheed had been my date the night Tony and I met in Vegas.

"Well, you certainly lead a complicated life."

If only you knew. . .

Then I came back, really back. I told Tony I was sorry, too.

"You must think I'm a slut."

"I don't think that at all," he assured me. "We didn't plan for this to happen. Okay, maybe I hoped *something* would happen. But I didn't expect anything like last night."

I don't know what I'd expected. I email a guy I met in a bar. I go to a museum to look at nude statues and then invite him up to my hotel room. I knew what Barb would say.

Hello! What did you think would happen?

Tony moved next to me and lifted wet strands of hair from my face.

"You have my number, Isis. You know where I am." He continued in a matter-of-fact tone, as if he were explaining one of his mathematical axioms.

"I come with baggage—a lot of it—starting with instant motherhood. And Princeton is not Las Vegas. I'd love to give us a shot—if you can't fix it with this guy. But I hope you can fix it. I honestly do."

I didn't know what to say. I didn't expect anything he was saying.

"I like him, Isis. He took it a lot better than I would have. Some guys would've tried to kill us both. He was humiliated but kept his cool. You've got to respect that."

"Humiliated?" *Is that how men think?*

Carthaginian

A score of men, full-bodied and strong like warriors, stood naked near the platform. Shackles around their ankles bound them together; their hands were chained behind their backs. The hot sun blazed down without mercy. Greek Alexandrians kept to the shade of the half-circle portico; I was reminded of a theatre with standing room only.

I saw him right away. Massive chest, thighs like tree trunks, his limp manhood longer and thicker than most men's when erect. His matted hair hung in heavy locks; his beard was long and filthy.

"Who is the beast?" I asked my slave Ajax.

He went into the crowd and returned.

"He is a Carthaginian general, Mistress. Captured in Syracuse."

The crowd booed when two giant Nubians pulled him to the block. Bits of garbage flew through the air; some splattered on his massive chest, while a few pieces hit him in the face. He didn't flinch but sneered at the crowd, holding himself proud as Hercules.

The bidding started. I tipped the parasol to signal I was in. The crowd stirred.

"Please, Mistress. May I be allowed to speak?" Ajax's eyes were wide with alarm. "Carthaginians are not suitable as house slaves. They cannot be trusted; they murder their masters in the night. Even in the mines, they cause trouble and refuse to obey. They are only useful as galley slaves."

I saw the doomed rowers on Athena's ship, chained to their oars, facing their death by angry waves or fire. Those were the lucky ones. Most galley slaves died slowly of malnutrition and exhaustion, thrown overboard when they could no longer row.

I tipped my parasol again to bid against a tall man in miner's garb. The crowd watched as the bidding went back and forth, neither of us relenting. The price went beyond what a galley slave was worth. A slave in the mines met death even faster. But still the man insisted, and I met every increase.

And then, as in every auction, there was a final bid. It was mine.

"Arrange to have the Carthaginian delivered to the villa," I ordered. "See that he is fed and bathed. Keep him chained at all times."

My whole body ached from the jarring bumps and jolts of the chariot trip; I ordered Dead Sea salts added to a hot bath. A slave massaged my stiff muscles with lavender-scented oil from *millefiori* bottles fused from tiny colored-glass rods. Exhausted, I slipped into the steaming water.

I must have dozed. Jason touched my shoulder.

"Mistress, the cook and Ajax are arguing. Ajax has told the others they must sleep in their quarters, but they won't enter, because the new slave is there."

"Send Ajax to me."

When he arrived, his face was tight, his voice high with anxiety. "The household is most unsettled with the presence of the Carthaginian. They call him the Crocodile."

"Is he restrained?"

"Yes, Mistress, he is chained in the slave quarters."

"Does he speak any Greek?"

"I cannot say, Mistress. He has not spoken."

"Test that column. Push as hard as you can. Ask another to help you."

When I was assured that the pillar supporting the portico around my bath was solid, I ordered Ajax to bring the Carthaginian.

Dousing the small brass lanterns around me, I watched from the shadows while they shackled his massive legs to the marble column. My slaves had managed to braid his long hair; they must have been terrified being that close to him.

"Leave us," I commanded.

Ajax and the other slave hesitated, glancing at each other.

"Wait outside. I shall call when I need you."

His face above the bushy beard was bruised; battle scars covered his arms and legs. His massive bull chest strained the cloth of the *chiton*. Scabs from a whipping streaked across his cantaloupe-sized biceps.

I flashed on the red welts my whip had raised on his flesh that night in the Persian tent.

A long moment passed while I studied him, wondering what I would do, now that I he was here. Wondering if he spoke Greek. As was his way, he took the initiative.

"It would seem that the tables are turned, Ishtar."

"Yes, General, indeed they are. You owned me once—and now I own you."

I rose slowly and deliberately from the bath; the water licked at my thighs. Pulling the pins from my hair, the mass of blonde waves fell around my shoulders.

The General didn't look away or lower his eyes as a slave should, but stared straight at me, lust on his face. He even smirked. I could have ordered him killed for less.

But I didn't want him dead. I wanted him to suffer. My revenge was for him to look at me and crave what he could never have.

I draped a thin shawl around myself, not to cover myself—the sheer cloth clung to my wet body—but to be more seductive, as *hetaerae* prefer the tease of a transparent gown over nudity.

The General's erection bulged under his *chiton*. I let my eyes linger on the swollen mound before I stepped slowly out of the pool and stretched on a divan covered in soft fur. The silk of my shawl tugged at my flesh like a second skin. My golden hair streamed around my shoulders.

"I would command you to bathe me as I once bathed you, General, but that would pleasure you, not punish. What am I to do? You were the predator and I the prey. You would like nothing better than that, I suppose—for me now to 'prey' upon you?"

The General chuckled; his dark eyes glittered from under thick lids.

"Are you so sure about which of us was the predator? Who lost his life?"

I should whip him for such insolence, but a whip in my hand only thrilled him.

I sipped unwatered wine, regarding him over my cup; the *Pharos* flamed behind him. He never turned his eyes away but challenged me, thrusting his swollen monster of manhood toward me in defiance.

A fresh breeze came up, and I felt a chill; his eyes went to my nipples pointing through the sheer cloth. Even chained to the pillar, he unsettled me. I covered myself with a heavy turquoise wool shawl and took a more businesslike pose on the sofa.

The General watched every move with hooded eye; he didn't try to hide his hunger. He held himself straight as the column behind him, his massive chest heaving with each breath, his giant feet spread as far as the shackles would allow. A slave necklace glinted in the tangle of black hair at his throat. He hadn't yet been branded on the forehead.

"I did not want to kill you, General, but you gave me no choice. In time, I would have run out of ways to please you. Was that not the attraction? To see what new tricks I could invent? But a sweet thing tasted too often is no longer sweet."

He smiled, but only one side of his mouth turned up. He found me amusing. I found him maddening. I should have left him for the mines.

"Admit it, General. You would have done the same in my place."

"That is where you and I are different, Ishtar. A man seldom kills a woman who pleases him—and you pleased me very much. Who knows how long we might have had together? Maybe one more night—maybe all our lives."

I took another sip of wine, studying him. He stared back.

"You are not going to force me to kill you again, are you?" I demanded.

He only chuckled and shifted his weight slightly so that his chains rattled. His erection was still huge.

"A man like you should never be in chains!"

In spite of my efforts to be in control, my voice was too full of accusation. It was his fault to end up like this.

He eyes travelled the length of my body.

"Your breasts are full. Your belly is rounding. Are you with child?"

I blinked. I had thrown up this morning and was tired before the day began. Why hadn't I hadn't thought of it?

He maneuvered to put me on the defense. I ignored his question and returned the subject to him.

"How *did* you end up a slave, General? Are Carthaginians not like Spartans? Rather die in battle than surrender?"

"I believed she was you. I let down my guard," he said with a shrug.

I stared at him, stunned by his admission. I'd never realized the full extent of his hunger for me.

"She had emerald eyes like yours, green as a cat. It was the eyes that fooled me. But she was a spy and drugged my wine. When I woke, I was in chains on a ship."

"So you were undone by your penis!" I laughed. "The Gods, too, are fond of a joke."

I drank more unwatered wine. Warmth spread through my cells. The wool shawl slipped from my shoulders, and the General's eyes followed. I pulled the shawl back up to cover me.

"What am I going to do with you?"

"Unchain me," he answered without hesitation.

"They say you cannot be tamed, that Carthage is a land of savages. My slaves won't sleep in their beds for fear of you. They call you the Crocodile."

He smirked again. He thought us fools. Fear of him was yet another of his pleasures.

"If I undo your chains, what is my guarantee you won't slit my throat—and those of my household?"

"You might trust my word. There are those who think it means something." He grinned. "But then, there are others who might wish they had been more wary."

"I saved you today from the mines or a warship galley, General. Do you not owe me something? Even in your brutal, vengeful world?"

"I owe you nothing. You did what you did for your own reasons, whatever they may be. Only you know them."

"I bought you to save you! Can you not understand how much it saddens me to see a man like you die on an oar?"

"And what kind of man is that, Ishtar? I am not one to fetch your curling irons and bend to your every whim. There are only two ways I can serve you. I would gladly do both with no disappointment on your part."

He shifted his weight. The chains rattled. For a terrified second, I thought I saw the pillar move.

"I can protect you. A woman with your beauty and position always needs protection."

His eyes wandered down my body, pausing on my breasts and then my thighs.

"We both know how else I can serve you."

I suppressed an insane impulse to free him so he could ravage me into submission. Suddenly exhausted, I wanted nothing more than to sleep. I rang on the brass bowl.

"Have they given you food?"

"I could have more," he answered.

Ajax must have been waiting right outside the door, because he entered immediately. Jason was on his heels. When Jason saw the General chained to the column, his hazel eyes grew enormous.

"Come, Jason," I said gently. "Do not be afraid."

The General's hooded eyes followed Jason as he came to me and settled on the floor beside my hand. The two of them stared at each other, Jason with round eyes and the General from beneath heavy lids. He looked first surprised, then suspicious when I stroked Jason's curls.

"Tonight the Carthaginian will sleep in the grain storeroom," I told Ajax. "Chain him and lock the door. Let him eat his fill and give him beer, but only with his food. We shall see what tomorrow brings."

Revelation

The General, hands chained together in front and ankles shackled, was sitting up. He probably woke at the first sound on the other side of the door. The storeroom was dim, but thin slats near the vaulted brick ceiling allowed in air and some light.

The storeroom was narrow; not more than six feet separated the long walls. Dirty straw covered the rough stone floor. The General's pallet barely squeezed in among the coarse sacks filled with grain. I sank to my knees across from him, watching his every move.

He watched mine and said nothing. Small pieces of gravel, loose grain and straw ground into my knees. I lowered myself onto a sack, curled my legs up close and leaned back against the hard wall. My hair in a thick braid was a rope on my spine.

"I am aware of the risk of being here with you," I said softly.

He said nothing. Not a muscle moved in his powerful frame. He could strangle me in a heartbeat, with his bare hands shackled in front, or with the chains that held them.

"I need your help, General."

There was just enough light to see his pupils dilate when I said I needed him.

My eyes filled with tears, and I rested my head on the wall, closing my lids, almost wishing that he would strangle me, that I wouldn't have to deal with what was coming.

"I have nowhere else to turn."

He shifted a little. I could see each scar on his face. His legs stretched out in front of him with monster feet stuck up at right angles from the floor, as far apart as the chains allowed. The skin around the shackles was covered with open sores and crusty scabs. I wondered how long the rough metal had rubbed his wrists and ankles. Since Syracuse?

"Tell me what I need to unlock your chains."

"Do you trust me that much?"

"I have no choice. If you kill me, I shall know nothing of the events that follow. If you do not kill me, then you will help me."

"Have you not left out a third possibility?"

I knew his hunger for me; I had foolishly taunted him in my bathchamber, never dreaming that this moment would come.

"I am at your mercy, General. Have you not long desired to have me once again in your power? Whatever you do is on your conscience, if you have one. I am staking my life that you do—and that you have feelings for me."

"You have even more guts than I gave you credit for."

"I shall free you from your chains, General, but you must agree to do one thing for me. You must give me your word."

"Who do you want me to kill?"

How tempting. I thought immediately of Ptolemy and how his death would make my life easier. And save Jason's.

"I do not want you to kill anyone. On the contrary, I want you to save someone's life."

He didn't try to hide his surprise. He never hid his feelings from me; he was that confident.

"You must take Jason and leave at once. Do not tell me where. No one must know where. Ptolemy's torturers can extract any secret; in the end, everyone talks."

I found a chisel and hammer in the tool room, wrapped sacking around the metal to dampen the sound and handed them to the General. He was lightning fast; the chains fell away.

He rubbed his wrists and his ankles and then, so quickly that I had no time to react, grabbed me by the throat with one giant paw and pulled me to him. His thick fingers encircled my throat.

I choked and put my hands on both sides of his head, not sinking in my nails or trying to scratch. I didn't struggle but went limp as a cat surrendering to a dominant.

My look told him I couldn't breathe, and he relaxed his grip. His face was only inches away; I saw each tiny red capillary in the whites of his eyes. His beard had a few strands of gray. His breath was sour with a hint of stale beer.

With a jerk of his forearm, he pulled me full into him and kissed me with such force that my lip split, and I tasted blood. His hunger sucked the air from my lungs. Opening my lips, I let him devour me but didn't give back. I might have been unconscious, I was that passive.

The more pliant I was, the more he crushed me against him. His arm locked around my waist; I feared he might snap my spine. Knife-like pains pierced my tender breasts. At my rounded belly, his monster manhood menaced.

Oddly, I was calm. He could choke the life from me with one hand, but his desperate need oozing from every pore gave me power.

Then, much like Black Falcon on the ship, he buried his face in my hair and inhaled my scent. Vulnerable. He was so vulnerable.

"We have no time," I urged. "Listen to me. Listen to why I came."

His hand around my throat relaxed more, but not enough for me to move.

"We had a child, General. Ishtar and Sher. Conceived in the desert. In your tent."

He stared at me. I wondered if he understood.

"A son. *We had a son.* And I believe our son's soul is Jason. Think! How else could I love him so deeply—and have done so from the first moment?"

He sank back, releasing his grip on my neck and his arm from around my waist.

"A son?" he asked dumbly.

"Yes, *your* son. And he needs you. Ptolemy wants him. He *will* have him, if we don't act. Do you wish him to be defiled by these perverted Greeks and then cast aside, broken with no hope ever to be a man?"

By his face, I thought he still didn't comprehend. He stared at me with empty eyes. Minutes passed. He seemed incapable of decision; I had never imagined him so weak.

"You must act *now*," I insisted. "Do you hear me? Now!"

I tugged at his arms to pull him to his feet, but he was like the carcass of a bull.

"A son, General. A son! You can save him!"

I was thinking of slapping his face, when a light came into his eyes—a look of wonder. He suddenly stood, dragging me to my feet with him.

Quietly opening the door, he took the chisel and pried off the iron bands of the bolt, catching them in his hand and scattering them silently on the floor of the corridor. He wrapped his shackles, chains and the iron tools in grain sacks to muffle any sound.

Silently we made our way to my bedchamber. The light on the sea told me the sun was near the horizon.

I kissed Jason's sleepy face, saying, "You must go with the General. Obey him in all things. Never tell anyone your name. Never mention mine."

I kissed him again, this time on the forehead. "Be brave. We shall see each other again, I promise you."

With Jason on his back, the General dropped without a sound over the balcony to the ground. He didn't look back and was gone among the trees and bushes before I shed my first tear.

Rhakotis

R hakotis, the Egyptian Quarter, was crowded with noisy men, mysterious women and running children. Garish images of Egyptian Gods jumped out from flat-roofed, mud brick houses crammed up against each other. Even the poorest hovel had crude ankhs painted on the walls. Eyes-of-Horus were above every door.

Scarface led the way down a narrow alley that widened into a square with a teeming market of spices and food stuffs. Skewers of meat roasted on open charcoal fires; black smoke billowed to mix with the heavy scent of frankincense and myrrh. Vendors called out to me in Egyptian as we hurried by. Everywhere were the sounds of Egyptian; I heard no Greek at all.

I plastered myself to a cobra-covered wall to avoid a cart loaded with fish. I stepped on a dazed snake in a small tattered basket. Chickens squawked and water birds screeched. A little monkey tethered by a rope to a blind beggar squealed and grabbed at the hem of my cloak.

The light was failing fast; trade carried on without pause by lantern and torch. So many people jammed the streets, it might have been midday.

Then I saw Goliath standing guard like a giant statue, his arms crossed on his massive chest. When he saw me, his eyes glowed, but he shook his head slightly, warning me not to react—to say nothing.

He had to bend to open the short door into a mud house with

no windows on the street. The Eye-of-Horus stared back at me from above the lintel as I passed through into a dark room. Thick walls muffled almost all sound.

It took a few seconds for my eyes to adjust to the dark. Closed double doors and shuttered long windows faced me on the opposite wall. I guessed an inner courtyard lay behind. I heard the cackling of hens and the cooing of pigeons.

He had been behind the door when it opened. I felt his heat before his touch. He unwrapped my cape slowly, as if opening a delicate and much anticipated package. Leaning back into him, I relaxed my head on his chest and rubbed my temple against his jaw. His breathing was fast and shallow in my ear.

He loosened my braid; my hair tumbled onto my shoulders and covered his bare arm holding me across my chest. Then he wrapped a handful of my hair around our heads; it tickled our faces like a mass of spider webs.

Still leaning against the door, he moved his hands over my breasts, down my midriff, along my waist, across my belly and over my hips. He caressed my thighs, on the outside, up the inside, everywhere he could reach. He memorized every curve of my body with the tips of his fingers.

His fingers went under my hair and moved it to the side, exposing the skin on the back of my neck. He kissed every inch from my shoulder blades to the base of the scalp. When he settled at the union of my neck and shoulder—the magic door that opens all doors—he sucked gently and then licked. His breath, hot and moist, sent chills everywhere. My canal throbbed.

I pressed into him, rocking back and forth against his iron manhood at the curve of my spine. He gently massaged my full, tender breasts. The slightest touch on my nipples, hypersensitive with early pregnancy, jolted me. His thumbs circled the tips slowly through the soft cloth while I sang out O-o-o-o-o-o into the dark.

Only then did he untie the silver twine at my shoulders; the light linen fell like silk in one long slide to my ankles. His hands stroked my belly and caressed my loins. Finally, he slipped over my mound into the wet.

He explored my valley and caressed my lotus; his fingers dipped into my canal. He loosened his loincloth. I stood on his feet to be higher and closer. He put his hardness between my legs.

One arm encircling my waist, he lifted me up and back into him—his fingers still exploring—and entered me from behind. I gripped his forearm at my middle, hooked my other arm around his neck and moved with him. There was nothing between us; we shared the same skin.

The door rattled as our bodies rubbed against it. The thought of Goliath listening and guarding on the other side entered my mind for a millisecond and then was gone.

There was nothing in the world for me at the moment except the euphoria of being one with Black Falcon.

We never lighted a lamp. The narrow bed had fresh straw and a blanket smelling of sun. Black Falcon lay on his side, supported by his elbow, his head resting on his hand. He traced me with his fingers, along my face, my jaw, down my neck, and over my breasts. He counted my ribs and caressed my mound, memorizing me again.

My fingertips trailed across his chest and down his biceps. I explored every feature of his face—his black eyes deep as a desert well, his sharp cheekbones, his proud nose with narrow nostrils. Even the hard lines etched around his perfectly carved mouth were beautiful to me.

He lifted strands of my hair and pulled them through his lips. Once he held a curl under his nose and inhaled deeply.

"I have never seen hair such as yours—like spun gold, but alive."

He bent and kissed me tenderly and then tickled the end of my nose with the lock of my hair.

"I had to see you," he said simply, switching to Egyptian.

I was afraid to ask why he was in Alexandria, afraid he would tell me that it was for his 'cause' and that I was a convenience he worked into his schedule.

"How is the slave boy?"

I considered telling him, but I'd vowed to tell no one. I had to think of Jason. The abbreviated truth served me well.

"He is no longer with me."

"That surprises me. I thought you would never part from him."

"I do not wish to speak of it."

He looked hard at me for a moment, and I thought he might ask more. But instead, he went back to memorizing with his eyes and his fingers. I felt him grow hard again.

"Your body is fuller now," he teased. "Did we not feed you enough on the ship?"

His harsh face was so tender in that moment, I wanted more than anything to believe he was the father.

"I am with child," I said, bracing myself for his questions.

"You are carrying my son?"

His ego stunned me; he immediately assumed the child was his—and a boy.

"She might be a girl," I dared to suggest. But I was relieved he had no questions for which I had no answers.

A rapping on the door signaled it was time to leave. He said nothing about when I might see him again. Goliath had to peel me from his arms.

"Tell no one about tonight. No one," Black Falcon warned. "For me, for you—and for the life of my son."

The door closed between us, and I followed Scarface back down the narrow, winding streets still jammed with Egyptians.

Emerald Scarf

The island prison lay just offshore. I had seen it every day from my balcony as I reclined on my sofa, eating my breakfast, enjoying the change of colors on the water. I never dreamed of the horrors that went on there.

Black Falcon was there now, somewhere in the dark, waiting to suffer a rebel's slow, painful death in the Hippodrome. Captured at Rhakotis. Because he had come for me.

A low building of marble with the usual columns and statues rose a few feet from the sea. Blue Beard didn't tie our skiff onto the dock but came ashore in a tiny cove on the far side of the island. The rocks were steep; he took my arm to drag me up. I tripped once on my long cape, but he kept me on my feet. When his cape opened, I saw the flash of steel in his belt.

Once we were at the building, Blue Beard wiggled his fingers, and I placed six more coins in his square palm. He grunted and disappeared around the corner.

I waited in the dark of the portico. Somewhere I heard laughter broken by an excited shout. I couldn't make out how many voices. My heart hammered in my chest. My mouth was as dry as the desert; there was no saliva when I tried to moisten my lips. I couldn't swallow; an invisible giant hand gripped my throat, allowing nothing to pass.

When he came back, he signaled for me to follow and put his finger to his lips. Glued to the walls of the villa, we moved silently toward a lighted open doorway. Laughter erupted from inside. From the sound of their voices, the men were deep in their cups. I thought I heard the clink of dice, followed by shouts.

A few yards before the light, we entered a small doorway that opened onto a narrow stone corridor. At the top of steps leading into blackness, a bulky guard with massive thighs and biceps stepped into our path. I pulled the folds of my hood over my face; the dark green cloak hid everything except the tips of my sandals.

Blue Beard signaled I should go with the guard and ducked into an alcove to wait. I could only hope he would be there on my return.

The guard stopped at the bottom of steps slippery from sea damp and moss. My nausea returned at the mixed stench of urine, feces, blood and rot.

He motioned for me to hold out my hands. When he started to untie the thong holding the leather amulet, I grabbed his wrist and whispered "No!"

But he peeled my fingers loose, and I was forced to let him fumble at the knot until the amulet fell from my wrist into his hand.

O Aphrodite! Please do not forsake me—not after coming this far.

Then he opened my cloak and ran his hands quickly over my body, not out of lust, but to see if I carried a weapon. He grunted when he felt the weight of my purse. My hands shook so hard, I don't know how I opened the pouch to give him three heavy coins. Apparently satisfied, he grunted again and motioned for me to follow.

The gate to the damp cell was not locked. I thought the creak of the iron hinges more deafening that the oarlocks on the boat. High up near the ceiling, a tiny window with iron bars let in the sounds of the sea. I caught a whiff of salt over the foul odor of blood and urine. Shadows flickered on the wet walls from a single torch burning outside the cell.

"Alone," I insisted.

The guard grunted again and shrugged his shoulders. I heard his heavy footfall on the stairs.

Black Falcon was chained to the wall at a height that didn't allow him to sit. I thought he was unconscious until I was next to him, and he turned his battered face toward me. I think he was blind. It was impossible to see if he had eyes. But he had a tongue.

"You?" he mumbled in a wondering tone.

I don't know how he knew.

"Me." I said simply, kissing his chest and tasting dried blood.

Hundreds of slits covered his skin. I stifled a sob.

"Let me smell you," he pleaded. "Let me smell your hair."

I lowered my hood and raised a lock of hair to his once proud nose, now smashed into his face. I couldn't imagine he could smell anything but blood. The lips I worshipped, now battered and bleeding, parted to show shattered gums where teeth used to be.

"Don't raise my son a Greek," he slurred. "Promise me."

"I promise." I whispered into his ear. I felt his agony right through to my bones.

We had little time. Every moment I was here was too long. I looked frantically around the cell to see anything I could use, but there was nothing. The chains at his wrists and the shackles at his ankles were too short.

I slid off the emerald silk scarf that covered the bruises from the General's fingers and quickly formed a loop. The tears streamed down my face as I slipped it over his head and around his neck.

"Forgive me, my love," I begged him.

I yanked with all my strength. I pulled with every muscle in my body. He thrashed back and forth, but he didn't cry out. I think I pulled too tightly for him to scream.

He fought me. He struggled for his life with what little strength he had, kicking his legs in wild spasms and jerks. His bloodied feet rose and fell on the floor, first one then the other. Bits of foul dusty straw flew in the air when his legs crashed down and bounced up again.

Then finally, his heels digging and sliding in the filthy straw, he slowed. Terrible gagging sounds came from his open mouth, and I thought the guard would surely come.

Desperate to end it, I braced one foot against the wet wall next to him and pulled with everything I had. I used the wall as leverage, my body leaning backward, my foot slipping in the slimy goo. I stumbled once, and then regained my footing.

"Please let go," I pleaded. "Give in. *Please* give in!"

His arms twisted in the shackles above his head, and his legs still jerked in the chains. He wouldn't stop trying to draw breath. I willed him to surrender as I pulled harder on the scarf. My whole body trembled; the muscles in my arms and thighs quivered uncontrollably. Choking back tears, I myself struggled to breathe.

"We shall be together again, I promise you. Please go now."

He shuddered. Both legs jerked at the same time. Then his right leg twitched once and went limp. His whole body went limp. Black Falcon, at last, was still.

I could scarcely see through my tears as I fumbled with the green scarf, sliding it from his neck and twisting it back around mine. The silk burned hot against my skin.

I doubled over from the pain in my chest. A vivisection surgeon's knife at the Medical *Akademy* might have opened my ribs and ripped out my living heart. Clenching my fists to stop my shaking hands, I swallowed the vomit in my mouth.

But Black Falcon felt pain no more. I touched his battered face and bloodied lips one last time with my fingertips. He was at peace; his soul had passed into another dimension. How many lifetimes would go by before I would meet him as Rasheed?

The guard was coming down when I started up the steps. He looked past me into the cell. From where we stood, Black Falcon looked as he had when I entered—unconscious.

My hands shook so hard when I handed him the pouch with the remaining coins, that I was sure he would suspect something. But he only grunted and led me up to the corridor where Blue Beard waited.

Antinous of Kos

A shiny-scalp priest with kohl-lined eyes opened the outside gate of the Temple of Amun for me, and Antinous and the guide leapt to their feet. The guide was in a hurry to return to the inn in Siwa; Antinous and I slowed our pace to let him go on ahead.

Antinous could barely wait for the man to be out of earshot before asking, "What happened?"

"Please do not ask me what I cannot say."

He was silent for much of the descent from the craggy peak. I imagined that he thought of what he would have asked of the Emerald Tablet in my place—how to build a dome that stands, how to explain the passage of seasons.

Dry earth and small stones crunched under our leather soles. The stars blazed over our heads.

We were about halfway down the path when he stopped and took me by the shoulders. His grip was firm, that of a wrestler. Instead of his usual detachment, he was intense and wholly present.

"How do you know the Oracle, Athena, and how does he know me? You must tell me at least this."

I searched for a way to explain our souls meeting in different lifetimes that wouldn't sound crazy to a nonbeliever like Antinous, but there was no explanation other than the truth.

"We knew each other in another lifetime three hundred years ago. Here in Egypt. In Saïs. The Oracle was my father, Hermes

Trismegistus, and you were his assistant. You helped him create the Emerald Tablet."

I didn't consider telling him that we also knew each other in the future. Already the past would be more than he could accept. I expected him to be shocked. Maybe I thought he might laugh. He didn't share Plato's belief in the transmigration of souls.

But it seemed that even Antinous had succumbed to the magic of the Temple of Amun.

Instead of arguing the implausibility of consciousness surviving death, he asked, "And what was I to you?"

"You were my husband."

Of everything I'd told him, that seemed to stun him most. I had the sense our marriage in the past came as a revelation explaining the connection between us he must feel. A few seconds passed while he studied my face.

"Did I make you happy?" he asked most seriously.

"How could I be anything but happy with you?"

The oasis was silent save for the song of the wind rustling through palm fronds. In the starlight, Antinous might have been carved from marble, his beauty was so pure.

"Now I understand your questions about my marital status," he said matter-of-factly. Then he added, "And your unease with Leandros."

Brutally honest, that's Antinous. But without harmful intent. To him, the world was a collection of facts and observable behavior. Emotions and feelings were but one part of the equation.

I didn't intend for him to see me react to his mention of Leandros, but there isn't much the brilliant Antinous doesn't see when he chooses to.

He touched my cheek and said gently, "There are many kinds of love, Athena."

"Yes," I answered, "I know."

There in the still of the night, perhaps a little high on the magic of the Oracle, Antinous kissed me as a lover for the first time in this life.

But instead of the wild exuberance typical of him, his lips pressed on mine in a kiss as sweet as poetry. His hands moved tenderly across my shoulders and up the sides of my neck; his fingers gently combed through my hair.

I leaned into him, my tongue in his mouth, and he pulled away.

"Not like this," he said. His tone was husky but firm; his mind was in control.

I imagined his pulse rate only slightly above normal.

He kissed me again softly; his lips were a cool breeze on mine. Surrounded by curling lashes, his eyes were all pupils. In the starlight, his curls were more silver than gold.

"I would have you, Athena, knowing that you could never give me all. Would you have me, knowing the same?"

The specter of the beautiful boy-god Leandros slithered between us.

When I didn't answer, he smiled knowingly and took my hand, leading me through the swaying palms under a glorious field of stars.

Tomb of the Crocodile

It happened so fast, I didn't have time to scream. A cloth went over my mouth and nose. I breathed something acrid into my lungs, and then the world went black.

I slept, but my dreams gave me no rest. I was back in the yellow silk bed beside the sea, but the four shadowy men now brandished small, sharp-edged knives. A blade flashed silver in the moonlight and pierced my right eye. I awoke from the blinding pain in my dream to the vivid pain of Zavan's special knife.

His ogre face was etched with the same evil as when I last saw him in the Persian camp. He hovered over me, holding the nasty small blade between our eyes, turning it from side to side to reflect the light from the torch burning beside us. Warm liquid oozed from my eyebrow; I didn't need to see it or taste it to know it was blood.

"Sorceress," he hissed. "You think I do not know your tricks? You may hypnotize the others, as you bewitched the General, but you do not fool me. Your power is in your green eyes. When they are gone, it is gone."

I squeezed my lids in hopeless defense; I saw Black Falcon's bloody slits where his eyes had once been.

How could the Tablet have failed me? I had asked for so little.

Zavan grabbed hold of my face; his coarse fingers dug into my flesh. I twisted back and forth and tried to bite his wrist. He stabbed me once in the left cheek—deep.

I felt the cold tip of the blade on my tongue. More blood flowed.

I couldn't think of the Tablet's mantra. Only the white glow of terror filled my mind.

"Let her go, Zavan."

Zavan released his grip immediately at the sound of the voice and jumped to his feet.

"General," he exclaimed.

"Move away from her, or I kill you where you stand."

Zavan had to be as shocked to see the General in the cave as I was, but he spoke as if three centuries hadn't passed since we were last together in that desert Persian camp.

"But, General, this is the Hathor whore who butchered you. Do you not wish revenge?"

"I want her—and in one piece. I said move away."

In the dim light of the torch, the General could have been a gorilla from deep in Nubia. He crouched. His arms swung low. On his toes with knees bent, a heavy broad sword in his hand, he poised to pounce.

Zavan hesitated and then stepped away from me. The tiny steel blade in his hand was no match for an iron sword. Zavan's weapon was death by a thousand cuts; the General could take off a head in one stroke.

In a movement so quick it was a blur, the General wrested the knife from Zavan's hand and shoved him against the wall, his massive forearm pressing on Zavan's throat.

Zavan gagged and put up his hands, palms out in the sign of surrender.

"If you have harmed her more than I can see, Zavan, I will take you apart limb by limb. Stand here. Do not move. Do not test me."

The General knelt, untied my bindings, put one arm around my back and the other under my knees and lifted me from the ground. Zavan didn't move from the wall.

"I kill you not today, Zavan, as I wish to do. You saved my life once in battle. The next time we meet, you die."

With that last warning, the General carried me out of the tomb.

Three bodies lay outside. Dark blood pooled on the pale sand. Ajax's throat had been slashed so deep, his head was attached only at the spine. I hung onto the General's neck and clutched in my hand the amulet with the poison vial.

Comet Ride

The General had a problem, and we both knew it. How could he get me on the ship without my cooperation? He had no leverage with which to threaten me. He could gag me and bind me and put me in a sack, but not without a struggle. He would have to knock me out.

"Are you going to hurt me?" I asked.

He had tethered the horses to stones; they nibbled at scruffy shrubs growing between rocks. The coarse-woven linen of the Berber gown was soft against my skin after the scratch of the wool cape. I couldn't see the wounds on my face, but the slit on my arm showed no sign of infection or swelling.

"What will you do if my child is a girl? Kill her, as is your custom?"

He glared at me. I wondered how far I could push him. I even wondered if I could overpower him and pour the poison from the vial down his throat.

"Would you really rather die than go with me?" he asked suddenly.

He must have been thinking about my words all day. I put my hand on his massive forearm scarred from a life of battle. His skin was dark next to mine; tiny black hairs rose in gooseflesh at my touch.

He closed his eyes. Dust coated his thick, wavy beard. His bull's chest rose and fell. Black fur covered his grizzly bear shoulders.

"I have a life in Greece, General, given only to a handful of women in the world. I am burdened with responsibility, but I am respected—and as free as a woman can be."

He didn't open his eyes.

"You once said you could never bend to my every whim," I whispered. "Could you expect me to bend to yours?"

"Would it be different if I offered you other than Carthage?" he growled.

His question took me off guard. I hesitated, trying to imagine where a Carthaginian renegade and a Greek priestess could go.

"No."

His sigh was heavy when he stood to his feet. His massive tree trunk thighs, fuzzy with curled black hairs, were within reach, but what could I do? I could hardly overpower him. I found myself focused on his hands clenched into powerful fists and his thick fingers that could crush my throat with one squeeze.

"Will you live with the father of your child?" He didn't look at me.

"No," I answered immediately.

Black Falcon was gone, Hektor married. I would return to my life as priestess. Then I held my breath when the words sunk in. Had he truly said *will?*

"That, at least, is some consolation," he grunted. His lips formed a bittersweet smile around words tinged with irony. "I told myself that if I could not have you, no one could. It seems no one will."

It took me a moment longer to dare let myself believe that he spoke of letting me go. He turned abruptly and sat on his haunches, facing me. I thought he might yet kill me right there on the sandy rise overlooking the sea.

"I lied to you, Ishtar."

His face was inches from mine. I could smell his breath, not sweet, a little sour, but not unpleasant.

I waited, staring at him, not daring to breathe or blink for fear of him changing his mind.

"Jason is not in Carthage. He is in the port."

"Jason is *here*? He is *here*!"

I can't explain my reaction. I couldn't control the shaking. I leaned into the General, put my arms around his neck and sobbed into his chest.

At first he stiffened. Then he put his powerful arms around my waist and crushed me to him, lifting me off the ground even while he crouched.

"Thank you! Thank you!" I cried into his mouth.

And then I kissed him. We breathed together, filling our lungs with each other's air. I don't know if I ever loved any man more than I did in that moment.

He spread the cloak on the hard, rocky ground and lowered me gently, careful of my arm, careful not to brush against my stitched cheek. As he lay me down, I saw on the horizon the sliver of the crescent moon with the brilliant evening star Ishtar at the tip of its horn.

With great care, he pulled the Berber gown over my head and kissed my breasts and my swollen belly. He leaned into my ear, his coarse beard brushing my stitched cheek, and spoke so deep from his throat that his words were more growl than speech.

"I wish you had let me see my son grow in your womb. I wish you had let me suckle your milk."

I untied his sash, letting it fall across my loins. With my cut arm throbbing, I pulled his tunic over his head and buried my face in the mass of black hair on his chest. I breathed deep of his animal scent.

My fingers barely reached around his engorged manhood. I didn't feel the sharp edges of rocks poking through the wool, except to register pleasure. With the General, it is always that delicious sliding back and forth between pain and rapture.

When he lifted my hips, I locked my legs around his waist and hung onto his neck, suspended above the desert floor. My mouth hung on his, our tongues deep in each other's throats. I forgot the stitches and begged him to devour me. Our feral cries frightened the horses; I was vaguely aware that they whinnied wildly and tugged at their tethers.

He was at my gate, pushing like a log into my canal.

I called out to the Goddess when he split me to ram up against the bottom of my womb. My legs around him tightened; I lifted myself into his thrust. The skin popped on my arm as the wound spread, but pain was so utterly confused with pleasure that I purred in delight.

He tore his mouth away from mine and, like a raged bull, snorted in my ear. Tiny droplets of his saliva sprayed my face. I bit his earlobe until I tasted blood and then licked and swallowed and sucked more. The harder I sucked, the harder he pounded me. I grabbed handfuls of his hair in my fists and pulled myself still closer into him.

His arm across my back arched my spine. My breasts crushed into the hot tangled hair of his chest. My head went back with my thick mass of waves swinging in the dust.

Suddenly his hand was around my throat, squeezing so tight I couldn't breathe. I gasped and choked, and still he didn't let go. I thought he was going to kill me, but when I looked into his eyes, I didn't see a killer.

I let go of his hair, and he loosened his grip. Our eyes locked. Then he squeezed again, and this time I felt the thrill.

I knew it was wrong; I knew it was sick. But still I felt it. He saw the pleasure in my eyes and squeezed harder.

I frightened myself more than he frightened me.

Frenzied, I pulled at his hair. I couldn't breathe; his hand crushed my larynx. The world went fuzzy and then sharpened in the purest and clearest of colors before exploding into radiant white light.

At the edge of losing consciousness, I dropped my hands, and he released my throat so I could breathe again. Even though he had let go, I still throbbed where each of his steel fingers had pressed.

He drove into me again and again, pushing me to my limit while every cell screamed for more. He gnawed at my neck like an animal, sucking the skin with his thick lips as if he could draw blood through my pores. I scratched his hairy back with my nails. Each time I dug in, he snarled and crushed me in his arms.

We developed a rhythm. When the pain was too great, I loosened my grip on his hair. I became passive to his dominant. When I wanted more, I pulled hard again. He unleashed a fire I thought could never be quenched.

The pressure started low in my buttocks, like a warm flame spreading down my loins and over my belly, burning hotter and hotter until my lotus erupted in a *Kundalini* wave that travelled up through my womb, stopped my breath and exploded in my ears. A ride on a comet.

When he climaxed, his great gorilla body shook with such force, I thought his heart might stop. His animal growls were savage in my ear as he heaved and trembled.

I let go of his hair when he relaxed his arm holding my back, and my shoulders fell to the ground. But my legs, with ankles locked, still gripped around his waist. He supported his massive weight on his forearms and knees; his head hung down with his long, coarse hair in my face.

We panted together as wild animals after a chase. We should have been drenched in sweat, but the droplets dissolved into the desert air before beading on our skin.

When our breathing calmed, he lifted his head and looked into my eyes.

"What a pity we have to wait until another lifetime to soar to the stars every night."

He kissed me tenderly with his fat thick lips, and then even more gently, kissed my wounded eye and my stitched cheek.

"You will always be flawless to me," he whispered next to my mutilated earlobe.

But when he looked at my arm, he frowned and found water to wash away the fresh blood. He reapplied a stream of honey slowly and carefully, precisely as the priest had done.

"Why did you deceive me about Jason?"

"I hoped for your gratitude when you saw him safe."

I should have been angry he lied, but instead I *was* grateful—for Jason, for my freedom, for the lessons I learned from every game he played. Today he taught me the dark secret that I could feel shame and thrill at the same time.

The stars shone in the wine dark sky. A fiery red moon with the cool evening star sank below the horizon before he handed me my robe.

"It is time to go," he said. "To Jason."

Late that night, when Jason slept, the General closed the bedchamber door in the tiny inn with thin walls. I put my hands on his bull chest, making him promise only one thing—quiet. He bound my mouth with a cloth and then his.

Goodbye Hektor

As the sun set in a blaze of red glory, a gilded yacht sailed through burgundy waters into port. It was Hektor. I judged the restrained and elegant opulence of his custom *bireme* to be Eugenia's taste.

He was the perfect gentleman when he saw my face.

"*Kallistei!*" He raised his silver *kylix* in toast, as he had that evening long ago at the *symposion* in Korinth. "To the most beautiful."

"It will heal," he assured me. "Small scars cannot detract from your beauty, but you should bathe and change at once. It pains me to see you in rags."

He led me to a luxurious suite, complete with marble bath and yellow canaries in gold cages. The sweet scent of gardenia filled my nose.

"I come bearing gifts," Hektor joked.

"When do you not?"

My two chests carved with my name—Ατηενα Κοριντηοσ, Athena of Korinth—stood by a bed covered in rose-colored silk and piled high with down pillows. I resisted the urge to lie down.

"Leave us," I told the slaves.

Hektor smiled, glancing at the bed.

"Eugenia told me about my child," he said as he poured dark wine into a second *kylix*.

He handed me the silver drinking cup embossed with Dionysus embracing Ariadne. We both took a sip, looking at each other over the rims of our cups.

He didn't waste any time taking the *kylix* from my hand and setting it back on the ebony and gold table. With a seamless movement of long legs and arms, he moved right next to me, taking my chin in his fingers and lifting my face so that I looked directly into his eyes.

"I have thought of nothing but you," he whispered in my ear. In his smooth, expert way, he started to lift my robe to ease over my head.

I took his hands firmly in mine and held them.

"No, Hektor."

"Why not? You please me more than any woman. I know I please you. What else is there?"

"It is not so simple for me."

I took refuge in a cushioned chair with low straight back and massive, unforgiving arms mounted with fierce, gold lion heads.

"Hektor, there is something you must do for me."

"Always that," he said glumly, picking up his cup of wine again. "You have no trouble asking for my help when you need it."

"I want you to adopt Jason. Ptolemy would not dare harm your son. Would you do that for me, Hektor?"

He straightened and turned away, taking a large swig of wine.

"Jason. Always Jason," he said resentfully.

"I love him with all my heart, Hektor, but he cannot be with me in the Temple. Men are not allowed in the sacred area. You, of all people, should know that."

It was not hard for my soft voice to conjure up those intimate, forbidden moments we had shared in my office high above the Gulf of Korinth.

I rose and went to him, putting my hand up to his smooth, newly-pumiced cheek. He softened ever so slightly.

"Hektor, please. Jason is part of me. If you truly love me, then you must love him, too."

"What of *my* child? What happens to *him*?"

I didn't tell him, of course, that paternity was in question. I wanted to say nothing that might sabotage my child's happiness.

"If the child is a boy, you and Eugenia may adopt him as your own. You may choose his name; he need never know about me. But you must vow he speak Egyptian as well as Greek—and worship their Gods if he desires."

Forgive me, Black Falcon! His dying wish was for his son not to be Greek. I had to live with a compromise position, but it was the best I could do for a child who might not even be his.

"If my child is a girl, I shall raise her in the Temple. She can grow to be her own person without the permission of a father or husband."

The air in the plush cabin was thick with his disappointment. He sat down on a low tripod stool, long legs bent at the knees, leaning forward with his forearms on his thighs, hands clasped together, knuckles white.

He said nothing; he glowered and refused to look at me. I'd even say he pouted I feared he might not agree to my terms; he was a man used to having his way. But when he finally sighed, and I saw resignation in the slump of his shoulders, I knew I'd won.

"I brought along something else of yours," he said flatly.

He turned his face toward the bed. "There. Under the green silk."

A wrapped rectangle leaned against the tapestry wall. I didn't need to fold back the cloth. I knew. The Red Mirror.

Jason was safe. I could go home. Really home. The Emerald Tablet was giving me all that I asked.

"I love you, Hektor. I shall always love you. You must believe that."

I resisted running my fingers through his rich reddish waves and barbered curls. I resisted kissing his lips, letting my love and gratitude flow into him, easing his tension.

My heart nearly broke as I let myself dream, for a breath, of the life Hector and I might have if we were free.

But we weren't free. There was his wife, Eugenia—my best friend

Barb in another life. There was the Temple of Aphrodite on the *Akrokorinth*.

I stood close to him, but not so close as to invite him to take me in his arms.

"You showed me, Hektor, that life must be enjoyed. You gave me the greatest pleasure when I needed it most."

He looked at me then, and seeing the glimmer of hope in his eyes, I quickly added, "But tomorrow I sail to Cyrene with the morning tide, and from there to take the first ship north to Greece. Tonight I return to the inn."

I didn't tell him, of course, that I sailed with the Carthaginian slave.

He didn't try to talk me out of it. He didn't move to kiss me or convince me with embraces. His long, beautiful body was so tense, he would shatter into a thousand pieces if I were to touch him.

He bit his bottom lip and turned his face away, avoiding my eyes. I think he didn't trust himself to look at me.

"You refuse to be with me because of a decision my family made before I was born," he said bitterly. "I had no choice in my marriage. Where is the justice in that?"

As always with Hektor, my resolve softened.

"Greece is yet another world," I said very softly, leaving the door open a crack.

I think he was too lost in his misery to hear me, because he didn't seize that tiny hopeful opening as I found myself wishing he would. Why else would I have offered it?

He, who believed most in seizing the moment, did not make his move. It seemed our fate was sealed. I raised his long, graceful fingers, the ones that went straight to the Spot no other man knew, and kissed the tips.

"I pray, Hektor, that the Goddess gives you a son."

Goodbye General

"Where will you go?" I whispered to the General as he licked my spine.

"It is not only Carthage that fights Rome. There are many who are willing to pay handsomely for my skills."

He took a fistful of my hair and pulled my head back to look into his eyes.

"But wherever it is," he growled, "it is after Cyrene."

The Red Mirror reflected back his long, thick black hair mingled with my blonde.

I gave myself over to the moment. Pleasure—and pain. That was the General.

But I didn't fear him. In fact, I wasn't afraid of anything anymore. My worries surely were over. I had the Emerald Tablet; I knew the mantra that unlocked its power. I had chosen the Protectors and given each a faience medallion engraved with a septagram. All except one, that is. I had not yet named the seventh.

The General mounted me from behind and held his hand over my mouth. I cried out when he rammed his thick log in me and bit down on his palm to taste blood.

O comet ride! O delicious stars!

How easily I might have passed from this life in that moment. With a single thought I could be back home in Las Vegas. But not before Cyrene. Oh no, not before Cyrene.

I prayed to the Goddess for headwinds to slow our sail.

Rasheed

When the knock came very late at night, it was Rasheed.
He leaned against the stucco wall of the hallway, dressed for a business meeting in a dark blue suit with starched white shirt and muted olive green paisley tie, the color of his eyes when he's moody. He was always impeccable, like he'd just stepped out of GQ magazine. I tried to remember if I'd ever seen him without a suit—well, except naked, of course.

He stood upright the instant the door opened. His black hair glistened in the overhead lights. The shadows sharpened his cheekbones. For a heartbeat, my mind filled with the terrible image of his mangled face in the prison dungeon. How much memory did Rasheed have of Black Falcon?

He stared at me, and I stared back. I'm sure I looked stunned; I felt shell-shocked. I didn't move to open the door wider.

"Are you going to let me in?"

The light that had passed across his face when I opened the door was gone. He looked very serious. I don't think it had occurred to him that I might not welcome seeing him.

I actually considered shutting the door like he shut the taxi door in Copenhagen. Too bad he wasn't standing in the rain.

"I need to talk to you, Isis."

To be honest, I was torn. One part of me wanted to rip his clothes off and pull him on top of me. The other wanted to slip a scarf around his neck and choke the life from him—and not from mercy.

"You told me in Copenhagen there was nothing to say."

"I was wrong. Have you ever been wrong, Isis? Have you never regretted a mistake?"

The scene in New York with Tony and Hector flashed for a moment. I still hoped Hector would forgive me—give me another chance. But I was not in a forgiving mood with Rasheed.

"Why are you here?"

"Don't make me do this standing outside, Isis."

"Why not? You left me standing in the rain."

But of course, I wanted to hear what he had to say. Most of all, I wanted to see him grovel. How many times did he think he could humiliate and reject me before I got a backbone? *Thank you, Barb!*

I opened the door all the way and stepped back.

We stood in the narrow, mirrored entry with our reflection repeated into infinity. Rasheed put his hands on the mirror wall on each side of my head. His face was inches away. Neither one of us blinked. His piercing eyes were almost brittle, like green glass.

They shouted, *Stop it!*

As hard as I tried, I couldn't ignore his heat; his special Hathor Power for men oozed from every pore. It would have been so easy to slip my arms under his suit jacket and slide them along his narrow waist. If he had touched me, I don't think I could have resisted dissolving into him.

He leaned forward to kiss me, and I ducked my head under his arm and moved toward the living room. I was not going to give in that easily. He'd hurt me. No! He'd broken my heart. And now he thinks he can show up at my doorstep, breathe heavy on me, and I'll melt.

If I asked him to have a drink, it was an invitation to stay. My hands shook, and I hated them. He followed me into the room and looked around. Rasheed had never been to my home, never sat, like Hector, in the gray leather chair.

Without invitation, he lowered himself to Barb's spot on my

red sofa. He stretched his legs out on the zebra carpet; his Italian handmade shoes didn't have a scratch. His thigh muscles pulled at the cashmere of his slacks. When he lifted his arms and clasped his fingers at the back of his head, I saw the bulge in his crotch.

I dropped into the gray chair to keep myself from unzipping his pants and straddling him.

Rasheed looked at me. Silence sat like a fat elephant between us. I could see he was assessing the situation, but I couldn't read anything in his face or eyes—not even desire, although I knew he wanted me. He was here. I saw the bulge.

"Every time I see you, Isis, I realize I'd forgotten how beautiful you are."

That was the first time Rasheed ever told me what Hector used to tell me all the time—not about the forgetting, but about being beautiful.

"Thank you Rasheed, although it's not a big compliment to be forgotten."

"Don't play games, Isis. It doesn't become you. I've never forgotten you for one moment, and you know it."

That edge of impatience was in his voice; Rasheed didn't like to waste time with words.

"And how would I know that, Rasheed? You disappear and reappear without explanation. I don't know what you feel. Or think."

"I think you and I belong together, Isis. I think that after everything we've been through in the past, we deserve to enjoy each other."

I was afraid I'd burst into tears. There was no guile in his face or voice; he spoke the truth, pure and simple, in words that until now, I had only dared dream.

"What you and I have, Isis, we don't have with anybody else. It might be different with another; it might even be good—very good—but someone else wouldn't work for me. It has to be you."

Not long ago, I'd have given everything I had—or ever hoped to have—to hear Rasheed say I was the one, that he couldn't live without me. But things had changed. I'd changed. Not totally, of course. I still craved his touch. I still craved his lips—but at what cost?

He reached into his pocket and slid a royal blue velvet sachet across the glass surface of the coffee table.

"It belongs to you. It should be yours."

Inside was the Hathor ring, the one from the auction in Copenhagen. My hands shook when I tried put it on my right middle finger. Too tight.

Rasheed reached over and slipped it on my left ring finger. It fit.

"I had it sized," he said simply.

Engagement ring? I stared at him.

"Come to Dubai with me," he said as casually as if he invited me to New York.

"Dubai?"

"Yes. I want you to be with me. I want to be with you."

"Isn't that in the Persian Gulf? Don't women wear veils there?"

I was so focused on the idea that he invited me to what I saw as a modern day Carthage, I forgot he was asking me to live with him.

"Some do, yes," he answered with a laugh. "But you won't."

It was the first time I saw him laugh. The harsh angles of his face softened. He was so handsome and warm when he smiled. Trouble is, he doesn't smile often, except for his special half-smile when I'm in his favor. Would that change if I went to Dubai?

"I live in a high-rise, Isis. We have TV and air conditioning, even restaurants. It's not that different from Las Vegas."

He had to be kidding. Did he expect me to wait in his glass and steel skyscraper in the Middle East while he disappeared to who knows where, doing who knows what? We sat only a few feet apart, but the distance between us seemed suddenly vast.

Before I could stop him, he slid down the sofa and took the hand with the Hathor ring, raising my fingers to his lips. I felt his wet tongue and remembered each time he tasted my body. I felt him in each secret place. Goose bumps rose on my arms; my face flushed.

My breasts throbbed for his electric touch, and I couldn't stop my nipples from rising in the white silk of the Chinese pajamas.

"I won't try to deny that I feel you in every cell of my body, Rasheed. I can hardly breathe when you're in the room."

He moved toward me. I pulled my hand away, and he sat back into the sofa again. I could see he was confused and maybe a little shaken. I found the strength to press on.

"But that's not enough to build a life in Dubai. I have a new career. I won't ask you for permission."

I stopped.

He studied me. The tic at his eye when he's losing control of events was very slight, but I saw it. He looked so much like Black Falcon in that moment, so much like River God.

"And I couldn't live with your jealousy," I added in a rush of bravery.

Rasheed put his hands behind his head again. He didn't say anything, but stared at me, clearly weighing the implication of my words. Then he looked over at the Red Mirror before looking back at me, hands still behind his head, elbows sticking out, legs stretched under the glass coffee table. The bulge was gone.

"Are you naming your terms?"

"Yes, maybe I am."

He dropped his arms, putting his palms on the sofa on each side of his legs. A light in his eyes flashed. I think he might have been both surprised and amused. I don't know what he expected when he showed up, but I don't think it was this.

"I would be free to travel when and where I need." I added quickly, "For business."

He cocked his eyebrow at that.

"No questions," I told him. "It'll go both ways."

His slow nodding of the head was almost imperceptible as he considered my proposal.

"Okay, Isis. But I have one condition myself. In business you are free, but no other men. I couldn't live with that."

"That means you'd have to trust me."

"I don't have a good track record, do I? It's not easy for me, but I'm willing to try."

I'd gotten everything I wanted. But the problem with 'trying' is that it doesn't mean you succeed.

"I need time to think, Rasheed. If I decide to give us a chance, you must agree to a trial period—say three to six months—with no talk of long-range commitments. With no pressure."

He laughed out loud. If he knew how he melted me with that smile, he'd smile all the time.

"I'd agree to almost anything right now, Isis, and you know it."

But there was one last nagging, frightening detail I couldn't overlook.

"What about those men in Copenhagen? I don't want a life looking over my shoulder."

His jaw set, and his eyes turned smoky. A black cloud moved quickly across his face but was as quickly gone.

"They've been taken care of."

I stopped myself from asking how he'd taken care of them. No questions from him and no questions from me. I already could see how this wasn't going to work and wished I had the excuse of needing permission from the Goddess.

"Are you finished? Any more demands? I'm giving you everything you want—even time to make up your mind."

"I'll let you know if there's anything else," I said with a grin.

He returned my smile before sliding to his knees on the carpet in front of me. I started to reach for him, but his hands slid under my silk top to my waist and stopped everything—my breath and all thought. No one had a touch like Rasheed.

His hot palms moved up my ribs, and I felt sparks like static electricity. His lips were only inches from mine, but still he didn't kiss me. He didn't say a word. He let his hands talk as he stroked the length of my smooth, strapless back.

I ran my fingers through his thick black hair and then traced his sculptured lips, rediscovering each curve, remembering with vivid sensation each of his kisses in every crevice of my body. As always, he mesmerized me; I couldn't define where Rasheed ended and I began.

He pulled me closer, sliding his knees between mine, pushing them apart. He put his face in my valley and licked me through my silk pajamas and panties, sucking on my bud—teasing me.

A current shot from his lips straight through me. All my muscles and nerves seized at once.

He licked my nipple through the silk, then pulled gently with his teeth until a rock hard point stood out in the wet, dark circle. He licked again, but only once, and then slowly traced his tongue around the edge of my ear. His hot breath on my neck sent chills down my spine.

"Now can we have what we both want?" he whispered.

I wanted to be nowhere else.

Hasta la Vista Hector

My cell rang again, and it was Tony. Hector stood out of the chair, came over to me and took the phone from my hand.

"Give us a moment, Tony," he said and ended the call.

He put his hands on each side of my face and lifted my head so that I looked straight into his eyes. My cell in his palm was cold on my cheek.

"I do not understand what is in your head, Isis. You have nothing to fear from me—*nada. Te amo.* Why would I want to harm you?"

He appeared utterly sincere. I tried to probe deep, but couldn't see evil. It would be easy enough to check if Hector had a place in Tahoe. There *are* such things as coincidences. Not everything has meaning.

"I said I would wait until you were ready, Isis. I must admit I never imagined so much competition. But *porque no?* If I want you, why would the others not want you, too?"

He kissed me so gently and with such love, I wanted nothing more than to let him wrap me in his cocoon and protect me from everything. As always with Hector, my resolve wavered. If I couldn't trust Hector, who was there?

His tongue went in my mouth, and he pulled me into him, his long arms strong and confident. Hektor's stunning virility was there; it had probably been there all along if I'd let myself feel it. His Apollo power drew me like a comet to the sun. My Spot throbbed;

I ached for the touch of his fingers.

But he stopped. He took hold of my upper arms and held me out from him. He stared down at me, searching my face, looking for answers in my eyes. I knew he was waiting for me to say what I wasn't going to say. What I couldn't bring myself to say.

When he saw that the words weren't coming, his lips pursed slightly. The red specks in his eyes floated on a glistening sheen.

"Call me when you make up your mind, Isis."

He handed me my cell phone.

"I think Tony is waiting."

He leaned down and stroked Aisha swirling at his ankles, before he closed the front door quietly behind him with a final-sounding click.

Part Three

The Black Scroll

Dreams

I t began again with a dream. The vague evanescence coalesced into a *film noir* scene of black shadows and high-contrast bright white. Save for a blue promise of sky at the top of the abyss, the only color was the girl's glossy red hair. Her long waves, the coppery auburn of an Irish Setter, swirled as she swam through air.

First we were two, and then we were one. Her panic gripped my throat. In that crazy way of dreams, when one sees oneself from the outside, I watched her struggle, like a soul seeing its body at the moment of death.

Closer and closer, four pairs of hands on long rubbery arms stretched down through the shadow.

Turning desperate, glittery emerald eyes on me, she begged, "Save me."

I reached out to snatch her from forty grasping fingers. But just as my hands pulled her toward me, her fiery tendrils snaking all about like Medusa, the dream dissolved into sunlight, and I opened my eyes to the Red Mirror.

Goliath

Not until we arrived at the auction block did I fully comprehend that I was a slave—or at least, about to be sold as one. I surely had known from the moment I opened my eyes in the cage, but the mind deceives and distorts and lets us deny until, finally, reality becomes impossible to ignore.

For as far I could see, scores of men, women and children, herded into bunches, heads hanging down, stood stoop-shouldered with ropes around their necks. In the roar of the marketplace, they were eerily silent.

While I watched in horror, knowing my turn would come, two wretched women were hauled to the block and stripped naked. The one poor thing had pendulous breasts; the second was painfully thin with a gaping overbite.

"Look at those cow tits! I'd pay to suck those."

"Keep those horse teeth away from *my* cock."

"Put a bag over her head, and I might fuck her up the arse!"

Next up was a delicate boy of about eight with golden curls and the face of a cupid. He stood all alone on the wooden dais, sobbing for his mother.

In the front row, two scrawny grandfather-types went at each other with the ferocity of jackals. The crowd went wild, whistling and cheering, shouting out wagers. Four centurions elbowed their way into the mob, grabbed the old men by the back of their necks and dragged them away with arms flailing and feet kicking up clouds of dust.

It took a few minutes for the booing and stomping of feet to settle before the auctioneer could return to the bidding.

In the end, the child was sold to a Roman lying behind the curtains of a litter. No one saw his face. His head slave had done the bidding.

A blue-skinned blond giant flung the howling boy over his shoulder, and the head slave barked, "Make way for a Roman citizen!"

The crush parted before the litter and then closed ranks again when it passed into the endless sea of milling brown wool and hard faces.

Next up was a group of ten broken men of indeterminable origin—ageless, faceless, human only in form.

"Show us more women!" the mob demanded.

"Bring up that redhead over there."

Hunks of bread flew through the air. Then small stones. A dozen soldiers banged on their shields with swords until the rock throwing slowed to a few pebbles and then ceased altogether.

Six of the starved wretches went quickly to one buyer for three thousand *denarii*, five hundred a man. Four more were sold for three hundred each. Mine prices. All dead in a month.

A ripple of interest quieted the crowd when the black giant was pulled to the podium. They knew something special when they saw it.

Two slaves in loincloths dumped buckets of water on the giant's front and back. For a few fleeting moments his long athletic muscles, more navy than black, glistened like onyx. The water evaporated quickly in the heat, leaving a fine white haze of salt on his smooth chest.

"Look at these shoulders and the power of those legs!" shouted the auctioneer.

Using an ebony camel crop with brass tips on both ends, the auctioneer slapped my giant's biceps and thighs while turning him in a full circle by the rope around his neck. He then forced the Nubian's lips open to expose strong, straight ivory teeth set in blue-black gums.

"This beast was born for the Arena. Don't insult me with anything less than three thousand *denarii*."

The bidding ended with five thousand *denarii*, and the giant was led down from the block. He passed so close by me that I could see shiny beads of sweat pooling in the hollow at the base of his throat. Just at that spot—so green against his ebony skin—hung a glassy medallion etched with a seven-pointed star. A septagram.

I grabbed his arm, and we looked straight at each other. He blinked and then blinked again. I could see every red capillary in the white of those wide, surprised eyes.

Goliath recognized me, but by the baffled look on his face, I saw he didn't know from where.

"Help me," I pleaded, although I had no idea how one slave could help another.

A soldier wrenched my hand away, but Goliath's eyes and mine stayed locked until a rough tug on my arm pulled me in the direction of the block.

I had no reason for hope, but I no longer felt alone. It couldn't be coincidence that Goliath was the first I should meet in this life.

I was back in the Circle of the Protectors.

Slave Auction

Viewed from the top of the block, the mob was impossibly more vicious. It was from that vantage point I saw how many they were and how utterly vile their faces.

A voice cried out, "*Praecantrix!*" And then another and another. "Witch." "Witch." "Witch."

The sun, a white orb in a white sky, blazed without mercy; it flailed my flesh. Blinded, I saw only light. When I raised my bound hands to shield my face, the auctioneer knocked them down with his brass-tipped baton.

"Strip the witch!"

"Strip her! Strip her! Strip her!"

They kept at it, baying louder and louder like packs of dogs barking in rough Latin and their harsh-to-the-ear language I didn't recognize.

This is not happening. This isn't real. But, of course, it was.

A northerly breeze sprang up, bringing cooler air from the sea. I took a deep breath and braced myself to be stripped.

But the auctioneer didn't tear off my gown. Instead, he stood back and grinned a broad, gummy smile with all his front teeth missing. A few strands of straw-colored hair were pasted with sweat to his cheeks and forehead. The rest of his hair gathered at the back of his neck in a straggly ponytail.

With grand theatrical gesture, he raised his arms for silence. The soldiers beat in unison on their shields with the flat side of their sword blades until the mob calmed.

He moved up close to me, making a great show of stroking my hair with his filthy, black-nailed fingers and rubbing back and forth across my breasts with his crop. The mob cheered and screamed again for him to strip me.

"You say witch," he shouted. "I say *enchantress*. Who will hold this head of red hair between his thighs tonight? Whose cock will she suck?"

"No bids til we see her naked!"

I looked straight ahead, fixing on a mammoth bronze statue of a Roman emperor with his arm outstretched in an orator's pose, his finger pointing right at me. *Wake me, Barb! Wake me up!*

But I didn't wake up, of course. I still heard the auctioneer.

He lifted a lock of my hair, ran it under his nose, dramatically inhaling the scent and, with a flourish, sucked on the tip, making smacking sounds.

"Now this goddess is not some weeping virgin who'll cower in your bed. This whore knows how to please a man. She likes the thrust of a cock, no matter where."

The crowd surged forward. I was terrified they'd storm the block, but a handful of soldiers repulsed them with spears and shields. Fistfights broke out among those jockeying for the front rows. Soldiers dragged frenzied men away. The mob shoved forward again. More soldiers arrived, locking shields to form a wall at the foot of the platform.

"Ten thousand *denarii!*"

The opening offer came from an arrogant-looking Roman officer with a nasty scar running the length of his left cheek. He stood to my right with two other officers a little outside the crowd. I got the impression they'd been passing by and stopped.

"I see we have a connoisseur today," boomed the auctioneer. "A man of discerning taste. Do I hear—"

"Twelve thousand." This bidder didn't shout out; he didn't need to. He was that close.

Striking in a savage way, he was all lean muscle for his age. Primitive, colorful geometric designs covered his knee-length tunic. Red mud matted his beard; feathers adorned his braids. His yellowish eyes stared up at me with the non-blinking gaze of a man who spends his life in the vast solitude of the desert.

"Thirteen thousand!" The third bidder was a balding, porky little Roman in a red-trimmed white toga. A painfully thin slave with knobby knees and elbows held a green parasol with gold fringe over his head.

"I have thirteen thousand. Do I hear fourteen?"

"Fourteen," agreed the officer with a nod. One of his companions said something, and all three laughed.

"Fifteen thousand for the redhead and five thousand for the girl-boy." The surprise bid came from the back in the direction of a pair of octagonal stone pavilions. I couldn't see who.

The spectators were clearly enjoying themselves now. Men laughed and joked, shouting out wagers, betting on who of the four would go highest. The auctioneer was quite beside himself; he obviously never envisioned the bids would soar so high.

"I have twenty thousand *denarii* for both females," he crowed. "Who will say twenty-two?"

"Twenty-two thousand *denarii*." Desert Man's eyes bored into me, but I refused to look at him.

I felt him probing, trying to get into my head. I pushed him away. He pushed back. His mind was terrifyingly strong. Of all the bidders, I feared him most.

I concentrated everything on the fat Roman under the green parasol. Too pleased by far with himself when the crowd cheered him on, he was a man I could manipulate. A man hungry for flattery is easy prey.

I gave him my most provocative look. Across the space between us, my smoldering eyes promised him everything.

"Twenty-five!" he called out bravely.

Convinced that his exorbitant bid would be the last, I began already to scheme his seduction.

But the bidding wasn't over.

"Thirty-five thousand *denarii!*" The stunning counterbid came from the mystery man in the back.

He had moved closer, close enough that I saw his thick chestnut waves shining in the sun. I don't know how I'd missed him before. He was tall—taller than most—and stood with that easy, confident stance of an athlete. Hector. He'd come through the Red Mirror again to save me.

"Thank you, Universe," I whispered.

"I have thirty-five thousand! Do I hear higher?" The auctioneer looked to the fat Roman who, giving me a sorrowful look of regret as if to apologize, shook his head.

There was no counterbid from the officer. He and his two friends were walking away.

"And you," the auctioneer put to Desert Man. "Do I hear thirty-six?"

Silence. Over and over I chanted, *Don't bid. Don't bid. Don't bid.*

"Going once," the auctioneer cautioned. "Going twice."

I held my breath, staring straight ahead, fearful that if I looked at him, he would counter. But he didn't, and it was over.

"Sold! Both females to the tall stranger for thirty-five thousand *denarii!*"

Once down from the podium, not a breath of air came off the sea. The marketplace began to spin; I was hit by a wave of nausea. It took all my will to move one foot in front of another.

Water. I needed water. Hector would soon give me water.

But that wasn't what the bare-chested Egyptian slave with a shaved head and *kohl*-lined eyes was saying to the sales agent.

"Have them delivered to the villa of Marcus Quintillus."

"There must be a mistake!" I shouted.

For a moment, no one reacted. I suppose they were stunned that a slave would dare speak without being spoken to.

"Where is your master?" I grabbed the Egyptian's forearm. "Take me to him."

The Egyptian tried to pull away, but I refused to let him go, digging my fingertips into his arm.

The soldier holding the rope around my neck hit me in the temple with his fist. The sky went bright white and then dark. Edges around objects grew fuzzy. I heard everything as if were coming from far away. Then in a sudden rush, the sound of the market travelled down a long corridor to explode in my ears. Edges hardened again, and the world came back into focus.

And when I saw clearly once more, Hector stood not ten feet away.

"Why?" I begged him. *Why?*

He stared at me for a moment then turned his back to leave, but not before I saw the look of triumph in his eyes.

"Hector!" I screamed after him. "Hector!"

But he kept going and never looked back.

Domina

Her bedchamber in the villa by the sea was dark as night, stifling hot and smoky with a cloying cloud of myrrh. I could see daylight as a faint glowing line around thick shutters. Tall bronze lanterns cut with stars and crescent moons cast dancing patterns on the mosaic floor and glazed red walls.

"Closer!" Domina commanded from across the shadows.

Major Domo, head slave of the household, pushed me forward into a hazy halo of amber light.

"Leave us."

She reclined on a sofa with a raised gilded armrest. At her feet lounged a leopard with a golden collar. The leopard was chained, but I saw at a glance that the silver chain was long enough for the cat to reach me.

"Turn around."

I did as she commanded, pivoting slowly.

"Closer."

I stepped up next to her couch, so close the leopard lay only inches from my feet. It hissed, curling its lips to show me sharp teeth the color of ivory. Forcing myself to breathe evenly, I blocked visions of those teeth tearing at the soft flesh of my throat. The hiss became a low, rumbling growl.

"Untie your right shoulder."

Slowly, so as not to provoke the cat, I loosened the cord, and half of my tunic top slipped to my waist. Domina's eyes widened just a little, but her breath came faster. Under the shimmering silk of her gown, hard nipples rose.

In the dim light, her lips were blacker than black against her stark white, lead-painted face. The light falling on her hollow eyes and cheeks cast dark shadows that gave her the face of a corpse. But she was very much alive. Her mouth hung a little slack; the pointed pink tip of her tongue appeared between crooked teeth.

"Your skin is like milk," she breathed softly.

If my heart raced, so did hers; her breasts rose and fell quickly.

"Untie the other shoulder," she whispered.

Just as cautiously as before, I loosened the second tie and the rest of the tunic tumbled to my waist.

For a long moment, Domina was silent, taking in with hungry eyes my white glowing breasts, moistening her lips with that pointed reptile tongue.

Try as I might to control my breath and heartbeat, blood pounded in my temples. My palms were wet with sweat. It wasn't her lust that frightened me; I'd seen lust before. It was the not knowing what it would take to satisfy her appetite that unnerved me. And the leopard. I'd seen that before, too. It was an ugly end.

"Æsa!" Domina hissed.

An Amazon with thick blond braids to her waist appeared from nowhere.

"Yes, Domina."

"The black one—and the Gaul."

Silence. The leopard shifted position and began to lick its paw in an idle, languid way. Long, curving claws unfurled. The growling ceased. For the moment, it seemed to have lost interest in me. My eyes kept going to the pink tongue and the razor claws.

"Look at me," Domina snapped.

She tried with her burning eyes to sear my soul, but I refused to let her inside.

"Where are you from?" she asked sharply.

"Hispania."

When her eyes narrowed, I added, "Domina."

"Say something else. I want to hear you speak."

"What does Domina desire me to say?"

She studied me, no longer mesmerized by my breasts but looking me hard in the face.

"They tell me you were born Roman?"

"Yes, Domina."

She considered me with new interest; in less than a heartbeat, she'd morphed from lustful to curious.

"I heard you tell the cook that you murdered a man."

"Yes, Domina."

"Well," she demanded impatiently. "Who?"

I hesitated. There were a dozen stories I could invent but none with the shock factor of the truth. I wouldn't tell her all, though. All would be too much.

"My father," I said evenly.

She reacted with all the fear and revulsion I'd hoped for. I might have put a deadly asp to her face, so quickly and completely she recoiled. The leopard tensed; its ears lifted. Yellow-green eyes watched me warily.

But my moment of advantage was fleeting; I hadn't counted on the men.

Suddenly they were there. Two beasts in horrid pewter masks with huge round eyeholes and thick wicked lips.

The one was a black giant. In the gloom of the darkened chamber, I at first saw only his glistening skin and thought with joy and hope, Goliath!

But when he came into the light, the eyes of a sadist glittered from the mask.

The Gaul had skin so blue, he glowed. His wild straw hair was braided loosely into long ropes twisted with colored glass beads that caught the flicker of the lamps.

When they saw me, naked to the waist, their already monstrous penises swelled. Their broad, bare feet were silent on the mosaic floor as they moved next to me, one on each side.

With the arrival of the men, Domina morphed once more. I had thought she wanted me for herself, but I now saw that she was one of those who takes her pleasure from watching.

"You. Black One. Take her from behind." Her voice was husky and terrifyingly breathless.

I knew that if I looked at her, she would be aroused, flushed under her white makeup, nipples rock hard in her silk gown.

But I didn't look at her; I couldn't tear my eyes away from the blue Gaul. Staring back at me was a black soul of pure malevolence.

"Make her squeal," Domina whispered in a small, little girl voice.

The black giant grabbed me by the hair, forcing my head down, bending me at the waist, hauling up my tunic, ripping away my loincloth.

"You. Gaul!" Domina panted. "Down her throat."

I felt the searing thrust of the black giant in my anus at the same time the Gaul rammed the back of my throat. I gagged and retched; bile burned my mouth. Pinned between the two men, I couldn't move.

"All the way in," she screamed. "I want you all the way in."

My mind shouted, *This isn't real! The real me is on the other side of the Mirror. This is only my mind. There is no pain.*

But the pain was real enough. A log tore me; I choked on my own vomit. Would I drown before I was split apart?

"STOP! Stop at once!"

At the sound of the odd, half-man half-boy voice of Marcus Quintillus, the black monster and the blue Gaul dropped me and went to their knees.

Dominus. Master of the house. Master of all, even Domina.

I collapsed between them, sucking in great gulps of air, my body shuddering. Warm liquid, surely my own blood, oozed on my lower buttocks and down my inner thigh.

I was on my hands and knees, head hanging down with long flaming hair sweeping the floor, blocking the room, shielding me from evil.

"Get her cleaned up," Dominus ordered. "I shall not touch that which reeks of these foul dicks."

"Fool!" Domina shouted. "She is a murderess. She could be an assassin! You know nothing of this Alexandrian who sent her. He is Greek! Who can trust a Greek?"

"Enough, Wife! You may yet have her again, but not before I am finished."

He snapped his fingers and said, "Let me see her up close."

To walk was agony, but I forced myself erect as Major Domo dragged me to stand in front of Dominus. He was not much taller than me, with thick lips in a doughy face pitted from the pox.

I kept my eyes down, as was proper for a slave. I had to tread with utmost caution. If I were to survive, I needed his protection.

"Look at me," he commanded.

My expression was blank; I showed him nothing. But behind my mask, I searched for clues as to what kind of man he was—in the rate of his breath, the pulse in his temple, in the blinking of his eyelids.

The length and quality of my life—and perhaps the length and means of my death—depended on his needs and the value he placed on me.

He took his own time trying to read me with his cunning, nakedly ambitious eyes. I had no sense that he desired me, at least not as a man normally craves a woman.

"Keep her away from knives," he grunted finally to Major Domo. "If you value your life. If we all value our lives."

Marcus Quintillus had seen something in me of worth, and whatever it was, I was spared, at least for now.

Convivium

The *triclinium* was dark. The sea was black. One by one, a new brazier glowed until the gold lion fountain in the center of the flickering orange circle turned fiery. I heard the pulsing rhythm of a native drum and the undulating wail of a single flute before I saw the musicians.

Coalescing from the night, they were there quite suddenly with skin so black I wouldn't have seen them save for the scarlet turbans. They sat in hook position, drums between their thighs.

Unseen hands cast powder on coals, and the room filled with a perfumed vermilion smoke. The dense cloud lingered for a few moments before clearing.

The woman was a vision of greased ebony flesh, tall as any man, all toned muscle, not a hint of fat on her long limbs, narrow hips and flat belly. Gold bangles encircled her ankles and wrists; huge gold hoops hung from her tiny seashell ears. Her oiled black hair, cropped close to the scalp, glistened like an obsidian helmet.

But it was the python that stopped my breath. It coiled up her never-ending leg, around her long midriff and between her high, tight breasts with hard nipples. In her right hand, she held the great snake just below the head. Its mouth yawned in a bright flash of pink showing no fangs, but two rows of tiny sharp teeth curved backward to latch onto its prey.

A flutist trilled high, hypnotic notes on a slender wooden pipe. The sway of the dancer and the rippling of the snake were one with the music. There wasn't a murmur in the dining room; even the retching had ceased.

The two slaves from Domina's bedchamber, the blue Gaul monster and the black giant, wearing the horrid pewter masks, moved into the circle of orange light. The Gaul took the snake's head from the woman's hands.

Whether it was the music or the effects of a drug, I couldn't say, but she was in a trance. Her eyes rolled back in her head. Only the whites showed. A fine sheen of sweat glistened over her polished ebony flesh. Her nipples were copper points.

The blue Gaul put the snake's mouth to one of those copper nipples, and the python began to nurse, its powerful muscles rippling in long, undulating convulsions.

The woman writhed in agony. The black giant held her shoulders from behind. His erection was like that of a stallion. I felt the pain of it tearing into me as if it were happening again at this very moment.

Bright blood began to trickle down the woman's breast.

It was the sight of the blood that inflamed the guests. They were agitated, most sitting up, straining forward. Domina was too much in shadow for me to see her face, but I imagined her hungry eyes.

The black giant slowly penetrated the woman, sliding his monster penis into her anus in time with the music, always swaying, keeping pace with the rhythmic contractions of the snake.

With great force, the Gaul pulled the snake from the woman's raw breast and, using all his strength, placed the head between her legs. The snake rippled in one long, crushing contraction. The black beauty's body convulsed. She screamed. And when she screamed, the dining room went mad. Two Romans reclining close by ejaculated into slaves' palms.

The black giant lifted her, impaled on his erection, by the back of her thighs and spread her long legs into the air. Red blood flowed down his black loins.

I wanted not to watch, to look anywhere but there, but I found myself mesmerized by the horror of the Gaul forcing the python head up her.

The woman kept screaming and screaming. The drums pounded faster and faster. The wail of the flute soared.

"Fuck her! Fuck her!" the room echoed.

Oh, if I could have, I would have merged with that wall. I would have put myself right out of existence.

Then the cries became, "Fuck her to death!"

I covered my ears with my hands but couldn't stifle the shrieks of agony or the applause of the guests.

The dining room kept shouting more and more terrible commands, until Domina herself rose from the divan and made her way to the fountain courtyard.

What a fool I was to think she meant to stop the show. What a fool I was to think her human.

It was only when she came into the orange circle of light that I saw she wore the dull metal mask with round terrible eyes and cruel mouth. In her hand, the shiny steel of a dagger flashed like a tongue of fire.

Swiftly, without any hesitation, she drew the blade across the soft underside of the woman's jaw open in mid-scream. And then, before I could squeeze shut my eyes, she slashed again, right down the belly to the groin. Wet, coiled pink intestines tumbled to the floor.

I so wish I truly had a witch's sight to have known what Domina would do. Then I could have spared myself the image that I shall never erase from my mind.

I couldn't watch the woman die, but I heard the guests roar. Like her crimson blood coming in a sudden rush, I shall never forget their cheers.

When I dared open my eyes, the son dressed in the formal *toga praetexta* with purple stripe of a boy not yet a man stood next to me. He took my hand and put it on his hard erection standing up in the wool.

I vowed then and there that, no matter what, I'd never again go through the Red Mirror.

Major Domo

The sound of a key in the lock woke me. I sat up. The light from the kitchen, dim as it was, blinded me for a moment before my eyes made out Major Domo's devil shape. A fiery-red aura from the cookfire glowed around him.

He stepped in and closed the door without a sound. In his hand he carried a rod as long as his forearm. I could only make out the gold tips on the ends. A rod like Domina's. Maybe it was hers.

He must have remarkable eyesight. Or he'd memorized the room while he still had the light, because he was on me at once, shoving me against the wall with his forearm at my throat. I reached out to scratch his face, but after my days of slavery had no nails.

I groped with my fingers for his eyes, and he pressed harder. I choked. My legs thrashed; my bare heels scraped on the rough floor. Twisting my hips, I tried to dig my toes into his genitals, all the while beating at him with my fists.

"Where is your magic now, *striga?*" It was too dark to see his face clearly, but I heard the wicked smirk in his voice.

With his other hand, the one that held the rod, he pulled up my gown and ripped away the loincloth. I tried to press my legs together, but he had his knee in my groin.

"I'll not give you the privilege of my cock in your cunt. I shall let you taste my little friend."

I felt the cold metal on the inside of my thigh and started to scream, but fast as lightning, his palm covered my mouth. His forearm no longer choked me, but his hand crushed my head to the wall.

We fought each other, me with my useless fists, him with one hand on my mouth and the other looking to open me, to shove the stick up me. I struggled, digging at his eyes with my fingers, clutching the wrist at my groin with my left hand.

The fork! Where was the fork? My right hand searched frantically on the stone until I felt the tip of the tines, and then the handle.

At the very moment he found my canal with the rod, I plunged the sharp prongs into his neck. He went rigid. His eyes were huge, so huge that in spite of the dark, I saw the shock there, only inches from my face.

But still he didn't stop. O Gods! I felt the rod pushing at my cervix.

With all my strength, I shoved at his heavy body, struggling to push him away.

He let go of my mouth to put his hand to his neck. My thrust must have hit his carotid artery, because blood suddenly spewed in a hot fountain, streaming down his neck and flooding me.

"Die!" I hissed. "Die, you bastard!"

In his effort to pull out the fork, he released pressure on the rod. I grabbed his wrist again and tried to pull it away. But even with blood pumping from his artery, he overcame me. The rod was deep in me again.

Whack!

His heavy body collapsed across my lap.

Standing next to us, holding in her hands a clay *amphora* big as herself, was the girl. I don't know how she carried such a weight, much less lifted it into the air to bring it down on his head.

And then, as if the effort had drained all her strength, she dropped the *amphora*. It would have shattered on the stone floor and caused a terrible racket if it hadn't landed on Major Domo's still legs.

The giant *amphora* teetered for a few seconds before sliding silently to the floor and rolling a foot or two. The girl stopped it with her foot.

I shoved off his dead body and jumped to my feet, wiping my bloody hands on his tunic.

"*Adios*, asshole."

His face was forever imprinted with an astonished look asking, "How could this happen?"

"His keys," I whispered."

The girl bent, rustled about at Major Domo's belt and stood again with a ring of iron keys in her hand.

Tiptoeing across the silent kitchen, we squeezed through the slightly ajar door into the night garden. The damp air was pungent with the scent of rosemary, lovage, savory and mint. Overhead the stars blazed in a canopy of wonder. Close by, slow waves tumbled in the magnetic seductive rhythm that is the Mediterranean.

The Universe blessed us, and the third key turned the lock in the green door in the white garden wall. Framed in the rectangular doorway were iridescent dunes with waves crashing behind them.

This was the moment of no return. There was only one outcome for a slave recaptured. Crucifixion.

The girl and I took each other's hands and stepped out.

At the bottom of the shallow rise with rocky crops, the beach was broad and white as snow. We headed into the waves, running together through the foaming surf, turning to the west, away from the lightening horizon, away from the city, away from the villa of horrors.

Horse Tamer

It was his presence that woke me. The third of the horsemen who had taken us from the beach outside the villa. Startled, I sat up straight, immediately tense, ready to defend myself.

He lowered himself to his haunches, pointing first to the sun and then to my sunburned arm. As he surely handled a skittish colt, his gestures were solicitous and unthreatening; his honey-colored eyes assured me that he meant no harm.

With slow, deliberate movements, he removed his unbleached wool cape and gently wrapped the heavy rough cloth around my shoulders, pulling it delicately into place to cover me.

The corners of his mouth turned up not quite in a smile, but his eyes held mine for a long moment before he stood and went back to grooming the horses.

He had lean, caramel-colored muscular calves. Geometric tattoos encircled sturdy ankles and strong wrists. Broad shoulders narrowed to slim hips. On the whole, his body was strong with no surplus. He wore his rich honey hair, a few shades darker than his eyes, in feathered braids like the other two men.

I watched him curry the mare, stroking her steaming black coat, whispering soothing words into her ear. I couldn't remember anyone who'd treated me with equal tenderness as he treated his horse.

When we were ready to ride again, the tall honey-eyed Horse Tamer signalled that I was to ride with him.

Assuring me again with his eyes, he expertly twisted Shinuba's emerald sparkly scarf into a turban, covering my forehead. After wrapping the final swath across the lower part of my face and over my nose, he tucked the end into a fold above my temple. Only my eyes showed.

He then lifted me astride the stallion and mounted behind me. I took a handful of the horse's mane to steady myself. He slid his left hand around my waist, taking the reins in his right.

There was nothing more natural than leaning into him, his arm tight around me. I relaxed back into his chest and belly. I felt him grow hard. He dug in his heels, and we set off, the girl behind us with the second horseman and Desert Man in the lead.

Each time we stopped, he dismounted and held up his arms to help me from the horse and set me carefully on my feet. Each time we remounted, he lifted me astride and then climbed on behind me, pulling me back into him.

The Milky Way arched in a broad hazy river across the heavens. Orion, the Pleiades, the Big Dipper pointing to the North Star—I looked for the guideposts I'd known all my life and in all my lifetimes.

Desert Man snored. The second horseman, the sullen one, rolled to his side with his back toward me. Ever so slowly, I tugged away the heavy cape and then wrapped the girl with the blanket.

My bare feet made no sound on the sandy ground. A shadow might have made more noise. I barely breathed. My heart drummed in my chest; in the still of the night, I thought surely he must hear it beat.

He was awake. Hands crossed under his head, lying on his back, he looked up at the stars, just as I had.

I slipped the emerald scarf from my head and pulled the pins and threads from my hair; lush waves fell around my shoulders.

My body ached all over. I felt pain everywhere but still I lowered myself onto him, draping the cloak over us. That's how starved I was for tenderness in this nightmare world. How desperate I was not to be alone.

His calloused hands might have been gloved in velvet, his touch on my bruised body was that soft. In the dark under the cloak, I found his lips and kissed him with a yearning that told him how I craved the loving care he gave his horse.

Those velvet hands stroking my back calmed me as he'd calmed the mare. With a magic touch, his fingers sensed where they gave pleasure or pain. And there was a lot of pain after Major Domo.

In my ear, he whispered sounds that didn't form words. I felt safe. Safe in the hands of a wizard.

Cradling me in his arm to protect my tender skin from the hard ground, he eased me from on top of him to my side. I moaned softly, and he breathed, "Sh-h-h." But he never stopped stroking me.

I wanted nothing more than to envelop him, for him to drown in my warmth. I needed for him never to want to leave me. *How else would I survive until Barb brought me back?*

The desert was so quiet, the camp silent in sleep. We clung together, me grinding into him, and him hard against my belly. Then like the wizard he was, he suckled my breast, the heel of his magic hand kneading my womb, and I surrendered. A wave began to rise and rise and, when it crested, I tumbled in a satin sea.

There was no time or space. I wasn't in Libya. I wasn't anywhere. Elektra wasn't anywhere. For the first time in her star-crossed life, she knew the pleasure of orgasm while pleasing and being pleased.

He kissed my tears away, and I kissed him on his chin, down his throat, all over his chest and across his flat belly. With the tips of my fingers, I traced the taut muscle from his knee to his groin, circling slowly, taking my time to touch. I toyed and massaged, never hurrying, following his breath, setting the pace to the thump of his heart. Squeezing, tugging and caressing until his body convulsed in a shuddering release I felt as my own.

My eyes had adjusted for me to see the imprint of my septagram medallion pressed into his chest. Surely, he must now belong to me.

The amulet was a sign. A sign of a new beginning.

If this was not magic, I don't know what is.

Lemta

Inside the Cave of Bats, under the pointed dome of the Hive, Lemta of the husky vibrating voice reclined on rich carpets and stacks of pillows. Her pearlescent skin, I believe even paler than mine, glowed white as the glyphs dancing around her head. A wild mane of curly hair, black as black can be, gave her a savage jungle look. I couldn't determine her age. She was neither young nor old.

In that mystical, alien tongue of the Berbers, she ordered the horsemen to leave. Her black eyes gleamed at me with the uncanny light of all-seeing. I kept my gaze level but without my usual boldness; this woman was too potent to challenge.

She waved me closer with an impatient flick of shiny talon nails. My mind went through a dozen possibilities as to what Lemta might want of me, none of them reassuring.

"I am not clean," I told her.

Her lips curved into an amused little smile, then she nodded to the Maiden who rang on a bronze bowl. A red door opened in the black wall, and a young woman about my age, dressed in an ankle-length ivory wool tunic like the Maiden's, glided into the Hive. A few low murmurs in Berber were exchanged in a hush.

The salve they applied to my bruised and cut feet brought instant relief; the stinging simply stopped. I held out my hand for the ointment jar, took some salve on my fingertips and then reached to soothe my anus. At a word from the Maiden, a fragile petite woman with liquid brown eyes diluted the cream with almond oil and massaged it gently into my sunburned skin. My body tingled with a slight chill before going numb.

Once bathed, oiled and dressed, I joined Lemta on the cushions. The downy folds of the ivory tunic caressed my breasts and loins.

Lemta's eyes, bottomless black pools in the low light, travelled without shame down the length of my body.

So she was, after all, like the others. To satisfy her shouldn't be difficult; I didn't sense a sadist. But if she wanted me, I had my price. Answers.

"You have not told me why I am here. "

"You are brazen," she observed. "I like that. It is a good thing to have courage."

She leaned back, relaxing into the scented pillows, radiating an electrifying sexuality impossible to ignore. Great sensuous waves rolled off her. I felt myself pulled into her tide, helplessly drawn to the inexorable ebb and flow that she, and she alone, controlled.

Unbearable moments of silence ticked away; a slight hum in my ears buzzed louder and louder. Her perfume, a heady scent of jungle gardenia infused with an alien, alluring spice, rose off the satiny pillows. My head whirled. My vision blurred, my lips numbed, and my tongue grew thick. I felt hot as fire and then ice cold.

They'd drugged me!

"How is your skin now?" Lemta oozed in her low, hypnotic, undulant voice drawing me closer and closer to her.

She reached out to trace her long, hennaed fingernail down my arm. "Do you still feel the sun?"

Unnerved, I jerked away, not because she was a woman—women had found diversion in my body for as long as I could remember. My mother had seen to that.

It was fear of *her* touch, falling under *her* spell that terrified me— the surrendering of my soul.

She laughed, but not cruelly, and the intensity between us relaxed a fraction.

"You are very beautiful, just as I expected." She wet a lock of my hair with her tongue and ripe lips. "Such glorious hair. Like living fire."

Again, I wanted to ask how she knew of me, but my tongue was thick, too thick to form words.

And then nausea consumed me, and I no longer cared. I succumbed to an irresistible need to lay my head down—to lay my whole body down.

"Do not struggle," I heard her say from far, far away.

I closed my eyes. The room began to spin. My heavy lids refused to open.

Her hand was hot, hotter than my burning skin, too hot to touch. I tried to pull away, but she gripped harder.

Her moist lips, close to my ear, breathed, "BERBELBÖCH CHTHTÖTHÖMI."

I lost all strength. Or rather I lost all will to resist.

I was no longer in my body but floating beside it, studying the fluttering of my eyelids, wondering at my long red hair on the pillows snaking out from my head like Medusa.

Time passed; I can't say how long. I was aware only of deep silence broken by the squawks of the birds. I thought if I opened my mouth to speak, I, too, would squawk.

Then Lemta was talking, and the low vibration of her voice drew me back into my body.

"You have had carnal knowledge of one of the men," she accused.

"Is it a crime to know a man?" I slurred.

"*This* man, it is."

"Why?"

"Because he is *my* man."

Her husky rich voice went gravelly, and I opened my eyes.

Gone was her glowing milky skin. Gone was the wild mane of raven curls. Dull gray frizz hung lifeless around razor cheekbones and a skeletal jaw. Creased lips sunken in a ravaged face mouthed her words.

I'm sure I stared at her in horror. Horror was what I felt.

She laughed a toothless cackle and, stretching out a black-veined hand with twisted fingers, lay her pointed yellow index talon on my forehead, right between my eyes. Blinding white light flooded the Hive.

I was back in the abyss of my dream, struggling to rise to the top toward the promise of blue sky. My fiery hair flowed around me; my skin was deathly pale.

But instead of hands on rubber faceless arms stretching through the dark, there was only the Horse Tamer looking down with honey-colored eyes. He reached out for me, taking my wrist, and I swam upward, weighing nothing.

I thought he would pull me from the black well to kiss me, but just when I was within reach of the blue, he showed me his face that wasn't his, but Lemta's. Lemta the hag. I screamed, but my scream was the squawk of a bird.

I tumbled further and further until there was not a trace of blue, but only blackness. Blackness, that is, until I crashed through the Red Mirror, shattering the glass into a thousand shards.

The Maiden

"Are you ready for another voyage?"

"Quite ready."

It was a solemn ceremony. Lemta, the Maiden and a dozen acolytes held hands in a circle around me, droning over and over in a slow mesmerizing hum the chant of Shinuba.

"ANA A A NANA A A NANA."

They had loosened their hair from the thick braids. Heads rotating far back and far forward in wide circles, in time with the chanting, they swung their long waves around and around. Their voices grew louder, the rhythm faster, the arcs wilder.

I lost myself in the chanting. Colors, muted before in the lamplight, burst into bright neon. Floating symbols and glyphs throbbed.

Lemta held a silver chalice to my lips; embossed septagrams rimmed the edge. I closed my eyes and swallowed a full mouthful, holding the potion only an instant on my tongue. The taste was slightly bitter but not unpleasant. Warmth spread through my chest, filled my belly and caressed my thighs. My toes tingled; my fingers vibrated. Every cell ignited. My ears hummed with a low drone.

Then out of black nothingness, thousands and thousands of angry bees swarmed round my head. The roar of their wings deafened me. I felt one sting and then another; I had only seconds before the swarm attacked. In panic, with arms flailing, I tried to protect my face.

At the center of the black swarm, the Queen Bee—Lemta with giant wings—seized my wrists with her sharp-barbed forelegs.

My eyes flew open, and she was there, gripping my arms, pulling me close to her face.

"Do not choose this journey!" she warned. "Choose *only* the reality you control."

She placed her index finger on my forehead, intoning, "BERBELBĞCH CHTHTÖTHÖMI."

White light flooded my brain.

It was the Maiden who settled me on the pillows and removed my gown. Her touch was that of an angel as she bathed me in scent of jasmine.

She brushed my long hair and spread the fiery waves in a corona around my head and shoulders. The pillows were satin soft against the bare skin of my hips and loins. I sank further and further into the cushions, becoming one with their silkiness. Becoming one with the Hive.

I let her do with me as she willed, transfixed by her arranging my limbs, my arms over my head, the back of my hands on my flowing hair.

Her lush mantle of glossy black waves, luminous under the light as a raven's wing, tumbled over her shoulders and onto my nude flesh.

When the Maiden breathed, I breathed with her. We were two, and then we were one.

My breasts were white mounds with rosy tips. I felt her wet tongue. A shock wave rolled through me.

Another angel coalesced from the swirling Hive; her long, musk-scented waves mingled with those of the Maiden's. I felt her soft lips and caressing tongue on my other breast.

"O-o-o-o-o-o-o," I moaned in the ecstasy of their tenderness.

When I tried to caress in return, warm fingers held my wrists gently in place, above my head. I was allowed only to receive.

Gentle fingertips lovingly spread my thighs and opened me, massaging, stroking, exploring. Hot breath, then warm lips and a knowing tongue teased my womanhood. Tongues on my breasts. On my belly. Tongues dipping in my ears. Lips sucking my tongue. All with the same rhythm.

We were one, the women and me. One in the Feminine. One with the Mother. One with the Earth. One with Eternity.

I convulsed in a roll of waves cascading through my soul.

When I opened my eyes, it was into the upside-down face of Lemta leaning over me. Her lion mane hair hung in my face; I breathed in the fragrant, exotic, seductive herb that was her unique scent.

"You are blessed, our Sister," she whispered, stroking my lips with her long talon nails. "The world is yours. You must seize it. It is your destiny."

Nemo

For the first time in weeks—or maybe months—I saw the sky. The pale light of dawn blinded me when I came out of the Cave of Bats. I blinked, holding the back of my hand up to my eyes.

Three silhouettes stood on the ledge, all with long braids entwined with feathers. I recognized the wiry one by his thin legs. I no longer saw the man in middle because I couldn't tear my eyes away from the tall figure on the right.

I would have burst into tears if Lemta hadn't taught me always to be strong and never show what was in my heart.

Nemo, The Horse-Tamer.

Around his neck he wore the septagram that I'd given him and Lemta had taken away.

Silently, he wrapped the green emerald scarf in a turban around my hair, leaving loose cloth to cover my mouth and nose. He lifted me up and into his arms, cradling me, my feet dangling over his forearm. His honey-colored eyes didn't close until his lips pressed on mine.

I think we both closed our eyes at the same moment. I know we breathed the same breath.

No longer did I dread the long voyage on the desert. I saw the sweet passing of each night. I saw the canopy of stars.

I saw the future, and I liked very much what I saw.

Gareth Greene

Resplendent under the Chihuly glass ceiling, the Bellagio lobby was packed. A big group had just arrived. I pushed through the crowd, forced to walk past the Petrossian Bar.

Hector and Ingrid were gone, but I still saw them there, Hector's thick chestnut waves gleaming under the light.

"*ABLAMGOUNOTHO ABRASAX!*" I muttered, and Nordic blond Ingrid disappeared from the vision.

"Hey, man! Over here!"

Startled, I turned in the direction of the Barry White voice I never expected to hear in this lifetime. He was not fifteen feet away, his head towering above everyone.

Goliath. Fully dressed, totally in command of the room.

A sports cap with a logo was jammed on his head. A gorgeous black chick hung on each arm.

The crowd parted for another giant to join him, and they slapped each other on the back, both of them laughing.

A young kid of about twelve elbowed his way in and held up a pen and magazine. Goliath grinned, took the pen and scribbled.

"Who's that?" I asked a thirty-something guy next to me.

"Him? That's Gareth Greene."

When he saw the name meant nothing to me, he prompted, "Forward for the Chicago Bulls?"

Still not getting the expected reaction, he tried, "The highest-paid player in the NBA?"

I dug in my bag for a pen. "Have you got any paper?"

He handed me the sports section of USA Today, and I squeezed through to stand in front of Goliath, once a slave, now superstar Gareth Greene.

I beamed up at him and held out the pen and paper.

"May I have your autograph?" My look was pretty intense; I was willing with all my might that he recognize me.

A small furrow appeared in his brow. His complexion was smooth, flawless chocolate, certainly without any tribal scars.

"Do I know you?"

"Maybe," I teased. "Can you dedicate it to Isis?"

"Isis?"

I could see he struggled, trying to remember where he'd met the redhead with green eyes—or maybe where he knew the name Isis. He had no inkling that lifetimes ago I spent hours on the Nile daydreaming of fucking him.

When he handed me the signed sports section, I gave him my business card.

"Call me," I said brazenly.

He grinned. "You can count on it."

The two pouty young things on his arm looked none too pleased. Hector hadn't watched me walk away, but Goliath did. I felt his eyes on me until I was out the entrance doors.

Bath

Hot water steamed in my marble bathroom. Bubbles foamed. Aisha perched on the edge of the soaking tub, settling to purr after she had licked up so many soapsuds I was afraid she'd be sick.

I didn't intend to go so far as to collect dog feces or menstrual blood to concoct potions, but it couldn't hurt to hum the chants, could it?

If I used a binding spell, Barb might get over her anger.

If I chanted a leading spell, Hector might want me again.

I slipped into velvet, jasmine-scented water.

"ANOK THAZI N EPIBATHA CHEOUCH CHA ANOK ANOK CHARIEMOUTH LAILAM."

Aisha's green eyes grew wide. She made small growling sounds. Her thick black tail twitched.

Nemo appeared.

He was so real that I reached out to touch his face, but there was nothing there.

I felt him, though. His lips on my breasts. His hardness between my thighs. I felt the taut skin of his muscled back erupt into a thousand goosebumps, and I climaxed in a wave of contractions and sighs.

Cesari

The General was waiting for me at a quiet table tucked away in the back of the Petrossian, on the other side of the lounge from where I had been with Hector that afternoon.

With dramatic flourishes of her wrists, a neatly-coiffed pianist in a starched white blouse was at the grand piano playing a flowery rendition of "This Guy's in Love with You."

In front of the General on the round table, two short, cut crystal glasses with a couple of inches of amber liquid waited. Macallan, 25 years old—his preferred single malt whiskey at this time of day. Later on, he'd sip Lagavulin.

He stood up when he saw me with my hennaed hair, his black eyes shining in appreciation. With Old World polish, he moved to pull out my chair.

"You make a stunning redhead, *ma bella*. But then, you make a stunning anything."

He unabashedly delighted in the deep cleavage of my black sleeveless sheath. This was part of our game—my tempting and never delivering.

"I have a small gift for you," he said as soon as we settled.

The black velvet box opened to a necklace of plump Tahitian pearls joined at a seven-pointed platinum star set with a huge ruby. A septagram.

I looked up at him. His thick lips turned up at the corners.

"It's beautiful," I said in a hushed voice. I was afraid to touch it.

"May I assist you in putting it on?"

I lifted my hair from the nape of my neck. He took the necklace in his thick fingers and leaned across the small table. Our faces were very close. I smelled whiskey on his breath and a hint of mint. His eyes held mine for a moment before he focused on opening the clasp.

When his fingertips brushed my skin, goosebumps rose. He traced the pearls from the back of my neck to the front with his middle finger, then sat back with a satisfied look.

The pearls warmed quickly. The platinum septagram touched just below the hollow of my throat, in the exact spot the faience medallion had hung on Elektra.

"It was made for you." Then he chuckled. "*I* had it made for you."

His eyes went to the lapis lazuli Hathor ring on my right ring finger.

I saw instantly that he noted I didn't wear it on the left hand, as I did when Rasheed first gave it to me. The General never misses anything. But he didn't mention Rasheed. He didn't need to.

"You've changed," he said.

"I want to talk to you about our business arrangement," I said flatly and a little coldly. Colder than I felt.

His left eyebrow arched; his eyes stayed fixed, unblinking, on me.

"You wanted once to be partners, General. I want to explore that possibility."

"But you *are* my partner, Ishtar. Are you asking for a bigger commission?"

"I don't want a commission. I want a share."

He sat back, studying me. The half-smile was gone. His wrist turned slowly, swirling the crystal tumbler of amber scotch.

"A share of what?"

"Of everything. Isn't that what you offered at Tahoe?"

His lids lowered. He had that lazy look belied by a glint in his eye. A crocodile awaiting the approach of its prey.

"You *have* changed."

"I'm talking about business, General," I said sharply. "Nothing else. We're not going to do that. It's not an option."

He laughed out loud, tossing his head just a bit. "You had me on edge there for a minute, Ishtar. Balanced breathlessly on the edge."

Then he signalled the white-jacketed waiter for two more scotches.

"And the Emerald Tablet?" he asked slyly.

"No. Definitely not."

"Why should I make you a partner, when *you're* not willing to share?"

"It's non-negotiable, General. The Tablet is not part of any deal, just as I'm not."

He smiled and leaned further back in his chair. He was totally at ease. His massive bull shoulders barely bulged in the Savile Row gray worsted suit. A repeating yellow crest pattern dotted a maroon silk tie. His starched white cuffs held gold crocodile cufflinks with ruby eyes.

The server set two more crystal glasses with amber liquid between us and took away the empties.

The General sipped languidly on the scotch, watching me.

I held his gaze, all the while silently repeating *ANA A A NANA A A NANA* to steady my nerves.

I travelled back to his Persian tent. I was his sex slave then; my survival had depended on pleasing him yet never showing weakness. I think he went there, too. Or maybe he returned to another lifetime when he took Athena over the razor thin line between ecstasy and pain.

"Do you think you're ready, Ishtar?"

"More than ready."

"*Bene*," he said, raising his glass in a toast. "To us."

"*BERBELÖCH CHTHTÖTHÖMI*," I chanted in my mind.

Rasheed of Vegas

The General's men walked me into the lobby of my building, and I was just passing alone by the security station on my way to the elevator when the guard stopped me.

"You have a visitor. His name's not on the list."

As far as I knew, no one's name was on my list.

In his dark blue suit and starched white shirt open at the neck exposing a triangle of tan flesh, Rasheed sat on one of the plush sofas in the lobby, watching me. He looked so perfectly groomed, he might have been an ad in GQ magazine.

His hair shone jet black in the light; a dark look sharpened the angles of his face.

My first impulse was to burst into tears of relief. Oh God, I ached to have him hold me. But he just sat there, staring from his brooding cloud.

When it became painfully obvious that Rasheed wasn't coming to me, I took a deep breath to garner strength—and yes, patience. Conscious of the lobby watching, I put one foot in front of the other as gracefully as I could to cross the distance between us. At least Rasheed had the decency to stand.

"Thank you for coming," I told him in a soft voice. My eyes pleaded, *Don't make a scene.*

I couldn't believe we were standing like this. We who moved each other's souls. Yet he acted the jerk, rigid as a statue, so like River God below deck on his ship, humiliating me, forcing me to grovel. I wanted to slap his face.

"What are Cesari's men doing here?" Rasheed demanded.

Not "I missed you," or even "You've changed your hair."

Of course, he'd recognized the General's men. Rasheed and the General had done business together once. I never asked what. No questions with Rasheed. And it suited my purposes not to speak of the General; I didn't want to arouse Rasheed's suspicion.

"I told you I was scared," I breathed, reaching out my hand, taking his fingers in mine. "They're protecting me."

He locked eyes with me for a moment and then looked away. The tic in his eye was there, the one when he's struggling for control. After coming all this way, from who knows where, would he walk out of the lobby, leaving me to stand here alone?

I dropped my voice a register and murmured, "Come upstairs with me, Rasheed."

He melted a little; he wasn't quite so rigid. *His mouth softened.*

When I saw he was wavering, I leaned into him ever so slightly while I spoke, my tone full of reason but my body language promising everything else.

"Rasheed, everyone's watching. Do you know how ridiculous we look?"

Maybe it was his pride that moved him in the end, but finally he gave in. Like practiced dancers who move as one, we glided to the elevator, his Italian loafers squeaking slightly on the travertine tile. His palm on the small of my back burned fiery hot. My whole body was aflame.

Every eye followed us. The lobby was absolutely silent.

From behind the front desk, the concierge watched with an open mouth. A handful of residents waited without shame to see what came next. Orsini was on the phone with the General reporting this new development. The valet alone had the decency to pretend to be busy with some papers.

The gleaming rosewood elevator doors slid open, and Rasheed and I stepped in to go upstairs to do what everyone knew we were going to do.

The key turned in the left mahogany door, and I stepped into my foyer with mirror walls, mirror ceiling and polished gray marble tiles. Rasheed in all his glory was reflected around me.

I heard the door latch and waited to feel his arms encircle me from behind, pulling me into him like he'd done our first night, the night of the Wynn.

But nothing. No touch. No embrace. Crestfallen, I turned to face him. The angles in his face had hardened again.

"Don't be like this, Rasheed. Aren't you glad to see me?"

"Are you going to tell me why you were with Cesari's men?"

I lifted my fingers to stroke his clenched jaw; his left eyelid spasmed. He wouldn't look at me—his way of punishing, of trying to make me not exist.

"Look at me, Rasheed," I whispered.

He looked straight at me and took my fingers in his to pull them away from his face. His eyes were glassy green—hard and brittle.

"You're a child," I said and turned to go down the short hall to the kitchen laid out like the galley of a millionaire's yacht—rich mahogany cabinetry, shiny brass fixtures, black marble counter tops and bottle-green covers on the chairs.

I was standing by the open, glass sliding doors to the balcony when he finally came to me. He stood close but not touching.

Twenty-eight stories below sparkled a blue pool surrounded by palm trees and flowering pink oleander.

From the pool and tennis courts stretched the green fairways of the Las Vegas Country Club. Beyond was The Strip against the backdrop of craggy, dun-colored mountains.

Even in his anger and suspicion, Rasheed was impressed. His eyes drank in the vista of Las Vegas Valley and lingered a moment on the bronze glass tower of the Wynn a long stone's throw away. Surely he, too, was in that hotel suite, reliving the night we first met in this life.

I wanted him to peel off my clothes and lick my body all over. Like he did that night. Like River God. Like Black Falcon.

Instead, the air was so thick with his rancor that I could scarcely breathe.

"Someone tried to kidnap me last night, Rasheed. It was really close. Police. Ambulance. Everything."

Almost in panic, he looked me over from head to foot—I suppose to see if I had any broken bones that he hadn't noticed. Had he noticed anything except the General's men? He hadn't mentioned my red hair.

Rasheed was shaken but not enough to forget the General.

"What has Cesari got to do with it?" he asked gruffly.

"What was I supposed to do, Rasheed? I was grateful for his protection."

What was unsaid was that *he* hadn't protected me.

"Can't you be happy that I'm safe?"

Whatever battle raged within him, my words had the desired effect. Angles softened; the tic in his eye relaxed. His brittle eyes melted to jade. Reaching out, he lifted a strand of my red hair, turning it to catch fire in a sunbeam. I could see he approved.

At last, he kissed me. A long, deep River God kiss that sucked my soul right out of my body. Never in a hurry, his tongue slowly circled mine; he sucked on the tip, drawing me into his mouth slowly, deliberately.

He was the sun around whom I orbited, and like a star swallows the comet, Rasheed consumed me.

Leading him down the long mirrored hall to the bedroom, I stroked his face, outlined his lips with my fingertips and caressed his throbbing throat.

I wouldn't let him touch while I pulled my top over my head and unzipped my jeans, peeling them past my thighs, stepping out of them, all the while swaying my hips with the gyrations of a Persian dancer. Taking his hand, I guided his fingers under my panties and into the wet. His fingers deep inside, rocking on his palm, I licked his lips and loosened his tie.

After each unfastening of the tiny buttons of his starched shirt, I kissed another inch down his bronzed chest. His fingers made love to me, exploring, caressing.

When his shirt was unbuttoned, I took his hand from my wet and traced his fingers across his lips so he might taste me. With my palm pressing on his hard belly, I pushed him gently onto the bed. Taking my time, as he always took his, I eased the zipper one notch at a time, then pulled his trousers and boxers slowly past his bent knees and down to his ankles.

I kissed the length of his bare thighs, first up one and then another. His erection stabbed the air. But I didn't touch him. I made him wait.

His eyes devoured my every move.

Hips grinding, breasts thrusting, I swayed over him. He leaned back on the bed, propped on his elbows, feet still in Italian loafers with his trousers around his ankles.

My bra brushed his chest, then came near to his lips. But I didn't touch. I didn't allow him to touch.

Reflected all around in the mirror walls, body weaving and dipping, my fingertips lowered my panties down thighs, past knees, along my calves to the plush silvery velvet carpet.

With a silent snap, I unfastened my bra, and my breasts fell free. Rasheed took a sharp intake of air. His pupils were huge in the shadowy room; his jet hair gleamed. The afternoon sun coming through the plantation shutters fell in charcoal and ivory stripes across the bed.

Teasing his belly, brushing his lips, my hair swung from side to side in the compelling, hypnotic rhythm of the sacred dance of the Hive.

Rasheed was so tense I could have shattered him with one flick of my finger. He reached out, but I grabbed his wrists.

Don't touch! Not yet, I told him with my eyes.

Pressing him back, holding his wrists to the bed, I hung over him, letting his lips suckle for an instant one breast and then the other. Pulling away, leaving him with an open, yearning mouth, I buried my mane of flaming hair in his loins and took him deep in my throat.

I knew him so well; I knew just how far to go and when to stop. I didn't bring him to the edge; that would have been cruel. I brought him only halfway and then traced my tongue up his flat belly, past his slim waist, over his erect nipples to his lush lips.

All the while, I held his hands firmly on the bed.

"River God," I whispered in his ear.

I might have intoned my most powerful spell. He grabbed my ass, flipped me over and drove, panting and crazed, deep inside me.

"Oh, Isis, Isis," he moaned as his back arched and his body shuddered.

And when I heard him cry out my name as he'd never done before and in a voice I'd never heard before, I knew. He needed me as much as I needed him.

We were one. We had always been one. This time the Gods would not set us on our separate paths.

BERBELÖCH CHTHTÖTHÖMI.

I would have my will.

Rasheed of Malta

The Maltese sun slipped behind the ages-old stone parapets into a mauve, oily Mediterranean; light hovered between day and dark. On the nightstand by my bed, a solitary porcelain lamp with ivory shade burned.

Rasheed stood stiffly in the middle of the room. Stony, like a statue. If I placed my palms on his chest, would I even feel a heartbeat?

"Rasheed," I begged him. "*Please.*"

I put my arms around his neck, molding my body to his, refusing to let him shut me out.

"Thank you for coming," I whispered. "I know how you feel about Cesari, but I have to do everything I can to save him—to get him out of Libya. I owe him that much."

His left lid twitched like it always did when he struggled for control. Now he struggled to resist giving in to what we both wanted.

I rose on my tiptoes and kissed his lush lips chiseled by a master sculptor. They didn't yield. But I felt him harden against my belly.

I kissed him again, and he grew harder.

Emboldened, I pressed my pelvis into his and rotated my shoulders to rub my breasts against his chest.

He drove me to the wall. His fingers tore at my waistband. He dragged at the zipper of my new white jeans and, when it opened, he yanked my jeans and underpants to my knees.

I clawed at his hair, my fingers digging deep through the thick waves, my tongue down his throat.

His jeans were down his hard thighs when he shoved my bare hips hard against the wall. With no caressing fingertips, no wet teasing tongue, he plunged deep, ramming me, tearing at me as if to cause maximum pain.

Rasheed, the lover who never hurried, the lover who savored me as one does the finest of wines, pounded me and pounded me with black savagery. The painting on the wall banged and banged with each thrust.

His mouth was cruel without a trace of tenderness; I tasted the salt of my own blood. Swept up in his fury, I dug my nails into his flesh and pulled my mouth away to bite him in the neck. With my head back against the wall, mouth open, panting, I gasped air in deep gulps.

Then I heard myself whisper, "Hurt me."

His hand went around my throat. I gagged and met his eyes. I'd never seen this Rasheed. Furious. Vengeful. He terrified me. I tried to pull his hand away, but he held me in a vise.

He morphed into Major Domo, then into the General, and finally back to a Rasheed I didn't know.

He squeezed until I could take no breath.

Would he kill me? Does he hate me that much?

My mind shouted, *Strangle me now. You broke my heart. Finish the job.*

He shook all over in one massive shudder, then collapsed on me in a series of spasms, finally releasing my throat. I coughed and sucked in air.

His forehead pressed on the wall next to my head, his forearm on the other side. We were both spent; his chest heaved. I put my arms around the back of his neck, but he pulled them away.

"Is that what you want, Isis?" he hissed in my ear. "Is that what Cesari taught you?"

He tugged up his jeans; I slid down the wall, exhausted and shattered. He stood there for a moment, looking down on me. So many emotions in his face. Triumph. Resentment. Disappointment.

Disgust.

"Don't hate me, Rasheed. I am nothing without you."

He didn't answer but went out the door, never looking back. Was it me he crushed, or the General?

Ultimatum

I slept on the plane and woke as we landed in Paris. The General was talking quietly with Orsini. He came over when he saw I stirred. He smelled of soap and a faint hint of aftershave. He'd changed into fresh clothes. His hair was wet.

"I booked you a flight, Ishtar. You'll forgive me for not returning with you to Las Vegas, but we've got some unfinished business, don't we? If you don't object, I think I'll wrap this contract up on my own."

He had a most pleasant expression on his face. You'd never suspect what he'd been through just a few hours ago, tied up in the Cave of Bats.

I reached out and touched his rough cheek with my fingertips.

"I'm happy you're safe."

"You shouldn't have come back to Libya," he said sternly.

"Nothing could have stopped me."

"Careful, Ishtar." He raised an eyebrow. "I'm easily encouraged."

The others deplaned just ahead of me. I was stepping out onto the platform when the General blocked my way. I took one step back and bumped into the airlock frame.

His fingertips grazed the bare skin in the V of my shirt. Then he curled his thick fingers and thumb around the base of my throat, holding me firmly but not forcibly, in his grip.

My heart raced; my pulse must have been through the roof. I didn't want to look at him but did.

His face was so close. Tiny red capillaries laced the whites of his eyes. He had that knowing look, the one that stripped me of all pretense. *The ride on a comet, Ishtar. Who else can take you there?*

As always, he both repelled and enthralled me.

"I have men at your building. Don't forget what happened before we left."

He glanced significantly at Rasheed nearly down the steps.

"He can't keep you safe, no matter what he thinks. No matter what you think."

His lips were inches from mine; I was afraid he was going to kiss me and terrified Rasheed would turn and see.

"Did you use the Emerald Tablet?" he whispered. "Is that how you pulled this off?"

"I have my own magic, General," I managed to say levelly. "It works rather well, wouldn't you agree?"

He dropped his hand, but his sly smile told me I could keep nothing from him.

On the tarmac, a white airport van with the Charles de Gaulle logo on the door waited to whisk us away to the terminals. I looked back when we drove off. The General still watched from the top of the ramp.

I grabbed a change of clothes in a shop in the transit area and cleaned up in *La Premiere*, Air France's first class lounge. When I came out of the ladies room, Rasheed had settled into a plush brown leather chair. His legs were stretched out straight with ankles crossed, and his cell was at his ear. I took the seat next to him.

When he finished his call, I reached over and touched his cheek.

"I don't have to take this flight, Rasheed."

"Yes, Isis, you do."

His cell buzzed again. *"Nam."* He started rumbling in Arabic.

Rudely and cruelly, Rasheed talked for what seemed forever.

The instant he cut the connection, I demanded, "Why are you so jealous of Cesari? If I wanted *him*, don't you think I'd be with him?"

"I won't share," he said simply.

"We agreed, Rasheed. Remember? No questions."

"Not Cesari."

"It's *business*, Rasheed. I make a lot of money with him. I'm going to make a lot more."

"You lied to me," he accused.

"What about you?" I shot back.

"I have never lied to you," he said with a look of surprise. "I don't tell you everything because I need to protect you—and me. It's not the same."

I could have said that I never lied either. That I always told him the truth, just not all of it. But I didn't because we both knew my intent.

He walked me to the gate, but we didn't talk.

"When will I see you again?" I asked.

He took my face in his hands, studied my eyes, my nose, my mouth, memorizing each feature. He lifted a strand of my hair and held it up to the light. Then he gave me a River God kiss of tender, yearning lips that sucked my soul right into his.

"Get rid of Cesari, Isis. It's up to you. It's all up to you."

I watched him walk away, further and further down the concourse.

An Air France attendant at my elbow said, "First class passengers may board now, Mademoiselle."

When I looked back, Rasheed was gone. I'm certain he never looked back for me.

Canopus

Pipes trilled. A lyre strummed. The languid melody took its sweet time, each note lingering into the next pluck of the string. Fragrant jasmine and heady musk filled my nose. Egypt. I'd made the shift through the Red Mirror.

I felt a wet, sloppy kiss on my right foot and opened my eyes to a flabby little Roman with extraordinary ears standing straight out from his head. Strands of limp hair clumped on his sweaty forehead. Around his neck was a leather collar with a silver chain, the end of which I held in my left hand. In my right hand, I gripped a gold-tipped ebony rod.

The Roman knelt on all fours, his puffy, florid face just next to my bare feet with brick red hennaed toenails.

We were on a barge—a gilded, opulent ship with a golden cobra rising tall at the prow. Four gilded cobra pillars held a yellow and white striped awning above our heads. Lacy papyrus trembled in cobalt glazed urns; a dozen songbirds warbled from four golden cages.

I reclined in the shade against an ebony armrest on a divan upholstered in blue wool. In the eternal Egyptian fashion, my carmined nipples and mound showed clearly through the sheer, pleated white linen of my gown.

"You are forbidden to touch me without permission!" I snarled, yanking on the chain, pulling him close enough to whack his skull with the rod.

He yelped and tried to pull back while I twisted the silver chain around my wrist, dragging him, pulling tighter and tighter. He gagged; his fleshy lips opened and closed in desperate fish-like gasps for air.

"Now I shall have to punish you. Show me your ass."

Whimpering and sniveling, still on his hands and knees, he backed his rear toward me.

I snapped my fingers, and a tall Nubian in a white kilt, yellow headdress and green leather sandals handed me a whip of knotted black silk cords. His identical twin, right down to the tribal scars on his cheeks and the yellow headdress and green sandals, lifted the Roman's toga and tunic.

I struck with the whip. He mewled like a forlorn kitten. I hit him again with twice the force, and he cried out with a sob, urinating on the deck. His pasty flesh flamed with scores of angry red streaks.

"You filthy boy. Next time you wear a diaper."

With the third lash, delivered with all my strength, his engorged penis, scarcely longer than my thumb, sprayed white milk. He let out a high-pitched squeal and sobbed.

"I did not say you could ejaculate." I jerked on the chain and dragged him around to face me again. "Now you must pay a fine. Give me your ring."

He pulled frantically at a ruby ring on his pinky finger but couldn't get it past the folds of fat.

"Hurry up!"

Finally the ring came off, and with eyes cast down, he put it in my hand.

I slipped it on my thumb, turning the blood-red ruby to catch the light. The stone was high quality, masterfully cut and expertly polished. At least five carats. Its setting was gold, not pure, possibly mixed with silver. Electrum perhaps. My jeweler slave would tell me.

"Go to your corner!"

He crawled across the deck as far as the leash would allow, curled up and stuck his thumb in his mouth.

I let him grovel and whimper for a few minutes before ordering the slaves to remove his collar and leash.

"Bathe His Excellency," I told one of the twins, "and freshen his toga."

"Signal his barge," I ordered the other.

Soon I heard the creak of wood as the ponderous barge trailing astern pulled along our port side.

"Ship oars!" shouted the pilot. "Lash on!"

While the two crews struggled with ropes and oars, slaves mopped our deck and tied back the draperies. By the time his personal guard crossed the gangplank, a cleaned-up Imperial Tax Collector reclined on a plush lounge, sipping sweet Delta wine.

I stood respectfully for his departure. We all stood with heads bowed, except for the galley slaves, of course, who were chained to the planks.

"It has been a most gratifying afternoon, Lady Elektra. I trust I shall see you at our usual appointed time?"

"I am at your pleasure, Most Excellent Publican."

He waddled across the deck and over the wood plank with his guard in scarlet red capes clomping after him.

"Home," I commanded.

The coxswain beat the drum. *Thump. Thump. Thump.* Back muscles rippled, and biceps strained. Our silver-tipped oars dipped into the jade water, and we began to glide east along the Canal toward the Nile.

We made steady progress through glassy waters sprinkled with myrtle blossoms falling like purple snow. Hidden musicians trilled on flutes and strummed on lyres. The heady seductive scent of *myrrh* wafted along the shore.

At the approach of my barge, revelers sang and cheered.

"Elektra! Elektra! Queen of Canopus!"

Canopus. The Empire's Las Vegas. Nothing forbidden. Everything allowed. There was no sin for Romans.

When we sailed past a party of Roman cavalry officers gathered in a gazebo with a cobalt tile cupola, they raised their chalices in salute, whistling and shouting in Latin, "Dock here, Elektra! We have plenty of cock to go around."

I granted them the favor of a wave of my ostrich fan and blew them a kiss.

My galley slaves rowed on. In the water—catch. Through the water—drive. Out again—recover. All in perfect unison.

Rough bronze cuffs chained their ankles to iron loops in the decking. Each naked back bore crisscross scars from the whip. Two men had fresh flaming marks; black gnats swarmed at the dried blood.

I watched them idly, waving my feather fan.

I'm not certain that I saw them as human.

I'm not certain I was human myself.

Grand Wizards

By the time I'd finished bathing and the dressing slaves had piled my hair into elaborate twists and curls held in place with ivory pins, the *convivium* had begun.

My dresser slave Ghazel chose an ankle-length, gossamer gown of scarlet sea silk painstakingly woven from the long filaments secreted by clams to attach themselves to the sea bed.

Gold earrings in the shape of Eros with tiny wings dangled from my ears. Thick gold bands circled my upper arms.

Brutus appeared with the ruby pendant just as Ghazel was drenching me in oil of gardenia. With his usual genius, he'd fashioned an intricate filigree setting of tiny wires of electrum in the shape of a septagram.

"The stone weighs six carats, Domina."

Ghazel hung the necklace around my neck. The huge ruby in the seven-pointed star fell precisely at my cleavage.

"Well, Ghazel, what is your judgment?"

"Beautiful, Domina. The red of your hair lights the stone as the sun lights gold."

Like all Persians, she was a born poet.

I entered the circular dining hall to find my guests drunk and rowdy. Nude teenagers with fit bodies and heads of barbered curls carried trays of fattened crane stewed in salty *garum*. The cook's signature dish, braised peacock in honey, vinegar, pepper and cumin sauce, had already been served.

"Elektra. We feared you would not grace us with your presence this evening."

"My apologies, Excellencies. Even a goddess requires time to cultivate her beauty."

The generals rewarded me with a round of toasts and cheers.

Platon the *vocator*, yet another Greek, had seated each man on his own private *lectus* in anticipation of the presentation of gift slaves to follow the banquet.

The floor was littered with dozens of oyster shells and bits of half-chewed smoked sausage. With only a cursory glance to ensure every guest was attended by an adequate number of slaves, I picked my way through *sputa*, smiling seductively.

Draped in leopardskin and trimmed in silver, my *lectus* stood on a low dais at the foot of a triple-tall marble statue of me. For tonight, Ghazel had dressed my likeness in a matching scarlet gown of the same iridescent sea silk.

I nodded to Platon to serve the *piece de resistance*—a whole roast giraffe stuffed with antelope stuffed with wild boar, in turn dressed with fattened hares. Trumpets blared. Ten muscular men in red *chitons* entered with the massive bronze platter on their shoulders.

The generals burst into wild applause. "Brava, Elektra! Brava!"

Once my major domo Aeneas, through his network of spies, had sniffed out that our guests were Grand Wizards, he'd spared no expense. Their identity was supposed to be hush-hush, of course. Everything about the Mithraic Cult was veiled in secrecy—their secret handshakes, cave temples and bull sacrifices to the Zoroastrian Fire God Mithra.

But whatever cosmic forces these men believed in, I had my own magic. None was more potent.

At my signal to Aeneas, the music shifted to wailing flutes and throbbing drums. A cloud of blue smoke rose from the braziers and then cleared. Coppery ripe-breasted belly dancers shimmered in layers of silk. Silver bells jingled at their wrists and ankles. One by one, a sparkly-threaded veil fell away, revealing more, and then more, of their lush bodies.

The Grand Wizards cheered and made sucking sounds with their mouths. On the divan closest to mine, a man in his late prime with a shock of silver hair pulled up his gown and thrust his engorged penis in the air. I snapped my fingers, and a boy of about fifteen with a mop of blond curls rushed to take the Roman in his mouth.

With his usual efficiency, Aeneas had seen to every detail. Each of the eight Romans had five attendants—a feather boy to tickle his throat to induce vomiting, a nude pubescent girl to fan him, a child to shoo away insects with sprigs of myrtle, a Nubian *masseuse* and a eunuch to help him urinate into silver bowls.

But those were amenities to be enjoyed at any banquet. Our spies had ferreted out the depravities unique to each guest, and Aeneas had spent hours handpicking slaves to gratify those needs.

"Here is the list, Domina. Each guest and his taste."

For Cassius Maximus Gallus—a twelve-year-old German virgin with wavy, spun gold hair. For Lucius Caecina Vestinus—a Persian youth with coffee skin and raven curls. A *mènage á trois* with an audience shouting suggestions for Caius Julius Capito.

Marcus Tiberius was the sole guest who desired only to watch. His preference was two women, one blonde and one dark. Aeneas had noted that he liked it rough. The black-skinned Amazon would be equipped with an array of whips and nasty props.

A Syrian had given Aeneas the most trouble. His perversions involved animals—savage cats mainly, and certain breeds of dogs.

Soon tonight's guests would retire to private rooms appointed with sparkling fountains, marble bathing pools, lion-head beds, gold chains, ankle irons, handcuffs and whips with silk or leather thongs.

I nodded for the lanterns to be doused and more colored powders thrown on the braziers. The musicians quieted their instruments. The room fell silent with the hush of anticipation. Perfumed smoke snaked through the still air.

I waited. I let the breathless mood linger. I let them grow slightly restive before signalling Aeneas.

In single file, each preceded by a garlanded girl child carrying a lighted torch, the gift slaves paraded into the hall. Unlike the nude servers and scantily-clad attendants, these women, boys and girls wore hooded red linen robes that hid their faces and perfect bodies.

One by one, they were led to the Romans reclining on couches. On cue, Egyptian musicians shook *sistrums*. The seductive jingle of hundreds of tiny silver bells grew increasingly louder and more frenzied. Drums joined in. With a flurry of drumbeats and a wailing of pipes, the oiled and perfumed slaves threw off their robes to stand naked before their masters for the night.

There were grunts of satisfaction. Hands reached out for flesh. Attendants moved to guide guests and pleasure slaves to their private rooms. My job was done.

I lay back and closed my eyes, thinking of Hektor. Just hours before, spoiled Flavia—my Barb in this life—had come to ask for a binding spell to make him her husband.

"ABLAMGOUNOTHO ABRASAX," I repeated to soothe my headache.

Not long now. Soon I would be in my atelier, preparing my special potion of venom and herbs that would bring Hektor's privileged life to a painful end.

Roman General

"Do we bore you?"

Startled, I sat straight up.

A gold eagle glittered on his massive bull chest armored in a leather cuirass studded with silver. The tongued leather-lappet skirt reached to mid-thigh on legs sturdy as temple columns. Biceps bulged below pleated cap sleeves.

And the hands. I stared at them—big, square, powerful—with thick fingers that could crush a windpipe as quickly as another man might squash a fly.

The General.

Which one of the names on the list was he? Thinking to identify him by depravity, I blurted out, "What is your taste?"

He laughed. And when he laughed, I saw those square teeth of his.

"I have but one taste, Ishtar. You."

He plunked himself down on the other end of my divan, leaning back on the armrest and pillows, forcing me to move my legs so he wouldn't crush my feet. At least he didn't put his monster military sandals in my face. A slave hurried over with a high footstool.

He traced his finger up my calf, and I gripped his wrist to stop him. He chuckled, withdrew his hand and reached out to take a chalice of wine from a slave.

"How?" I asked without needing to elaborate.

The General and I don't need a lot of words.

"Talk of the green eyes, perhaps," he said with a shrug. "I wasn't sure it was you until today. When I saw you on your rather stunning barge."

He took a deep swig of wine, tilting his head back, then wiped his lips with the back of his hand.

"You are quite a star. A true evening star. All of Alexandria speaks of you. A living goddess, they say, capable of special powers."

He stared at me, expecting a response. I stared back.

"Is that true, Ishtar?"

"That I am a goddess?"

He threw back his head and laughed again. Another deep drink from the chalice. A slave was there immediately to top off his cup from a silver pitcher.

"Excellent wine," he commented.

"Thank you. I have my own vineyards."

"Of course. I would expect nothing less."

He studied me for a while from under hooded lids. I met his gaze. We engaged in a brief staring match, neither of us blinking.

"I made inquiries," he said finally in a too-casual tone. "It seems you have no history, Ishtar. Why is that?"

He leaned forward to touch the ruby hanging at the top of my cleavage with his index finger before slowly tracing a circle on my skin around the pendant.

Then he said unexpectedly, as if mentioning something he'd forgotten until now, "If you are good to me, I shall arrange an introduction to Emperor Hadrian."

Good to him? Did he intend to blackmail me into submission?

His eyes travelled the full length of my body, so provocatively and deliberately displayed to evoke desire. His gaze paused on my loins; he wet his lips with the tip of his tongue. In spite of my determination not to let him move me, my nipples rose to peaks in the red silk.

He shifted his weight, leaning forward, and before I could protest, slid his bear paws behind my back. He pulled me upright, into him, and put his lips to my throbbing nipple and my hand on his monster manhood. My breath caught in my throat.

"I see you still enjoy that," he whispered in my ear.

We both felt my heart race.

In one powerful, graceful movement, he scooped me up in his gorilla arms and rose to his feet.

"Where?" he snarled to a bewildered Aeneas.

Aeneas stood paralyzed, his already protruding eyes enormous in his startled face.

I absolved him by nodding my head. The relief that washed over him was so complete, that I wondered for a moment if he, like the Tax Collector, would leave a puddle on the floor.

In giant strides, the General covered the distance to the interior courtyard. We stepped into the peristyle garden; Aeneas threw open the door to the best of our rooms.

Without ceremony, the General dropped me on the bed.

"Get out," he barked.

"But—" Aeneas started to protest. He never left me alone with a client but always made certain the Nubian twins were present.

The General picked him up by the back of his tunic and threw him out the door, slamming it after him.

I heard the bolt slide in the lock. And then with the speed of a charging bull, the General was on the bed, his fingers around my throat, his other hand under my gown and between my thighs.

"I have waited lifetimes for this," he snarled in my ear.

I struggled. I gasped for air. I couldn't breathe. Bright lights flashed in front of my eyes, and he was no longer the General but had morphed into Major Domo.

I beat about his face, yanking at his hair, scratching at his eyes. He didn't stop. All I saw was the hated face of Major Domo, and I went wild.

In panic, I reached down along the edge of the bed. My hand found the hidden shelf.

The hilt of the dagger was in my palm, and then the point was at the General's jugular. When he felt the cold steel at his neck, he stopped. His hand was still at my neck, but I could breathe.

"Get off," I commanded.

He blinked.

I applied more pressure. The point dug deeper into his neck. A drop of blood appeared.

He released my throat.

I pressed harder.

Abruptly he leaned back with a look of profound surprise. And once he pulled away from the dagger point, I lost my power over him. If he wanted to wrest the knife away from me, I was no match for his strength.

But he didn't try to take the dagger. Instead he said quietly, "I thought you liked it rough."

"Not when forced. I do not like anything when forced."

Seconds passed. I heard the play of the Venus fountain with her gold-tipped breasts spouting water into a marble bowl. I could see the General was sincere in his confusion, but not about whether I would have used the knife. I'd ended his life once, in his Persian tent. Neither of us doubted that I'd do it again, if he pushed me too far.

Slowly, his eyes assuring me that he'd surrendered, he reached to take the knife from my hand. I let him have it, as I would a chalice of wine we shared. Then he sat full back near my feet and casually tossed the knife aside. I heard the muffled thud of its weight hit the carpet.

"Forgive me," he said. "I miscalculated."

"Is that how you want me? Is that what I am to you?"

A shadow passed over his face. For a fleeting moment, I saw pain in his eyes, but it was quickly gone. Vulnerable only seconds, he leaned back on an elbow and gave me one of his little smirks that says there are no secrets between us. But I'd surprised him, taken him off-guard with the ferocity of my resistance.

"So how do we decide, Ishtar? What shall be our rules? Do you whip me—or do I whip you?"

"No one whips me—ever."

"Then we have common ground. I have no desire to strike you in any way."

He traced the septagram with his finger, barely grazing my skin. I felt my pulse quicken. He saw the stirring in my eyes and stood out of the bed. Watching me watch him, he unlaced his leather military cuirass with golden eagle and leather lappet skirt and tossed the uniform aside in the same casual way he had the dagger.

His stallion erection stood straight up in the linen of his tunic. His thick military sandals still laced up his shins.

"*Come get it,*" his animal power dared me.

I rose to my knees on the bed, facing him. Carefully, as if unveiling a priceless artifact, I lifted the tunic. His penis was inches away. I wet my lips and leaned forward to take his huge glistening head in my mouth and down my throat.

He growled like a lion and dug his fingers into my elaborate hairdo with such force that the pins came undone. Fiery waves tumbled around my face.

I pinched the inside of his thighs, hard. He caught his breath and slowed, letting me set the pace. I licked and then nibbled gently while my fingertips massaged his balls covered in coarse black curls.

He growled louder. I wanted to make him roar. But more than that, I wanted to make him mine.

I could use a powerful man like the General.

Alternating tender caresses with strokes more and more forceful, I kneaded and pulled. My lips, my tongue and my teeth matched the rhythm.

His hips began to slide backward and forward, trying to force me to take him deep into my mouth. Without mercy, I pinched his inner thighs hard again. My signal that I was in control.

I imagined that his erection grew larger.

Just when I swallowed him all the way to the back of my throat, a high-pitched, blood-curdling scream shattered the air. Even through the heavy wooden door, the wail was piercing.

Another scream, this one longer and more terrible. His erection melted.

The General grabbed his *gladius* and was at the door in two strides, sliding the bolt open.

"Stay here," he commanded. "Lock the door."

The screams went on and on until I heard shouts. Then it was silent.

There was a knock, and the General said, "It is I."

Blood stained his arm and the tunic with little pleated sleeves. I glanced at the sword still in his hand. There was blood on the blade.

"Cassius Maximus Gallus gets…carried away at times." He told me this while putting on his leather cuirass.

I didn't ask why the screams had stopped—if he had gagged the girl, released her or put her out of her misery.

I didn't have to. I knew.

"I need to get Cassius back to Alexandria. He is…shaken up."

I tried to recall more about the girl. I could vaguely remember that she didn't speak Latin or Greek. Aeneas had purchased her only two days ago. Or was it three? I'd only seen her for a few moments. Just to approve that she would do, that she was the right type.

I sat there mute while he struggled with the leather thongs of his cuirass.

"Could you help me with this?" he asked.

I found myself lacing the front to the back under his raised left arm while he gave me brisk orders.

"You must keep this quiet, Ishtar. Hadrian disapproves of the killing of slaves without just cause." His voice was matter-of-fact. A young girl wasn't butchered tonight, only a slave.

I knew by his tone that he'd seen worse. A Roman General sees much worse than the girl in the room.

"I have found him to be progressive," he went on about Hadrian. "He even extols tolerance of Christians, if they live within the law."

He belted his *gladius* on his right side and adjusted the balance.

"Caesar is superstitious, though. Which brings me back to the introduction I proposed."

He looked at me in the way of a fellow conspirator.

"Hadrian has dreams, it seems. Dreams that disturb his sleep." He paused, lifting an eyebrow. "You can interpret a few dreams, Ishtar, can you not?"

He leaned down and kissed me on the mouth, putting his hand on the back of my neck, gripping me firmly—very firmly, not letting go when he pulled his lips away.

"Now you are not going to call that *forcing*, are you?"

As an answer, I grabbed the back of his neck, kissing him hard, my tongue down his throat.

"I shall be back to finish up where we left off," he said gruffly, "but not tonight."

He opened the door and stepped out, closing it firmly behind him. I could hear footsteps in the portico, and voices, but they soon faded.

Ebony and Ivory

My cell buzzed. I tore my eyes away from the Google search on Hadrian and his lover Antinous and picked it up, thinking it might be Rasheed. Too late, I saw the Caller ID showed 312 area code.

"Hello," I said impatiently.

"It's about time," said Gareth Greene in his Barry White voice.

"I've been out of town."

"Isn't that why people have cell phones?" But there wasn't anything in his playful voice that was accusative.

"I didn't have a signal." The truth. You can't beat it sometimes.

"Hey, did your being out of town have something to do with those bad guys? You ever find out who they were?"

"Not yet."

"But you feel safe now? I mean, you're back. Or are you back?"

"I'm in Vegas, yes. But just a short time. I came back to get... something."

"Time enough to see me?"

That took me off-guard.

"How much time are we talking about?"

"Time for a drink?"

I looked at the Red Mirror. I looked at myself *in* the Red Mirror. Not too bad. My hair looked pretty good.

I'd been waiting a long time, about 2,500 years in fact, to have Goliath; he was an itch never scratched.

"I've got an hour."

We do live more than once, but still it's a pity not to live each life to the fullest.

When I came out of the elevator, Gareth was standing at the security desk laughing with the guard Jack who held a piece of notebook paper in his hand with Gareth's autograph.

In a way Goliath the slave would never have dreamed of, Gareth gave me a blatant once-over from my shiny copper hair right down to my black high-heeled boots. I was all in black—a Michael Kors slinky, long-sleeved, tight-fitting top over black leather pants. A thin snakeskin belt with brass buckle showed off my waist.

On my wrist was a heavy Italian gold ID bracelet. I wore my Tiffany diamond studs in my earlobes.

"Nice. Very nice," Gareth said. His eyes said a lot more.

The lobby was empty except for the valet, the concierge and two powerfully-built men in dark business suits, one sitting close by the front door, the other by the door to the parking garage. Corsicans. The General's men.

I nodded to the one taking out his cell phone. He looked at me, then at Gareth, and started talking into the phone.

Gareth drove one of those big black shiny Escalades that I always associate with drug dealers. The sound system played smooth jazz.

Mixed with the new car scent was his cologne, more primal than spicy. I wore Sung—heavy, exotic, cloying sweet like a jungle gardenia.

"Where to?" he asked. "This is your town."

"I told you an hour. Someplace close."

"My place?"

We exchanged looks.

"If it's close."

Gareth had a condo in the Cosmopolitan with the best view in Vegas, looking right down on the Bellagio fountains and north up the Strip to Caesar's, the Venetian and the Wynn. The Paris balloon was huge in the night sky. The Eiffel Tower, which used to dominate the Strip, had dwarfed in the new scale of high rises.

Gareth's place was shiny black, just like his car. The scent of new leather was here, too. So was the incomparable sound system which he switched on with a remote. Barry White's slow, deep croon filled the room.

The lighting was subdued. An array of mini-spots recessed in the glossy ceiling highlighted some impressive African art.

A lounge chair was upholstered in zebra. A real zebra skin hung on the wall behind the glass dining room table surrounded by black leather and chrome chairs.

"Shall I take off my boots?" I asked when I saw the white carpet.

"At least."

I slid open the doors to the terrace and stepped out. The view took the breath away, even of someone like me who's seen just about every view in Vegas.

"Nice, huh?" he asked from two inches away.

He held two flutes bubbling with champagne.

"How often do you stay here?"

"Whenever I'm in town. I could be here more often." His eyes asked me if I liked the idea.

"I'm gonna be straight," he went on. "I wanna fuck you. I think I've wanted to since you stood there in front of me in the Bellagio lobby wearing that sexy yellow sweater."

And I've wanted to fuck you for about twenty-five centuries. I didn't say it, of course.

"I don't have a lot of time," I said as I unzipped his fly.

I reached into his jockey shorts and pulled him out. Oh God, he was as beautiful as I'd daydreamed on the Nile. His black glistening head was big as my fist. He just kept growing and growing as I stroked him.

He put the two glasses on the railing and scooped me up with his giant hands spread under my butt. I wrapped my legs around his waist, my arms around his neck, and pulled myself into him. His huge cock pressed against my leather crotch. I gyrated my hips, grinding into him.

"Oh baby," he moaned.

Like a pro going for the dunk, he didn't take many strides to get to his king bed on a lighted platform.

His hands were inside my tight shirt and his fingers in my bra before my back hit the zebra bedspread.

I twisted and growled. His other hand was between my legs, his strong finger rotating on the leather. I squeezed his thick, iron penis in my fist, milking him, matching the rhythm of his fingers in my groin.

I came. Suddenly and unexpectedly. My hand stopped, my breath caught, my vagina contracted and contracted; heat flashed through my womb.

"Whoa," he said. "Man, you're easy."

"Don't worry. I'm not done."

I rolled him over and unbuckled his belt. His mammoth penis stood straight up, a basalt obelisk to the sky.

I took him all the way to the back of my throat. Just once. Then I pulled his trousers and shorts past his ankles and dropped them on the floor.

He reached for me, but I pushed his hands to the bed and held them there firmly until he got the message that I was calling the shots.

Then I unbuttoned his black silk shirt, alternating each button with a lick on his bulb, or a suck on his balls, or a swallow to the back of my throat. I never did the same thing twice. I never let him predict what was coming.

"Oh baby," he kept saying over and over. "Where did you learn to do *that?*"

When his shirt was off, I swayed between his ineffable long legs hanging off the foot of the bed. I took my time, circling my hips to the throbbing beat of "Can't Get Enough of Your Love, Babe." With my fingertips, I removed each piece of my clothing with the delicacy of lifting a sea silk veil woven with golden threads.

First my leather pants, then my black top and then the black lace panties.

"Show me those tits," he begged.

I unhooked my bra and let my breasts fall free.

"Nice, baby. Nice."

And then, precisely as Isis had daydreamed of seducing Goliath on the Nile, I straddled him and placed him at my gate. He reached for my breasts, but I held his hands down to his sides.

Slowly—so slowly—I lowered myself onto his giant pedestal. I couldn't sink all the way. He was too big. My throbbing lotus screamed each time I moved up and down his shaft.

I dangled my ripe breasts in front of his thick lips, teasing him, never close enough for his tongue, offering him forbidden fruit that he must never taste.

Mesmerized, Gareth watched me act out my drama, happily playing his part, never imagining I was living a daydream 2,500 years old. I wouldn't let him touch me; he devoured every swaying tease with his eyes.

And when my aching bud fully flowered in its lust and the tsunami wave crashed in my surf, I threw back my head and howled, "O Goddess divine!"

"Far out," he shouted. "Far. Fucking. Out."

He grabbed me then and threw me onto my back and started pounding. He showed me no mercy, and I asked for none.

He shook all over in one final savage plunge and collapsed on me. We were both drenched in sweat. His male scent overpowered his cologne; I drank it in with deep gulps.

Finally he rolled onto his back beside me. He was glistening ebony against my glossy ivory skin.

"Where have you been all my life?"

I laughed and got up from the bed.

"You don't wanna know. You wouldn't believe it anyway."

"Hey," he called out as I headed to the bathroom, "You're not a real redhead."

"I'm not a real anything," I said as I blew him a kiss.

The valet didn't try to mask his surprise to see me stroll up to the glass doors an hour and fifteen minutes later. Even the Corsican gave me a look. Then the cell phone was at his ear, reporting to the General.

"When can I see you again?"

"I don't know, Gareth. I'm going out of town for while."

"That sounds suspiciously like a brush-off."

"My life's pretty complicated. Why don't we just wait and see what happens."

"You mean like, 'Don't call us. We'll call you?'"

"Let's not spoil a great time, Gareth. I'll walk myself in."

Emperor

Waiting aboard Hadrian's Imperial Barge was the General. He wore a gold muscle cuirass with white leather lappets and a gold helmet with a white brush. His monster sandals laced up the shin with golden twine. But all the finery and plumage didn't tame him; he throbbed with raw animal savagery.

With a grace that always surprised me, he took my hand and led me onto the deck.

"Be careful, my beauty," he said after undressing me with his eyes. "You are certain to make enemies among the ladies tonight."

Then he leaned into my ear.

"I shall come after the feast to finish what we started."

"I cannot say that I shall be free. You forget I am a businesswoman."

With that, he laughed a good-natured laugh and wrapping my hand around his forearm, said, "Shall we go and meet the Emperor?"

I was quite unprepared for the glory that was Antinous standing by the Emperor's *lectus*. His golden skin glowed. His eyes danced. Never had I seen anyone more radiant. So vibrant. So incredibly, enthusiastically imbued with life force.

Very much like the first time I met him in the cavern library of Hermes Trismegistus, Antinous was dressed in a sky-blue *chiton* in the classic Greek style, belted at the waist, with loose pleats falling to mid-thigh. Soft wool draped from under his right arm across his perfect chest to fasten on a muscular bronzed shoulder. His mane of blond curls was expertly arranged to suggest no arrangement at all.

And because he was Hadrian's lover, I hadn't anticipated the force of his masculinity or his reaction when I entered the Imperial cabin.

His face was instantly attentive. His eyes lit, but not with recognition; he didn't know me from another life. I met his eager look only briefly before quickly turning away. All the world knew Hadrian was besotted with Antinous; he was with Caesar always.

The General brought me forward to where Hadrian reclined.

"May I present to Caesar, Elektra of Canopus."

Hadrian proved not beyond arousal by a woman; his hungry eyes ate me up.

But he was tired. Haggard even. I'd envisioned him as the virile, confident man captured in bronze and marble with a full head of hair and a robust, wavy beard. This Caesar had scraggly tufts of hair combed over a bald spot. The manly beard was far from full and streaked with gray.

Yet he still had some vigor left. His eyes shone with delight as he looked me quite thoroughly over.

"So you are the beauty of whom my old friend boasts," he boomed in Koine Greek.

"Caesar is more than kind. I am but a simple woman whom the Gods have blessed."

I answered him in Greek, relieved to avoid Latin and the risk that he might detect the accent of Italica, our common birthplace. I wanted no questions as to my origin.

"Come. Be here close to us. Let us feast upon your beauty. My old eyes, alas, see not well from afar."

I relaxed onto the silk cushions of the divan to his right and, conscious of every eye on me, casually arranged my shoulders, hips and legs to present a seductive and inviting curve that narrowed at my waist and sloped along my thighs. My ripe breasts bulged the yellow silk; my oiled shoulders and arms glowed in the lamplight.

Great sensuous waves rolled off me and washed over Hadrian.

I beamed a laser of sensuality through him. His pupils dilated; his breath quickened. I cast a sidelong glance at the General, who watched me with a half-smile of amusement.

To the left of Hadrian, Antinous appeared mesmerized. He caught me looking at him and smiled altogether too warmly.

"Caesar," the General suggested, "I believe you shall find Elektra's ability to see beyond the veil even more alluring than her charms."

"Yes, so you tell me, my Moor." Hadrian's voice had the telltale huskiness of a man drowning in sexual possibility. Still his eyes sharpened at the General's mention of seeing beyond the veil.

"If Caesar would be so gracious as to give me something of his to hold," I breathed in a low vibrating tone.

Without hesitation, Hadrian took off his signet ring, the one whose insignia set in red wax carried the full force and might of Rome. A slave standing at his elbow passed the ring to me.

"*ANA A A NANA A A NANA,*" I murmured under my breath just loud enough for Hadrian to hear. My eyes were closed; I feigned the expression of one not quite of this world.

When I spoke, the timbre of my voice, tinged with wonder, was seductive as warm oil.

"I see a villa in the countryside. And rolling hills richly planted with olive trees. So gre-e-en." I drew out the word green as if in awe of the lushness. "The sky is immense. It goes on forever."

I paused a moment for dramatic effect before taking a sharp intake of air.

"Dogs! Dogs barking and barking. Hunting dogs. And horses. Such magnificent steeds."

I paused again before whispering, "A hunt."

Thanks to Google, I knew there were few things Hadrian loved more than a hunt.

In minute detail, I described a special valley near Italica where I'd been allowed once to hunt with my brothers. So rare was the occasion they showed me kindness that each tree, stone, hill and scent of that afternoon was vivid in my mind.

"Yes! Yes!" Hadrian cried out. "I bagged my first boar there."

Then he shouted to the General, "Great Jupiter, man! You were right. The woman has the gift of Sight."

"I see another hunt. A hunt for lions. A hunt yet to be. I see Caesar with Antinous. Chariots in the desert. The Egyptian desert."

Again I paused for dramatic effect before whispering in a hushed, urgent voice, *"Periculum!"* Danger!

Visibly shaken, Hadrian whispered "What is the danger?"

I hesitated, pretending a reluctance to disclose my vision.

"Tell me!" he ordered. "I command you."

"The loss of Antinous," I said gravely.

Hadrian sucked in a long swallow of air. His right hand trembled; wine spilled from the chalice. I glanced at Antinous, who seemed not at all disturbed. On the contrary, he gave me a small, knowing smile.

But Hadrian believed. I snapped my fingers for Aeneas to approach and gave him my ruby septagram necklace.

"It is not too late to alter events, Caesar. Wear this amulet on the hunt. It was crafted in my personal atelier under a waxing quarter moon in Aries with the sun in the 12th house. It shall protect and grant the strength to vanquish any peril."

"Ask for anything within my power, Elektra," Hadrian said solemnly.

"There is nothing I desire other than the satisfaction of assisting Caesar to live a long and fulfilling life."

"The response," he chuckled, "is that which I would expect from one who has the Sight to see what pleases me. And now, alas, I am told the guests impatiently await my presence. Shall we make our appearance at the *convivium*, Elektra?"

I pushed aside any angst of whom might be in attendance. I had come this far. And I had now an Emperor as ally. Surely the gods smiled on me.

But for extra protection, I murmured *ABLAMGOUNOTHO ABRASAX* and chanted *ANA A A NANA A A NANA* all the way to the torch-lit deck arranged with silk and fur-festooned divans.

Antinous of Bithynia

I have never had a woman," he told me.

He had a beautifully modulated voice, masculine yet sensitive. The voice of an orator—or an actor. A poet perhaps. His blue eyes without a trace of artifice held me transfixed. I couldn't stop thinking that in only a few days, this glorious Antinous would be no more.

I had the sense he saw the world through the eyes of a man who'd lived twice his years, if not three times. I certainly had no impression that I was standing in a dark corner inches away from a boy of nineteen.

His golden locks shimmered in a halo around his Adonis face. His lower lip was slightly fuller than the upper; they almost formed a pout. The cleft of Venus, goddess of love and beauty, scored his chin.

He had so little time left, I couldn't deny him. I put my palms on each side of his face and pulled him down to my lips. How sweet his mouth was on mine. Tender, tentative. My tongue found his.

Taking my hand in the way one would hold a priceless object, he led me below deck. Both of us on tiptoe, we moved stealthily along a narrow passageway with closed doors. His hand on the last door opened the latch, and we were inside. The cabin was simple and neat with none of the extravagance of a Roman stateroom. No wall murals showing satyrs frolicking with bare-breasted *maenads*.

One lone oil lamp burned on a wooden table laden with scrolls.

A single bed with a simple coverlet stood in the corner. The Emperor did not come here.

Antinous locked the door and turned to face me. His breath was hot and moist on my forehead; my lips tasted the salt in the hollow of his throat. I took his right hand and placed it on my breast, watching him. He caught his breath; his pupils dilated.

Still holding his hand, I guided his fingers inside my gown to my swollen nipple and closed my eyes. My head fell back, and I breathed a sigh of real pleasure, with no acting on my part. Antinous waited breathlessly for me to come back. Eyes fixed, totally in the moment, we swayed.

With the undulant molasses rhythm of the Hive, I inched my gown to my waist and slid his hand between my bare thighs just at the Gate to Pleasure. His eyes closed as his fingers dipped cautiously into my damp. He explored for the first time the dark, wet mystery of a woman.

We took our time; I wanted him to savor each moment, for each new touch to be divine. My lips were at his ear, blowing softly and then sucking gently.

Inch by inch, I slipped the yellow silk from my breasts. He drank in my white flesh and carmine nipples.

My hands on each side of his head, my fingers in his curls, I first wet his lips with my kiss, then guided him to my breast.

A born lover, he had the gift, tormenting me with his tongue, his finger deep in my canal. No wonder Hadrian adored him.

"And now," I whispered at the same time my hand caressed his pulsing erection, "I need you to come home."

He exploded. Hot semen sprayed my loins.

My lips went immediately to his; I kissed him tenderly, our tongues entwining. Not a minute passed before he hardened again.

I walked him backward to the bed, my hand slowly pumping him in a languid, easy rhythm that said we had time, plenty of time.

At the slight push of my hand on his chest, he lay back, and I mounted him, my legs straddling his thighs, my knees at his hips.

My palm wet with my saliva guided him into me.

"Ah-h-h," he moaned when my warm wet swallowed him whole. I put my mouth on his, murmuring, "Sh-h-h."

His hands kneaded my breasts; I kissed his lips tenderly.

"Thank you," I breathed. "Thank you."

He exploded again. This time deep inside me.

I pulled away from him inches at a time, backing down his thighs until my lips were on his limp manhood.

But limp not for long.

O Antinous, thrice-greatest! O glory of youth!

It took only the touch of my tongue teasing his balls, and he was iron hard once again.

He grabbed my ass and flipped me over, ramming me again and again. I lay with my arms over my head, palms up while he pummeled me.

Antinous was in another world. He snorted and raged, driving into me with all his force. I locked my thighs around his waist and rode him.

We were both drenched in sweat. My intricate hairdo woven with silver thread and pins came apart; thick red waves cascaded around my head to flow on the bed.

I couldn't remember the last time I'd been so thoroughly ravaged; I'd forgotten how delectable it is to be pounded and to do nothing but receive.

His hands were everywhere, exploring, memorizing, relishing a woman's softness—and wet.

When he came, he took me with him. Trembling, our bodies clung to each together. I found myself sobbing into his neck, with my hand over his mouth to quiet him.

Finally, he rolled over onto his back, holding me tight into his side with a grip that said he never wanted to let go.

With my fingertip, I traced his profile. The high, intelligent brow. The perfect nose, cupid lips, Venus chin.

I couldn't bear to think that such perfection would soon be gone.

I kissed first his top lip, then the bottom, taking it gently between my teeth and tugging.

"I am sick of Hadrian's touch," he said quietly.

My fingertips stroked his muscled, sculptured hairless chest.

"I have to pluck my hairs—on my chest, on my face," he said bitterly. "I must not show I have a beard. Everyone knows it is time—past time, but Hadrian will not let me go."

There was nothing I could say. An *eromenos* must become an *erastes*, a penetrator, when the appearance of a beard announces he's a man. The Greek code of conduct required it.

But as much as Caesar put on Greek airs, he was Roman. And a Spaniard at that. Only when Hadrian tired of him would Antinous be free. And I knew from Google that there was no time for Hadrian to let him go. Antinous had only days to live.

"The soldiers despise me. I see it in their eyes. I am not a man to them, but a plaything. Less than a girl. More despicable than a girl."

I didn't try to console him with silly words that both of us knew would be false; Antinous was too intelligent for platitudes.

He breathed in a long deep breath and then exhaled slowly.

"I am a man, Elektra. I can wield a sword or ride as well as any. Better than most. I want only to be what I was born to be."

He looked at me sharply, narrowing his eyes. "And you, Elektra. Have you never known love?"

"The gods withhold their greatest pleasure."

"Then I shall love you. And you shall love me."

How innocent he was of his fate, one far more tragic than any he imagined. I remained convinced that one act of daring might yet change events.

"Hadrian seems not in good health," I ventured cautiously.

Antinous, pure that he is, didn't take the cue. "I concede he looks ill, but I assure you he has the vigor of five men."

"It can be otherwise," I said softly, placing in his palm Eben's green and red vial. I closed his fingers around it, saying "Two drops only. It is painless."

His eyes widened in shock. "I could never do that," he protested.

"How badly do you want to be a man?"

He studied me. The cabin was so still, I could hear the Nile rushing past the cedar boards. The quiet was broken by the muted cry over our heads of a gambler and then drunken laughter.

"Not badly enough to do what you suggest," he answered gravely. "My affection for Hadrian has changed, but I shall always love him for what he has given me. What honor would I have if I committed so base a crime?"

"There is being a man. And there is being a knight. Why set the bar impossibly high? Death is coming. I see it. I do not wish it to be yours."

"Do not play your magic games with me, Elektra," he teased, stroking my cheek with his fingers. "I do not believe in visions. And neither do you."

"I must return, Antinous. We shall be missed."

"When may I see you again?"

I kissed him lightly on the lips. "Seeing should be easy enough, Antinous. But if it is more..."

He grabbed my face and thrust his tongue deep in my throat.

"You risk too much," I cautioned. "We could lose everything."

"I would give it all, Elektra—everything, anything—to be with you."

"Would you, Antinous? Would you give up your honor and use the vial?"

Red Viper

"Can you not see the tattoo on his neck?" I insisted. "The septagram on the left side? The man bears my mark as do these male slaves who accompany me."

The legionary looked first at my major domo Aeneas, then at my Celt bodyguard and finally at my Syrian. Their red-tinted seven-pointed stars showed clearly below the ear.

Then he obediently squatted down and brushed away blood and dirt to reveal Khan's tatoo.

Still he was obdurate. "I regret I cannot, Lady. My orders say *fugitivo*. He is to be crucified."

"There has been a mistake," I contradicted. "He is *my* slave, he did *not* run away, and I do not desire him to be crucified. Kindly give him over into my charge."

I spoke with the utter confidence of one fully expecting her commands to be obeyed.

He stood a little awkwardly for a moment or two. I could see he was confused; perhaps he had no precedent to follow. More than likely, he didn't have the authority to stop an execution, even if the owner of the slave interceded.

With a nod of my head, Aeneas discreetly passed him a small drawstring purse. It disappeared quickly into his leather cuirass.

"I really *must* return to Canopus, Sir. I expect guests."

Canopus. It said everything. I gave him my smile that promises the world.

"Perhaps you might like to visit my island, Legionary. The Temple of Elektra? Perhaps you might like to bring a friend?"

No common Roman soldier could dare dream of the pleasures my Canopus offered. Those delights were for the wealthy and powerful—for officers of the highest rank. Grand Wizards of the Mithraic cult.

And then, as I stoically watched a chain of human misery pass on their way to being flayed and nailed to crosses, I saw Rasheed. Perfect bronzed body still whole, naked save for the loincloth.

His expression was rock-hard, steeled to what he was about to endure. My head swirled, then the whole Hippodrome swirled, all of us in a vortex around him.

I yearned to stroke that proud face with chiseled jaw and cheekbone, to run my fingers across his bare broad shoulders and caress his naked muscular hips. I ached to massage his runner's thighs.

On his neck, from his shoulder to his left ear, coiled a flaming viper tattoo. On his forehead and cheeks festered the *denarii*-sized open sores of brands not quite crosses and not quite *ankhs*, but a morphing of the two.

"Centurion! What is the crime of the one with the snake tattoo?"

"The Red Viper, Lady? He is an assassin. Leader of a vile cult of those fanatics, the Christians. They say he slit the throats of at least one Roman and his wife. Most likely more."

"Who can stop his crucifixion?" I demanded.

"Stop it? Why no one, Lady. The Red Viper dies here in this field on the cross. But not quickly. We have orders he must beg for death and then live to suffer more."

Hadrian had promised me to grant any favor. But I didn't have time to reach an emperor. There was only one other who had the power to help. The General.

He could stop—or start—anything. Or so I chose in that moment to believe. Because without that belief, I had nothing. Rasheed had nothing.

The Moor

D o you question, *Eques*, that the Moor desires to receive me?" I leaned a bit forward, thrusting my cleavage into his face. Wetting my lips, I gave him one of my come-hither looks that expunged all doubt that a man—any man—should refuse to see me.

Hesitating, he blinked hard and tried in vain not to stare at my breasts bursting from red silk. There was a half-witted look about him that told me he would take too long to coddle.

"Hear me, *Eques*," I hissed sharply. "I should not care to be you when the General discovers he was not advised that Elektra of Canopus was here."

His jaw contorted in a series of grotesque facial tics while he struggled to make up his mind.

"Go now!" I snapped. "Tell the Moor that I am here."

He took a deep breath through his mouth. And then having at last found the courage to decide, he straightened his shoulders, thumped his right fist on his chest and turned on his heels to march with purpose to lead us to the pavilion.

Inside the tent, the General reclined on a couch carved with lion paws as feet.

He didn't give me a chance to speak before growling, "I sent word you should stay on your island!"

"I sailed before first light, Excellency," I offered in a quiet, husky voice. "I did not receive your message."

Each step that I took toward him was calculated to arouse. I chanted silently. My aura pulsed, sending waves of desire to roll over him.

Never taking my smoldering eyes away from his, I glided across the carpets, hips swaying and breasts stabbing the air, to uncoil on the divan next to his.

The green *palla* fell from my coppery hair, the *stola* slipped off a shoulder. Tilting my lush, bulging breasts into his eyes, I arranged the contours of my body to rise and fall in sensuous curves.

But instead of his pupils dilating and nostrils flaring as I anticipated, he snapped, "What is this charade, Ishtar? Do you expect me to believe you came here out of lust for me?"

"I expect you to want to finish what you started," I answered coyly.

"When I 'finish,' it shall be the beginning, Ishtar. And when it suits *me*."

My first reaction was to glare at him, but in truth I was grateful to get to the point. I had no time to waste with seductions. At this moment, the soldiers could be scourging Rasheed with one of their odious flails hung with small pieces of glass designed to tear away flesh. They could be cutting away at his manhood. They might be poised to gouge out his eyes with a hot poker. I'd seen all of this today—and worse—in the killing field.

"What do you want?" he growled. "What is so urgent?"

"I want you to stop a crucifixion."

His eyes, heavy-lidded like a crocodile until now, widened in surprise. "Whose?"

"A Christian."

He raised his eyebrows at my answer; it must have been the last he expected.

"What do you care what happens to those superstitious fanatics?"

"There is only one man who concerns me."

"A man?" He sounded puzzled; perhaps he didn't assign

Christians gender. "Who is he?"

"They call him the Red Viper."

"The Viper?" he snorted with a laugh. "I think not, Ishtar. No one can prevent his death. He killed a Roman."

I was fully prepared for his response and countered immediately, "Then make his death quick. You can do that. You have the power."

"And if I oblige you, what will you then do for me?"

"I shall do," I said without a trace of hesitation, "whatever you wish me to do."

"So you would be my slave?"

"No! I shall never be a slave——," I stopped before saying what was on my tongue.

"Again?" he supplied. "I do not believe, Ishtar," he continued in a too quiet voice, "that you realize how precarious your situation is."

With all my strength, I pushed away the vision of myself, naked, bound and bloodied, hanging from a cross. Once, in Hispania, a runaway slave had taken nine days to die. *O General! You are wrong. I do indeed realize.*

"Will you help me? Will you stop Red Viper's crucifixion? In return, I shall do whatever you desire."

"Easy enough promised now."

"You shall have to trust me."

With that, he laughed out loud. "I trust you only to be yourself."

There was a finality in his tone that told me not to waste more time here.

"Pray remember this, General," I warned him in a voice that left no doubt. "If the Red Viper is crucified and I still live, then one night when you least expect it—one hot night when your loins throb, when the taste of me is still on your lips—I shall thrill to watch you take a last painful breath."

Before he could speak, I was out the velvet tent flap. I had to do something fast before Marcus Quintillus found me.

I'm sorry, Rasheed, I called out to the cosmos for him to hear. I have not forsaken you, but I can't save anyone until I save myself.

Rufus Hektor Ptolemais

There was a ferocious intensity to Hektor's voice when he realized the woman waiting for him was not Flavia but me.

"I have never stopped wondering what happened to you. I have never stopped regretting that day."

I moved to make room on the bench. "Come sit beside me."

He hesitated a moment and then sat, giving me a puzzled, uncertain look. "Why do I feel I have desired you all my life?"

I leaned forward and kissed him tenderly on the lips. My hand went under his tunic; my fingertips slid up the inside of his taut thigh and under the loincloth to caress his full sacks.

"What can I do to right my wrong?" he begged.

"Do you still have the bill of sale?" I breathed into his mouth and then kissed him again, always with a great tenderness designed to relax him. "You didn't send it with me that day."

He pulled back, but my massaging hand didn't stop.

"Bill of sale?" he gurgled. "I…I do not know."

I took his sacks in my palm and rolled them gently together.

"Yes!" he blurted. "Why not? My accountant keeps everything."

While licking his lips, my breasts rubbing against his chest, I placed my palm over his nostrils that he might smell his own scent.

"Marcus Quintillus is in Alexandria," I said softly.

"What?!" he cried out.

"He recognized me," I whispered.

The tip of my wet tongue dipped into his ear. My hot palm

stroked his iron post. I put his hand inside my bodice and filled his palm with my breast.

"He has asked for my crucifixion." My tongue still circled his ear. My moist lips breathed my words, "But without proof of ownership, he has nothing."

Suddenly, my old Hektor was here. He sat straight up, alert and determined, eager to come to my rescue.

"I shall go to a magistrate at once! I shall claim you as my property."

"There is still the matter of the Major Domo's death," I cautioned.

"One slave slays another," he said with a dismissive shrug. "I shall pay compensation. You belong to me. Only I may determine your punishment."

"And that shall be?" I whispered, guiding his fingers up my gown to my wet.

There, lying on my back on the hard bench in the hidden little chapel to Aphrodite with blue dome, I cooed like a dove while his long fingers explored me, caressed me, dipping into my canal. He went to the Spot. The G-Spot that only his fingers found.

The world faded for a few blissful moments. Even the horrific screams of Rasheed were gone from my head.

I felt only warmth spreading through my pelvis, up my womb and down my buttocks. With my thighs wide open, my legs dangling on each side of the bench, I rode the wave of ecstasy to sublime.

"You are so beautiful," he crooned. "I could never tire of touching you."

He bent to kiss the base of my throat.

"To think you could have been mine all this time."

I loosened the ties of his loincloth and gently took his fingers wet with my fluids and traced them around his own lips.

With expert, practiced moves, I maneuvered his long legs, placed him at my gate and ushered him into me. He slid in, and slid out, and then in again.

I matched each thrust with a rising of my pelvis to welcome him. I contracted the muscles in my vagina to squeeze him each time he entered.

He went deep. He would have crawled inside me if he could. Then he pulled all the way out. His steel erection with glistening head stood up between my open thighs.

Coitus interruptus always, Flavia had told me when she asked for the magic potion to make Hektor hers. He would only make a son with a Greek.

I gripped his butt with one hand and guided him back to my gate with the other. Locking my legs around his waist, I pushed upward.

He moaned, resisting, trying to pull out. I gripped harder, thrusting my hips into him. I felt him weaken and then surrender. Once more he filled me.

My hands kneaded his butt muscles, tight from daily workouts in the athletic fields of the Library. His thighs were rock hard, the muscles long and taut.

Using all the little tricks I know so well—the pull and tugs on his balls, the teasing of my finger in his anus—I led him inexorably to where I wanted him to go. In a great shaking and trembling and gulping of air, enveloped in my warmth, he exploded inside my hot cocoon.

I waited what I thought was a decent passage of moments before whispering, "I must go."

"Are you not my slave?"

"You have not yet produced the bill of sale."

When I'd straightened my gown and my hair, I put my hand on his cheek.

"I would not mention this meeting to Flavia, Hektor. It is best she knows nothing of us."

I kissed him, my tongue deep in his throat.

"Can I count on you to take care of Marcus Quintillus?"

"What is your name?" he called after me. "How shall I find you?"

"I am Elektra. Ask anyone on the Canal the way to my island."

Roman Bath

The bathing pool in my *tepidarium* was heated to just above body temperature. Eunice dripped oil of gardenia from the silver spout of a cobalt-and-white glass flask.

Nubian women massaged my feet and calves, hands and forearms while Eunice loosened the weaving in my hair. She brushed the long mass one hundred strokes with a soft bristle brush backed with silver. When finished, she piled my hair on top of my head and fastened it with ivory pins.

Once in the scented waters with my head leaning back on a wooden headrest, floating in delicious warmth, I allowed myself to close my eyes.

Visions of a battered Red Viper filled my head. Defeated. Destroyed.

"Bring me the yellow flask and then leave me."

I swallowed three drops and waited. My lids closed. I counted imaginary stars until the Red Viper was a tiny figure far, far away.

My cells melted; I was one with the water. Then I didn't feel anything.

I can't say how much time passed. I felt a presence in the *tepidarium* and opened my eyes.

A naked bronzed God sat on the edge of the pool, facing me. Antinous.

When he saw my eyes were open, he slipped into the water and glided toward me.

"I told you I would come," he stated simply.

I wanted to ask how he got in, but my tongue was too thick to speak.

"You are the most desirable of all women," he murmured.

His fingers touched the base of my throat. I leaned my head back and felt his warm lips there.

Then his fingertips grazed my breasts rising up from the water, and I felt his lips again.

Down across my belly, over my shaved mound, his fingers travelled, followed always by his mouth.

He stroked between my thighs, down one loin and back up the other.

I spread my legs, and his fingers were in me.

"Tell me everything that gives you pleasure, Elektra," he whispered. "Teach me."

He didn't need instruction. His finger found my swollen bud and rotated. My nipples rose to aching peaks. His tongue licked.

My brain, the small part of it that wasn't numbed, shouted, "Danger! Don't do this."

I heard, but I didn't listen.

To lie in the warmest of scented waters, for a God to caress me, for me to be pleased and not please, was a temptation the drug rendered irresistible.

Antinous nibbled my neck. When hearing my moan of pleasure, he bit just a little harder, sucking the skin, teasing with his tongue.

All the while his finger rotated on my aching bud.

When the orgasm rolled through my womb, I cried out, lifting my pelvis to his touch.

"Again, Elektra," he breathed in my ear. "Let me take you there again."

Then his finger deep inside me found the Spot. The magic spot that only Hektor knew.

He felt me melt, and although never having touched another woman, instinctively knew why. His finger stayed exactly where it was supposed to, massaging with exactly the intensity he was supposed to.

"You are a goddess," he crooned. "I shall worship you forever."

Heat radiated from the Spot; a hot flush spread through my hips and belly.

"O-o-o-o-o," I breathed out as the wave crested. His lips brushed mine with a kiss sweet as poetry. A God. Yes, Antinous was a God.

He stood to his feet, his erection piercing the air. Scooping me up in his wrestler arms, he carried me from the pool to the yellow linen divan with gilded lion legs.

The room swirled; my head still reeled from the drug. For a brief moment, I thought I might be sick.

"Wait," I managed to whisper. And he answered by sitting on the divan beside me and pulling the pins from my hair to bury his face in my scented waves.

"Can you give me a vial with your smell?" he teased.

Only the slimmest circle of blue rimmed his huge pupils. His wet hair hung in ringlets about his face and neck.

I climbed onto his lap and straddled his thighs. Wrapping my legs around his waist, I guided him into my wet, pulling myself into his groin.

He went wild. Grabbing my buttocks with both hands, he sat on the edge of the divan, thighs spread wide and rocked me.

His erection deep inside, he stood to his feet and carried me, my legs locked around his waist, across the mosaic floor to a ledge holding an urn. Using the ledge to support my hips, he pommeled me and pommeled me against the wall. The urn crashed; I heard it break into a hundred pieces, but he didn't slow.

My mouth was on his, my tongue down his throat, when he climaxed with the bolt of a stallion. His body jerked once, then twice; he rested his forehead on mine.

"Oh Gods," he said, "there is nothing else like it."

He was careful to step around the shards of ceramic to carry me back to the divan.

"Give me a minute," he breathed.

A minute was all it took.

"How many positions are there?" he asked, rock-hard again. "I want to try them all."

On the third position, my head began to clear. This was wrong. Very wrong. I had to get him out of here. What if the General came back?

To hurry the climax, I reached between his legs to caress his balls.

He exploded, as I knew he would, and I allowed him to lie beside me for a few moments.

His curls had dried to gold. His flawless golden skin glistened with sweat. Never had I known a man more perfect. So lacking in guile, so pure. Innocent. Innocent of his fate.

The Greeks would claim that his beauty made the Gods jealous, and that is why They took him so young. The Romans say that he whom the Gods love dies young, with health, full senses and sound judgment.

But by coming here, I had my doubts that Antinous was of sound judgment.

"You must leave, Antinous. You risk both of us by being here."

"I have come on Hadrian's command, sweet Elektra. We set sail tomorrow for the South, and you are invited!" His eyes glowed with excitement.

"Do not go, Antinous. You must find an excuse."

"Why should I not go? I can see you every day."

"You tread a dangerous path," I murmured.

But I could see he was blinded—blinded by something more perilous than infatuation. I saw adoration.

Adoration drives men to foolish acts.

In that moment, a scene unveiled in my mind. A scene I'd not anticipated. A scene I would have done anything never to see.

If I couldn't alter events, Antinous would die in a few days. But instead of saving him as had been my intention, I saw that I would be the instrument of his death.

Dagger

I t was a splendid October day with the clearest of skies and most tender of breezes. The air was dry and warm but not hot. The sun kissed my skin without burning.

When I saw it was the General who stepped onboard, I found myself overcome with relief and went down from the poop deck to greet him.

"Are you a fool, woman?" he snarled.

"I try to avoid it."

"You do a poor job. I killed a Roman so that you might live."

By that I took him to mean Marcus Quintillus.

"Is he dead then?" I asked hopefully.

He answered by going into my cabin, plopping himself on my divan and shouting at Ghazel to bring wine.

I signalled for the Nubian masseuse, who removed his sandals, washed his feet in scented water and dried them with soft linen before rubbing his soles with warm almond oil.

"Leave us," I said, taking the flask of oil from the Nubian.

I started with his right little toe, rubbing it with oil, then between it and the next toe, and then pulling gently until I heard the gentle pop of a joint.

I rubbed warm oil into the next toe and the next. I massaged gently his calloused and torn big toe and then repeated every touch on the left foot.

His anger drained. I felt it flow through me and out the crown of my head into the warm, fragrant air.

Using my thumbs, I pressed hard into his calf muscles. My fingers found a tiny knot and massaged until it disappeared.

My thumbs on his inner thigh brought the erection rising from a mound to a pillar between the leather tongues of his lappet.

I put my mouth on him and took him deep in my throat, tunic cloth and all. When he grabbed my braids in his fist to push my head further, I bit down. With a cry of pain, he released me.

Faster than he could realize what was happening, I grabbed the silk rope stored under the divan and lashed his wrist to a little post in the armrest.

Startled, he watched me with open lips. I lashed the other wrist to a second post.

While he stared and panted, I tied his ankles spread-eagle to the foot of the sofa.

His erection grew taller, thicker.

I held his eyes while I moved his tunic aside, straddled him and poised above his throbbing manhood.

He breathed short quick breaths through slack lips. His irises were so black I could scarcely see his pupils dilate.

Slowly, so slowly, I lifted my caftan, exposing first my white thighs, then my shaved and carmined mound and gently rounded belly. Finally I pulled the robe over my head to bare my ripe breasts. He couldn't tear his eyes away from them.

Slowly, so slowly, I lowered myself onto his pedestal. We locked eyes again. He held his breath as I took him deeper and deeper, until I was filled. And then I pushed more, and then more, using all my weight to bear down.

Every cell screamed and stretched; I cried out in a frenzied release born of both ecstasy and pain. O comet ride! O flight to the stars! The General's great mass shuddered under me with the force of an earth tremor.

I settled into a chair just next to his spread-eagle legs, crossed my own bare legs and poured myself a chalice of wine. I made no move to loosen his ties.

He struggled against the ropes, twisting from side to side, trying to free himself, bellowing like the bull that he was.

I popped a big juicy purple grape in my mouth, chewed and then spit out the seeds onto the deep green Persian carpet.

"Untie me!" he demanded.

"Not until you tell me how Marcus Quintillus died. Did you make him suffer? Tell me he suffered."

"He was Roman!" he snarled back.

"He was a pig and deserving of slow slaughter."

From under my divan, from the same shelf that had held the ropes, I pulled out a steel dagger, double-edged, razor-sharp—a shiny blade as long as my hand. I didn't recall ever seeing uncertainty in the General's eyes, but I saw it now.

"Do you want to know what *I* would have done if given the chance?" I asked.

My chair was close enough that I easily lifted the hem of his short tunic with the tip of the blade. I tossed the rest of the cloth back, fully exposing his belly.

"I would have tied him down, just like this. Then I would have carved away at his balls, taking only tiny pieces until there was nothing left but a gaping hole."

As I spoke, the tip of the blade nicked at his testicles. The look on his face was priceless. I think he finally understood what I was capable of.

"His penis I would have taken off in one piece and stuffed down his throat. In the end, while he still gagged and choked, I would have disemboweled him."

With each step of my tale, I traced the knife. First his balls, then around his penis, then down the thick black line of hair on his belly from his navel to the black bush.

He looked quite terrified, more than I imagined possible.

I laughed out loud and leaned over to slice the silk bonds tying his ankles.

"What will you do if I loosen your hands?"

"I shall strangle you."

"Will you stop in time?"

"I have not decided."

"Then why should I untie you?"

"You have enough troubles without the Moor dying of starvation in your cabin."

I had to laugh. And while still smiling, I sliced the last cords with the dagger.

His gorilla hands were at once around my throat, dragging me to the lounge. Our eyes fixed. His were wild as one of the beasts tormented for the Arena.

I put my fingers in his short, curled hair and pulled his face toward me, pressing my lips to his, opening my mouth to swallow his tongue.

He pressed harder; my vision blurred. I could no longer kiss him. A flash of light exploded into a kaleidoscope of high-intensity color, stronger than neon, brighter than the sun.

Then a curtain fell and blocked out the light at the moment I climaxed.

This was death, I told myself. No more painful than this. Why does everyone fear it so?

But I didn't die. My vision came back, and when it cleared, the General was kissing my neck where his hands had been, his erection in me again, but not for long. He exploded when he saw my open eyes looking with wonder into his.

He raised up on his elbows, his face so near, our noses nearly touched. I saw each tiny capillary in the whites of his eyes.

"Is this finally to be our lifetime?" he asked.

"You tell me. You are the one who knows everything."

The Greatest Gift

Antinous loves you. I give you that," the General whispered in my ear. "But there is no hope for that love. Would it not be the greatest mercy to let death relieve him of his misery?"

"Can I not bring him one last night of joy? Can you not allow me a last time to see him smile?"

"Do you love him that much?"

"The Praetorian Guard would never suspect you," I whispered.

"You risk everything for him," he said in awe.

The longer I looked into his hooded dark eyes, the deeper he let me go. And in letting me go deep, he let me see his need for me. A need that frightened him. A need that, when I saw it and realized its depth, frightened me.

"And if I do this for you, what will you do for me?" His tone wasn't the arrogant or challenging one I knew so well. He spoke quietly and soberly.

"I shall try to love you," I answered immediately and with absolute sincerity.

He laughed out loud and then said amicably, "I guess that is the best I can expect."

In the middle of the night, while everyone slept, a small boat without lights, smaller even than a skiff, rowed by only one man, pulled alongside my barge. In the bow was Antinous. At the oars was the General.

Antinous reeked of wine and vomit when he stumbled on board. The General said nothing except, "Two hours." Then he rowed away toward the rushes of the river shore.

I bathed Antinous as a mother tenderly bathes her child. He wept in my arms while I kissed his curls.

When he had calmed, I led him to the divan and lay him down gently. Under my silk caftan, I was naked and oiled with jasmine scent.

I kissed his perfect mouth—gently, unhurriedly—with a touch so light my lips were the flutter of butterfly wings. He opened his eyes blue as the spring sky over Thebes.

"I love you, Elektra. I do not wish to live without you."

He was so very young; he wouldn't have the chance to learn that life goes on with a broken heart.

"Sh-h-h," I whispered. "Be nowhere else but here. Be here with me in this moment."

I lay beside him, molding my bare flesh into his on the velvet couch prepared with soft furs. The sweetest of incense burned in the glowing braziers.

I would not cleanse myself tonight; I would not wash away his seed. And if the Gods blessed me and my cycle followed its natural course, I might bear the child of Antinous.

"I love you, Antinous," I whispered when he entered me. "I shall love you for all time."

There was nothing I did not do for him; there was nothing he did not do for me. We were one soul in two bodies, then one soul in one body.

"Is this our goodbye?" he asked. "Shall we never watch the sun rise together? Shall I never wake in your arms and kiss the sleep from your eyes? Shall we never make love in the grass among spring flowers?"

"Imagine the sun is rising now. Can you not smell the flowers? Kiss my eyes."

I was strong until the last moment. But when he opened the door to step out of my world, I weakened.

"Leave, Antinous. Leave now," I begged him. "Take the boat and row. Get away!"

"What is a life without reputation or honor?" he asked in the purest and calmest of voices. "What is life without love?"

He took my face in the palms of his hands. When I looked into his eyes, I saw quiet resignation and no pain.

"If I step from here into the darkest abyss, I take the light of your love with me, Elektra. You are a goddess. You have blessed me. I carry your love to eternity."

I watched from the upper deck as they rowed away. Antinous sat in the bow, facing me. He never took his eyes away.

The General had looked only once at me. The rest of the time he kept his face forward, his eyes perhaps on Antinous watching me.

Finally the speck of their boat disappeared in the pre-dawn mist.

Goodbye Antinous

His perfect body was whole. The General, Goliath and I had stopped the priests before they reached the sacrificial altar. There, under the foul eyes of Seth and Anubis, in a tawdry river hut, surrounded by obscene incense burners in the shapes of demons, they would have wielded their ritual knives to harvest his organs while he lived.

"Antinous," I whispered.

He opened his eyes and turned toward my voice.

"Have I passed?" he asked.

"Not yet," I answered gently. "Soon."

"And I am with you. The gods are kind to grant me my wish."

Sweet Antinous. Even now, so close to the end, he saw kindness in the universe.

"I drank the vial, Elektra. The one you gave me for Hadrian. You were right. There is no pain."

I didn't bother to ask how long ago, for I knew of no antidote. Once ingested, death was inevitable.

"Will you hold me, Elektra? Hold me in your arms?"

Pulling his body into mine, I cradled him more like a child than a lover.

I kissed his parted lips. His breath was weak. As I watched, the potion drained him of another ounce of life.

"I go to eternity," he whispered, "with the vision of your fiery hair and green eyes to remember forever."

His eyes closed. He was so still, I thought he had passed. But he opened them one last time and breathed, "You are a goddess, Elektra. You blessed me with the greatest gift. I became a man with you."

And then he was gone.

I kissed his closed eyelids and his open lips. I stroked his golden curls.

"I shall see you again, Antinous. We shall love each other again." As I whispered, I hung my ruby septagram around his neck. He would take a part of me with him to the void.

Later that morning, the General woke me with a kiss.

"He has been found. By the Praetorian Guard."

"What did Hadrian say?"

"He said, 'The light of my life has been extinguished.' And then he wept like a woman."

I wept again without shame. I am a woman. I am allowed tears.

And through my tears, I saw the Red Mirror hanging on my cabin bulkhead and knew it was time, finally, to go home.

Goliath Redux

Gareth was so tall, his head was cut off in our reflection in the Red Mirror. His black silk shirt was open four buttons to show a gold chain on lustrous muscle. I saw Goliath's gladiator chest in a warrior's cuirass.

The giant bulge in his black cashmere pants throbbed at me. Behind us, also reflected in the mirror, was my wide, racing green bed.

I tore my eyes away. This was *not* what I intended. What had I said? *I moved past it.* I'd scratched the itch.

"It's hard for me to believe that we haven't been fucking our brains out through the centuries," he growled in my ear.

"I'm flying tomorrow to see someone."

"That's tomorrow," he crooned, massaging my tight shoulders in his mammoth hands.

Thick, hot, wet lips sucked on my neck. Against my will, my nipples hardened.

To give in or not to give in.

While I was deciding, Gareth took charge. Palm pressing on my womb, his long basketball player's fingers were between my legs, rotating on my clitoris.

"Relax, baby, " he whispered in his Barry White voice.

And so I did.

A series of dog-bark sounds woke me from sound sleep; Gareth snored. He stretched out on his back the full length of the bed and then some. In the low glow of the indirect lighting, his nude body shone black as polished obsidian against the snowy white Egyptian cotton sheets. How he managed to have a hard-on was worthy of the Mithraic Mysteries.

The god Min with erect penis. His pungent male sweat clung to the sheets. I stretched. Ouch! My hip. Goliath could be rough.

That's when I heard the sliding door to the terrace scratch along the track. I instinctively looked at the altar-niche where the Red Mirror should hang. Gone.

"The Mirror!" I yelled.

Gareth was immediately awake. He leapt from the bed and crossed the silvery carpet with the speed of a forward going for the dunk. We went through the open sliding door and onto the balcony in time to see the edge of the Red Mirror disappear over the railing.

Gareth lunged, caught the corner of the frame with his right hand, doubling from the waist to hang down. I grabbed his left biceps and hung on with all my strength, bracing myself against the wrought iron railing.

Twenty-eight stories down shimmered the swimming pool. One story below, balanced like a performer from Cirque du Soleil, a wiry figure in a black leotard perched on the railing of the terrace under us. He hung onto the other end of the Red Mirror.

Gareth pulled; the muscles rippled across his powerful shoulders. The acrobat-robber used his weight hanging on the Mirror to counter Gareth's strength. I thought that surely with the size and force of his hand, Gareth would wrench the mirror away.

But instead, in one long heartbeat, the Mirror slipped, slipped more, and then began a slow motion tumble to the tiled deck far below.

It took forever for the mirror to fall. I watched each twist and turn. Just as my dream in the Hive. And just like in my dream, the Red Mirror shattered into a thousand shiny shards of splintered glass.

Tony

For Tony it was never about power; it was about what was reasonable and fair. Noble. Noble through the ages.

"I have to decide."

"Not tonight," he said. "Tonight I have other plans."

The last log in the granite stone fireplace cast a reddish aura that licked the tips of his blond curls with fire. Tony's face showed traces of life's passage missing with Antinous. Otherwise, they were the same pure soul who loved in the same enthusiastic, joyful way.

I felt lighter, more hopeful when in his arms. The world was brighter. Less complicated. I was a better person. I believed I could be better still.

"What if I told you that we've known each other before?"

"I'd say I'm a lucky man."

"I'm being serious, Tony."

When he looked into my eyes and saw my gravitas, he pulled back, then rolled over to sit up straight beside me with his back against the chintz sofa. I sat up too, and he wrapped a giant crocheted afghan around our shoulders. Our bare legs, parallel on the braided oval rug, stretched toward the open hearth with glowing embers.

Even his toes were perfect, each one straight and just a tiny bit shorter than the one before, forming a precise diagonal from the big toe to the little.

"Remember, Tony, when we went to the Metropolitan Museum? How the statues were more than statues to you? How you felt like you knew them as people?"

He handed me a wine glass with the last of the Barolo.

"I remember everything about that day, Isis. Everything. That was the first time I recall being happy since Susan died."

"We were married once," I blurted out.

The words just came. I'd thought to take him along in stages, but I heard myself say what I'd wanted to tell him for so long, but never dared.

He blinked.

"In another lifetime."

Our faces were close enough that the blue of his eyes was the thinnest of circles around huge black pupils.

"I know it sounds crazy. I would have thought it crazy, too—not that long ago."

The furrow between his eyebrows deepened, the one he gets when struggling to reconcile disparate thoughts.

He didn't ask how, or what, or why. He didn't say anything. I wanted to crawl inside his head. His eyes had that detached quality of a mind separate from a body.

I rose to my bare feet and padded across the worn parquet floor to find my purse and take out a folded-up paper.

While he stared at the printout of a bust of Antinous at the Prado Museum in Madrid, I curled back down beside him on the braided rug.

"It's you. You can see that. I'm surprised no one has pointed it out to you before."

I was certain he was going to say that it was a coincidence. That the striking resemblance was due to an anomaly of genes programmed to produce eyes, ears and noses. That given the number of human beings on the planet throughout time, doubles were statistically predicted to happen. *Doppelgängers*. The Germans had a word for it.

But he didn't respond like I thought he would.

"I've had the strangest feeling since I met you. The first time in Vegas when you told me your name. Isis. And then in New York. It's never been like we were strangers who'd met randomly. Not for me."

"Then you don't think I'm some kind of nut?"

"You are definitely some kind of nut." His eyes twinkled; his face glowed. "A very delightful one."

Leaning into me, taking my chin in his fingers, he kissed me on the lips, his tongue probing just a little. Just enough that we both stirred.

"It explains so much, Tony," I argued earnestly. "Why we're instantly attracted to someone—or repulsed. Why people are drawn to a strange land—or a time in history. Why it's easier for some to play the piano. Or for you to do math.

He smiled and blew gently in my ear.

"It's all happened before," I insisted. "We're building on the past."

"Does that mean we have a future?" he asked, his fingers holding my chin again.

"It means we have now," I answered.

He smiled and quoted Epicurus, "We have this moment only. There is only here and now."

When he saw my surprised look, he laughed out loud. He had the exact, mischievous, heart-stopping look in his eye as young Antinous.

"I've been studying up on the Greeks," he grinned. "I may be more in tune with the universe than you think."

And then Antinous Thrice Greatest kissed my lips, my breasts, my belly.

His manhood first pierced the air, then me, driving deep into my wet, his palm muffling my cries.

O Aphrodite! O Gods divine!

Reunion

The leaden skies of London opened; slate sheets of driving rain pounded the pavement. *Thump, thump, thump* went the windshield wipers.

When our cab approached, he got out of an idling taxi. That Rasheed stood alone, in the rain, caused my heart to pound.

Who knew from where Rasheed had flown? No doubt a shiny city under harsh azure skies and an uncompromising sun.

I opened the door before our taxi came to a full stop.

Twelve, maybe fifteen feet separated us. I was reminded again of Copenhagen. Dark skies. Light rain. Taxis. Rasheed and I staring at each other across cold, wet space.

Rasheed had worn a suit that day. I'd been dressed to kill in black stiletto heels and pearls. All dolled up to impress him.

Today, here in London, I was a mess. Blue jeans and V-neck sweater I'd slept in. Drab hair unlike my natural color—unlike any color I'd ever had in any of my lifetimes—frizzed all over the place.

I stood there, knowing that a rapt Lars and Gareth watched the scene, maybe even holding their breath like I was.

I knew that Marcos and Gamel were watching, too. There wasn't much between Rasheed and me that they hadn't witnessed.

And then, there was no distance at all between us. Rasheed's arms were around me; his perfect mouth chiseled by a master sculptor devoured me. His tongue down my throat, his manhood a stone post at my belly, I melted into him. Where I ended and he began was impossible for me to know.

"Ride with us," I breathed in his ear. "We're going after Cesari."

I didn't need to say it, though, because the General was precisely why he'd come. *Get rid of him, Isis. It's up to you. It's all up to you.*

When Rasheed opened the door and I crawled into the back of the cab, I locked glances with Gareth.

Please don't spoil this for me, I begged with my eyes.

Gareth looked from me to Rasheed. I knew by the wonder on his face that he recognized the man he'd once worshipped. We'd both loved Black Falcon then and wept together at his death.

Of course, Rasheed knew Goliath. Rasheed always recognized the players in our drama of reincarnating souls; the past was a wellspring of anger and jealousy. Thank the Gods, I saw no signs of jealousy now. He suspected nothing between Gareth and me.

They nodded to each other in that special way men acknowledge comrades-in-arms, and Gareth slid over so Rasheed could take his place facing me.

Gareth turned out to be a man who took defeat as gracefully in love as on the court. He grinned and said, "So *you're* the lucky guy."

All the way to Q's, Rasheed leaned forward in the seat, knees spread, gripping my hands in his. Once, he raised my fingers to his lips and kissed them.

His eyes studied my face in the way Black Falcon had memorized the angle of my jaw, the curve of my lip, every freckle across my nose, sensing he'd not see me again.

I wanted to shout at him, *You don't have to do that. You can keep looking at me every day!*

We bumped along, four men, one of them a giant, none of them small, and me on the jump seat in the back with Gamel in the passenger seat next to the driver. Not even for the drive through London would Marcos and Gamel leave Rasheed's side.

Six of us. Only one more, Q, to complete the New Order. Seven Protectors on a magic ride to find the General and the Emerald Tablet.

Crocodile

By some bizarre stroke of synchronicity, the sun broke through a somber sky, spotlighting the General's parked Rolls.

Orsini waited by the car. As soon as he saw me exit the hotel, his hand reached for the door handle.

Had he killed Q?

We locked glances before I was swallowed by the dim interior, shielded from the sun's bright blessing by tinted windows.

His thoughts were shielded as well. I saw nothing in his eyes; they were expressionless as—and not far from the color of—the gunmetal canopy of clouds behind his head. We might never have been together in Malta, might never have together saved the General from the militia in the Cave of Bats.

The General loomed larger than life on the black leather seat. His bull shoulders and chest in a navy blue blazer filled my field of vision. A green glassy septagram glinted in the patch of black hair at the V in the neck of his snowy white dress shirt.

Stretching out his thick-fingered hand, he patted the black leather seat beside him. I caught a glimpse of the gold crocodile cufflink with the glittering ruby eye.

"Surely you are not afraid *now*, Ishtar? Not after we've been through so much together."

Orsini shut the door. I heard the lock click. I waited to hear the trunk open for my case, but a second or two later, he was climbing into the front seat.

I stared straight ahead, forcing myself to breathe slowly and evenly.

While I watched, an impregnable black glass window closed with a quiet electric whirring, and Orsini and the driver disappeared. Was the partition also soundproof?

"I need you to change your clothes."

The General's tone was so polite and his expression so mild that under any other circumstances, I might have characterized him as pleasant.

Inside the Harrods sack were slacks and a sweater. He held up another Harrods sack, smaller, probably with underwear.

Without a change of expression on my face, saying nothing, I emptied the larger bag and started to strip, toying with all manner of ways of undressing, inclined at first to change as rapidly as possible. But as I chanted silently to give myself strength, my movements slowed.

First the sweater. Teasing up from the hips, back slightly arched, I paused a heartbeat before lifting the soft black cashmere to expose my full breasts thrust up in the black French lace bra.

Then in one long, unhurried movement, I eased the turtleneck over my head. My hair crackled with static electricity.

I tossed the sweater to the thick carpeted floor and turned my eyes to the General. His pupils dilated when I gave him my icy emerald stare smoldering with promise.

He watched, as I knew he would, transfixed. His breath came a little quicker.

I slid my left fingers across to the right bra strap and, caressing my shoulder with my fingertips, slipped the black lace down my upper arm.

Without any hint of hurry but replete with suggestion, my right fingers dropped the left strap.

It wasn't much really. Two bare shoulders with straps hanging down. He couldn't see more flesh than before. But it was enough for the General's bull chest to heave.

Stretching behind my back, I unsnapped the bra but held the two ends together.

He heard the unfastening. I saw the electric jolt in his eyes.

Oh, how I would have loved to laugh out loud.

Spaniel eyes. Well, not quite. But he was close. I never dreamed I'd see him beg.

In the silence of the limo, the air throbbed.

I wet my lips with my tongue and released the bra, shrugging my shoulders lightly so the bra slipped to my ribcage, and my breasts fell free.

Oh, how he yearned to touch me. I could see it. I could feel it. But he played the game. He was enjoying the torture of my bare breasts just within reach, but off limits.

I'll admit to a perverse excitement. My engorged nipples ached.

Taking my time, I eased out of the slacks, pointing one foot, then the other to kick the soft wool from around my ankles and pile on the floor next to the sweater.

I held his eyes every second that I slipped down my panties— along the thigh, over the knee, slowly past the calf, then the ankles.

I thought he might actually weep when he saw all pubic hair gone. *A la arabe*, they call it in North Africa. Like Ishtar in his tent, like Athena in the desert, like Elektra on her barge. I'd stopped short of rouging the white, smooth, seductive, nude mound of womanhood.

Finally, my fingertips eased the black lace past my pointed toes to drop on the plush carpet with the black slacks, sweater and bra.

The General's breath was coming fast; his chest heaved. In a Herculean effort of self-control, his monster hands curled into fists.

Under us, the road bumped and thumped. Around us was charcoal nothingness. I suppose if I'd put my nose to the glass, I could have made out our surroundings. It was clear by the increased speed of the car that we were racing out of the city.

When I'd settled into a Goya pose, I held out my index finger for the little Harrods sack with underwear.

The bag was so tiny in his gorilla hand. Instead of taking it from him, I changed my mind and, stroking down my thigh, commanded in the sultry, breathless voice of Elektra, "*You.*"

Reaching into the green bag with his beast fingers, the General pulled out the black lace panties. His choice was my clue to arch my back and subtly square my shoulders, enticing him with my full breasts and erect nipples in his face.

His lips parted. Elektra would have owned a slave to satisfy that yearning, a young nursing mother with a throbbing nipple dripping with drugged milk.

With the undulations of a Vegas lap dancer, I shimmied the panties up my calves and over my thighs to my pelvis.

Why the General didn't pull out his god-sized penis and cram it down my throat or plunge it up me, I don't know.

Pure animal. Glorious carnal lust. Contained. *Controlled.* I can't explain what happened in the back of that limousine.

I had no plan. Chanting in my mind over and over the words of the spell Hermes had given me, BOR PHOR PHORBA PHOR PHORBA BES CHARIN BAUBA, I let myself go. I rode each moment and let it carry me to the next.

Some might think that the General and I were being swept to a foregone conclusion defined by fate. But I didn't believe it. I had a great deal of power over the conclusion, and I intended to wield it.

When I'd pulled on the new sweater and slipped into the new boots, the General rolled down the electric window and tossed everything—my boots, slacks, bra, Escada coat—all except my passport and the faience septagram at my throat—out of the car to scatter by the motorway.

I imagined the odds and ends of my things settling here and there on the motorway. The tiny emitters Lars had placed in my bra, right boot heel and in the waistband of my slacks, would no longer show as speeding dots on his laptop map, but stationary blips.

"You know what I need, Ishtar."

The General's deep, bull voice after such a long silence jolted me.

"And if I don't give it to you?"

"It won't be pleasant for your friends." He paused. His expression almost begged me to cooperate.

"Especially for Rasheed," he added unnecessarily.

"And what if I prove to be like you?"

"Then you have an Achilles heel. Just as I."

"I want to see him," I said. "I need proof of life."

"All in good time."

"So where do we go from here?"

"That depends on you, Ishtar. You command quite a bit of power, if you haven't noticed."

His black eyes twinkled when he said that; in spite of everything, he could smile at the irony of his own weakness.

Goodbye General

When I came out, the General in a white dinner jacket stopped weaving his bowtie and stared.

Shimmering white silk swathed my breasts. My shoulders and arms were bare in the halter top. Instead of the gold sandals, the new ones were silver.

His hard eyes, usually coal black and glinty, softened to smoky charcoal. Waves of yearning rolled across the room to break on my shore.

He went directly to a black velvet case on the dressing table and took out the Tahitian pearl necklace with the ruby septagram. I didn't bother to ask how he got it from the hotel room safe or even how he knew to look for it there.

He smiled and raised his eyebrows to ask permission, and I obliged by turning toward the French doors, lifting my hair.

His touch, I regret to say, was electric. His fingertips seared the back of my neck. As thick as his fingers were, he unclasped without effort the thin gold chain with the faience septagram.

I held out my hand, and he dropped the necklace in my palm.

His fingertips still seared when he fastened the black pearls. I felt his moist lips on my top vertebra, then the second and the third. Goosebumps rose on my shoulders; I shivered when his thick fingers trailed down my spine, past where a bra strap would have been, to stop at my waist and then trace around the band.

His eyes had a satisfied look when I turned to face him.

As much as I hate to admit it, I would have made love to him one last time. I would have worshipped his swarthy, furry body with my lips, my tongue and my teeth.

I would have engaged in every depraved, animal mating his wretched soul desired. White silk draping my body, I would have kissed his broad chest and fondled his stallion jewels to ready us for one last comet ride. I loved him that much, sick as it is.

"Don't think you've won," I warned him.

"I've learned, Ishtar," he said, "not to take anything for granted with you."

It was only in the last hours, I believe, that he'd fully realized what I was capable of. He was near surrender. So close.

I touched his rough cheek with my fingertips. Then I leaned into him, my eyes holding his, and kissed him lightly on the lips.

"Will you spoil now, all that we've had together?" I whispered. "You made me happy once. I think I made you happy."

Between us played holograms of our passion. The scene in his tent when I rode his comet to the stars. The twilight and rising moon on the desert when I crossed the line between ecstasy and pain.

The scenes that played the longest were ones of which I had no memory. Tender nights and savage afternoons in Canopus when we lived as Roman and wife. Those memories were his, and he shared them with me.

BOR PHOR PHORBA PHOR PHORBA BES CHARIN BAUBA, I chanted softly in his ear, not to elicit fear or control his will, but to ease the separation that we both knew was coming.

"Give me the Tablet," I crooned, wet tongue in his ear, gentle hand caressing his bull manhood. "Give me Rasheed."

I kissed his ear and sucked away the last of his resolve.

"Let us keep our memories, General."

Then I delivered the *coup de grace*.

"Let us keep hope for a future."

River God

Cotton clouds floated on the horizon. The sun was a golden disk high in an azure sky. Gentle swells rocked us as tenderly as a mother's hand does a cradle.

In the distance, the white triangle sails of Marcus and Gamel's yawl billowed. Not that far, really, but far enough.

We'd dropped anchor just offshore of a tiny, kidney-shaped emerald isle with an empty white crescent beach edged with feathery palms. A thousand shades of Caribbean turquoise stretched from our boat to the sandy shore.

If I imagined another coastline, one with white rocks and green cypress, I might have been back in North Africa the day Black Falcon gave me up for silver.

But there was no giving me up this time. Or escape from the boat.

Fresh out of the shower, wet wavy jet hair shining, Rasheed came up from below deck.

"Isis!"

I had a name, the name of a goddess. I also had a man. And what a man he was—a River God of bronzed flesh and snowy linen.

Only the white linen wrapped around his hips and ending above the knees wasn't a kilt but a towel.

He wore nothing above the waist except a small faience septagram disk hanging on a silver chain. Just like the one around my neck that hung on gold.

Rasheed's broad shoulders tapered in a triangle to a narrow waist where the bright pink traces of a bullet wound marred his perfect flesh. His thighs and calves were taut. The skin on his chest glowed like burnished stone.

I didn't have to guess if he wore underwear.

His mouth, exquisitely carved by a master sculptor, turned up at the corners in his seductive half-smile promising flight to the stars. His eyes were the warmest of jades. His face, once riven with lines of anger, had relaxed into soft angles blurred by tender kisses.

Trailing my fingers down the length of his arm, I watched the tiny hairs rise. Gooseflesh rose on my own skin, like a chill across my shoulders in spite of the tropical air.

"Now, Isis," he whispered, his breath hot and moist on my neck. "Now."

Not in a hurry—I'd never known him to hurry—he rediscovered every part of me. He kissed my toes, my ankles, the back of my knees, but waited to enter the Gate to Pleasure.

He kissed my fingers, my palms, my wrists, inside my elbows, the base of my neck, but waited to touch my breasts.

I thought of a thousand places I wanted him to taste but surrendered to his pace. He would find them all.

His magic touch. The touch of River God. It was mine.

O Aphrodite! I shall make sacrifice at your altar the rest of my days.

I didn't chant incantations from the Black Scroll. I didn't call upon Higher Powers. I didn't need to. There was nothing in the world for me at that moment except the euphoria of being one with Black Falcon.

Epilogue

I try not to think about what my life would have been if I'd chosen to gaze into Tony's enamel blue eyes shining with the noble spirit of Antinous. I don't let myself dwell on the idyll I might have lived with sunny Hector on the *estancia* in Argentina. I keep myself from imagining the dark depths and sharp thrills I could have explored with the General. How would it have been if I'd given Goliath a chance?

I made my choice. Maybe Rasheed will break my heart. Maybe I'll break his. But I have to try. You see, I never got past that first vision of bronzed flesh and white linen on the Nile. River God. I had to have him.

Can you understand why, in spite of the dangers, regardless of the risks, I gaze into the Mirror? If I have learned just one thing, it is that there are many kinds of love. And if I keep going back, I don't have to choose. I can have them all.

One man is not enough for Isis. Or one life.

Cast of Characters

Isis. Isenknebe Nefrusobek. Ishtar. Athena. Elektra

Her lovers

Present: Rasheed. *Past:* River God called The Commander. Black Falcon. Red Viper.

Present: Gareth Greene. *Past:* Goliath.

Present: Hector. *Past:* Hetmus-hor. Hektor of Naukratis. Rufus Hektor Ptolemais.

Present: The General called Cesari. *Past:* General Sher. The Carthaginian. The Roman General called The Moor.

Present: Tony. *Past:* Antinous. Antinous of Kos. Antinous of Bithynia.

Characters:

Crown Prince and his companion the Scribe

Qeb-ha the eunuch priest

Sit-Hathor (Isabel) the mother and High-Priestess

Maia the hand servant

Gamel and Marcos, Rasheed's bodyguards

Lars, Rasheed's friend

Eben the fortune teller

Barb the best friend

Hermes Trismegistus father and wizard

Jason the son

Major Domo the head slave

Domina the mistress of the house

Marcus Quintillus (Dominus) the master of the house

Nemo the Horse Tamer

Lemta the Sorceress

The Maiden

Aeneas the head slave

Ghazel the dressing slave

Hadrian the Emperor

Orsini the General's man

About the author

Born with wanderlust, forever living in a fantasy world, S. L. Gore escaped the prairies of Kansas to follow the yellow brick road on an odyssey that took her to Europe, Africa, Latin America and the Middle East.

Starting with a one way ticket to Iceland, she returned with a Viking husband, an art degree and speaking five languages.

A love of travel, classical history, languages, mysticism, food, shopping and romance led Gore to create the novels of the *Red Mirror Series*: **The Red Mirror, The Emerald Tablet** and **The Black Scroll.**

As a self-challenge to test her range, Gore re-cast the story of Isis of The Red Mirror in two more versions: **Isis Erotica** and a sanitized PG-rated version, **Isis BeachRead.**

Her non-fiction publications include the self-help manual **Sex and the Zen of Shopping:** *How to Live Rich by Shopping Smart* and memoir contributions to three **Life Choices** anthologies.

Expect a cookbook of Gore's own recipes plus those of talented, food-loving friends from around the globe. You can find samples from time to time on her blog.

The joyously married Nielsens have a grown daughter and a son and divide their time between a California beach house and a Las Vegas condo.

S. L. Gore's Books

Red Mirror Series ~ *One life is not enough*
Published by Tajine Publishing in print and eVersion

The Red Mirror (Book One)
 - Pharaonic Egypt, 525 BC
The Emerald Tablet (Book Two)
 - Greek Egypt, 215 BC
The Black Scroll (Book Three)
 - Roman North Africa, 130 AD

Lovers of Isis - *Red Mirror Series Vignettes* S. L. Gore
Published by Tajine Publishing in print and eVersion

Isis *Erotica* Sandra Gore
Published by Tajine Publishing in print and eVersion

Isis Beach Read Sandra Gore
Published by Tajine Publishing in print and eVersion

Sex and the Zen of Shopping: Live Rich by Shopping Smart
Sandra Gore Nielsen
Published by Tajine Publishing

Life Choices Anthologies
Published by Turning Point International
Navigating Difficult Paths: "A True Love Story"
Pursuing Your Passion: "The Muses Whisper"
It's Never Too Late: "Road to Vegas"

Tajine Publishing
2550 E Desert Inn Rd, #443
Las Vegas, NV 89121
702-279-6556
tajinepublishing@gmail.com

Author website: **www.SLGore.com**